**5 *cups*** "All Night Inn literally sucks you in from beginning to end." ~ *Coffeetime Romance*

"Imagine a world where Nightwalkers feed, Shapeshifters frolic and Spellcasters work their magic just beyond the realm of human awareness…once you enter you will never want to leave." ~ *Paranormal Romance Reviews*

**5 *Stars*** "All Night Inn by Janet Miller is a joyous walk on the "dark-side" of life." ~ *EcataRomance Reviews*

**5 *Roses*** "This is an exceptionally well-written vampire romance, which should be on every paranormal lover's reading list. Hurry! Get your copy now!" ~ *A Romance Review*

"Reminiscent of Charlaine Harris's Dead Series, this is a fun, well written book and I truly hope only the first of many more from this author." ~ *Eternal Night*

**5 *Hearts*** "Exciting and emotional, the love scenes pull on the heartstrings and are sensual and erotic." ~ *Love Romances*

**4.5 *Hearts*** "The plot flows smoothly, and I really resented life interrupting my reading, because the story line was so engrossing. ~ *The Romance Studio*

# Janet Miller

# All Night Inn

Cerridwen Press

A Cerridwen Press Publication

www.cerridwenpress.com

All Night Inn

ISBN #1419954075
ALL RIGHTS RESERVED.
All Night Inn Copyright© 2005 Janet Miller
Edited by Ann Leveille.
Cover art by Syneca.

Electronic book Publication August 2005
Trade Paperback Publication March 2006

With the exception of quotes used in reviews, this book may not be reproduced or used in whole or in part by any means existing without written permission from the publisher, Ellora's Cave Publishing, Inc., 1056 Home Avenue, Akron, OH 44310-3502.

This book is a work of fiction and any resemblance to persons, living or dead, or places, events or locales is purely coincidental. The characters are productions of the authors' imagination and used fictitiously.

Cerridwen Press is an imprint of Ellora's Cave Publishing, Inc.®

## About the Author

❧

During the weekday Janet is a mild-mannered software engineer who writes code and design documents. At night and on weekends she turns to the creation of offbeat stories about imaginary pasts, presents, and futures. But no matter when or where the story happens, there will always be some adventure, some humor, and meaning to the tale. For Cerridwen she's writing a new line of parafolk tales about modern day vampires, called nightwalkers, along with psychics and shapeshifters of all kinds.

Janet welcomes mail from readers. You can write to her c/o Ellora's Cave Publishing at 1056 Home Avenue, Akron, OH 44310-3502.

## Also by Janet Miller

෩

If you enjoy *All Night Inn,* are interested in a spicier read and are over 18, you may want to read the related story *Fangs for the Memories*, which gives you later glimpses of Sharon and Jonathan and is written under Janet's pen name of Cricket Starr. (Contains somewhat more explicit sexual scenes.) Visit our website for Ellora's Cave Publishing at www.ellorascave.com.

***And check out her erotic romances also written under the pen name Cricket Starr at Ellora's Cave.***

Divine Interventions 1: Violet Among the Roses
Divine Interventions 2: Echo In the Hall
Divine Interventions 3: Nemesis of the Garden
Ellora's Cavemen: Legendary Tails I *(Anthology)*
Fangs for the Memories
Memories To Come
The Doll
Two Men and a Lady *(Anthology)*

# *All Night Inn*

୭

# Dedication

༂

This is dedicated to my family who told me my writing was great even when it wasn't, and to my critique buddies and editors, who taught me to make it better.

I'd also like to thank all those vampire and shapeshifter authors whose work inspired me into making my own little parafolk world. Please don't stop writing.

Cheers!

## *Trademarks Acknowledgment*

~

The author acknowledges the trademarked status and trademark owners of the following wordmarks mentioned in this work of fiction:

Velcro: Velcro Industries B.V. Limited Liability Company

GQ: Advance Magazine Publishers, Inc. Corporation

Star Trek: Paramount Pictures Corporation

Martin Guitar: C.F. Martin & Co., Inc. Corporation

Cuervo Gold: Tequila Cuervo La Rojena, S.A. De C. V. Corporation

Tiffany : Tiffany & Company Corporation

Heineken : Heineken Brouwerijen B.V. Private Limited Company

Mercedes: Daimler-Benz Aktiengesellschaft Corporation

Lear: Lear Corporation

Jacuzzi: Jacuzzi Inc. Corporation

Cadillac: General Motors Corporation

Devo: Devo, Inc. Corporation

Metallica: Metallica composed of Kirk Hammett, James Hetfield and Jason Newsted, all U.S., citizens, and Lars Ulrich, a citizen of Denkmark PARTNERSHIP

Steely Dan: Steely Dan Corporation

# Chapter One

"You can't work here without my mark, Ms. Colson. No one can."

Sharon watched Jonathan Knottmann lean back in his chair, no doubt waiting for her refusal. His unblinking, disconcertingly blue gaze fixed on her face and his dark hair, so dark it might as well be black, fell across his forehead and down to his shoulders, wide under the simply tailored white shirt.

Once again she noticed what a good-looking man he was. Or would be, if he were a man. For a moment she considered giving up and escaping into the night, but this was no time to be timid. Jonathan might be a vampire, but he needed a bartender and she needed the work—no matter what it took!

"So mark me. I want the job and you're the only one in town hiring."

From the look on his face, she'd surprised him. "You don't know what you're saying."

He eyed her neck, and briefly his tongue appeared, touching his bottom lip, pulling it in. For an instant the twin fangs showed and glinted in the dim lighting of his office.

Sharon had noticed he kept the lights down, both here and out in the bar. She hadn't much experience with the paranormal, but she'd seen lots of movies and knew what to expect. Probably his eyes were photosensitive. Certainly it helped preserve his image as a normal human being. She expected that in bright light it would be easy to see the deadly pallor of his skin. He'd probably had long practice at keeping his lip drawn across his upper teeth, hiding the most obvious indicators of what he was.

Only that once did she see them. Instinctively she drew back and for a moment saw something like relief in his eyes.

*No, she needed this job!* Stranded in the little coastal town of Los Niños de la Noche, she was broke, dead broke, with a car to match. No way to repair her car, no way to raise any money short of finding work. Thanks to her landlord locking her out of her room, the clothes on her back were all she had in the world.

Sharon forced herself to meet the vampire's steely gaze. "I'll take your mark anyway."

His eyes narrowed and he almost smiled. He tapped on the table the single-page resume she'd given him, detailing the bartending experience she'd had in Los Angeles and her very few club dates as a singer. His deep voice had a soft edge to it, that of a foreigner speaking English. "You interest me, Ms. Colson. Tell me about yourself. Do you have any family?"

"I don't really have any. My father just died...I haven't heard from my brother in ages." Stuart hadn't been reachable for weeks now, probably abusing some substance somewhere in LA. As family he was almost as useless as he was as a manager for her career.

"Have you worked with parafolk before?"

"Parafolk?" She wasn't familiar with the term.

He nodded. "Parafolk are people like me, and others. Shapeshifters. Spellcasters. Similar types. The places you worked are all establishments for norms—that is, normal people."

"No. But I'm not averse to doing so." She had nothing against working with anyone if she could find a way to pay her rent and repair her car.

From hidden speakers came a soft melody, a female vocalist accompanied by an acoustical string instrument. Her potential boss turned his head to listen and a real smile appeared on his face.

Sharon broke in. "I'm actually quite good as an entertainer. I can sing and play the guitar if you have one handy."

His attention shifted back to her. "You don't have one of your own?"

She hesitated. "I had to pawn mine a few weeks ago. For the money to drive back to LA after my father died." Sharon leaned forward and placed her hands on the desk. "You've seen my references, you know I can do the job."

He leaned forward, his ice blue gaze intense. "Are you sure you know what you're doing, Ms. Colson? Do you know what it means to be marked by one such as I?"

He hadn't once referred to himself as a vampire, as if he wasn't comfortable with it. Sharon wasn't comfortable with it either but she wasn't about to let him know that.

"I know it means that you've taken blood from me and left the mark to prove it. It means I'm your servant, like the man you have working the bar."

"Marcus. He cooks for the inn, normally." Jonathan folded his hands, a delicate gesture, strikingly graceful. Something that might have been a happy memory eased the severity of his expression. "He's been with me for quite a while."

The moment passed and once again she was the subject of his intense stare. "It means those things, yes. Marking you would mean taking you as my companion and that is much more than a job. As my companion, you are there for me when I need you. In return you have my help, my protection. For a very long time."

He emphasized the last of that and briefly Sharon wondered how long "long" could be. Still, it was irrelevant. If she had to make a long-term commitment, a year or more, that was fine.

Marcus had told her about the mark when she'd asked at the bar about a job. She didn't often use her psychic ability to read people, but she had with him. Marcus was one of the good guys, friendly and pleasant in spite of the twin scars on his neck, the vampire's "mark". If Marcus was comfortable in his position with Jonathan, how bad could it be? Besides, her only other choice would be to try hitchhiking down the coast and abandon to her landlord the few things she'd kept after her dad died. Something froze inside her at that plan.

"Listen, Mr. Knottmann, I really want to work here. If you need a drink of me to trust me enough for the job, then so be it."

He winced. "It's not just a matter of trust, Ms. Colson, but safety. My place is frequented by parafolk after normal hours, when I'm closed to the general public. Most behave themselves, but an unmarked human could easily become a liability. Any employee I have must be seen as belonging to me."

Once again he appeared to study the brief resume in front of him, but Sharon felt a questing tendril, a mental probe aimed at her and immediately her mind slapped it away.

His head jerked up and his startled gaze drove straight through her. "You have mental powers."

"Some," she admitted. "Not many, but I can block a probe like that one."

Now he was truly interested. Again he eyed her neck, and this time she wondered if he didn't see it the way she would a long-necked beer bottle.

He spoke softly. "It's been a long time since I've had a woman companion."

*What did he mean by that?* A tremor of uncertainty shook her but she forced herself to stand still and allow his piercing examination. Finally a brief smile flitted across his mouth.

"Very well, Ms. Colson. We'll do a trial, I think. I'm short-handed anyway and could use you to work the bar tonight. I believe none of my more—*special* customers are likely to be around. If we're both satisfied in the morning, I'll hire you full time and we'll take care of the mark then. Otherwise, I'll pay you for the night's work and let you go. Is that acceptable?"

Sharon nodded then followed him back to the main room of the inn. She'd fallen in love with the place the minute she'd walked into the big open room. The decor of the All Night Inn was warm and inviting, dark wood paneling, worn but serviceable furnishings, scattered wooden tables and chairs, and booths with red fabric seats along the long windowless walls.

It was the kind of place people—and others, she reminded herself—could come to soothe their problems with companionship and drink. Best of all was the solid maple bar that lined the back of the room. On one side stood tall stools. On the other were the taps, glasses, bottles, bins of ice and other paraphernalia that were the mainsprings of her vocation.

Behind the bar a bear-like man, Marcus, raised his dark fuzzy eyebrows and promptly checked her neck when his boss told him she was taking over. With a shake of his head, Jonathan waved away his questioning look.

"Have you eaten, Ms. Colson? Marcus could bring you something."

To her embarrassment, her stomach growled, and the vampire and his companion exchanged amused glances.

"I'll take that as a 'yes'," Marcus said. "Be back in a bit." The man headed toward the kitchen with an air of relief at being excused from bar duty. Clearly he regarded his profession as cook with the same satisfaction Sharon felt for hers.

She went to check her reflection in the mirror behind the bar only to discover there was at least one difference in Jonathan's establishment from other places she'd worked. No mirror.

He seemed to be suppressing a chuckle when she turned around. "I'm not fond of mirrors, Ms. Colson." He reached over and gingerly moved a strand of her blonde hair away her face, tucking it behind her ear. "You look fine."

The brief caress of his hand left Sharon with an uneasy feeling. Not repulsion…for some reason, totally irrational, she wished he'd touch her again.

From the other end of the bar a couple of customers hailed her, and happy to have something other than her handsome, undead boss to think about, Sharon answered their call.

She did her best that night, working the bar with a professional zeal that surprised even her. Jonathan kept watch, silent, still as the grave, from the corner of the room. All night long she felt his eyes on her, and the patient quiet of his demeanor.

In keeping with the tavern's name, it was approaching dawn when the last customer departed. Marcus left the kitchen to sweep the floor while she cleaned the tables and finally the maple counter, polishing the smooth dark wood to a rich gleam. Ah, the joy of being back where she belonged. She was happy behind the bar of a well-kept tavern.

Still, bartending was marking time, a way to earn money—that's all. She was good at it, but it didn't satisfy her deepest desire, the need to make music. For years Sharon had yearned to find a place in the entertainment business. She'd been singing in the small clubs in Los Angeles when her father had taken ill, and with no one else to take care of him, she'd put her dreams on hold. Now, months had passed since she'd last performed.

Poverty and trouble had stolen her music.

"Ms. Colson." Jonathan came upon her so quietly she startled, dropping the rag. He watched silently as she recovered her composure. "You did well tonight. I have no objection to continuing your employment." He eyed the cloth on the counter then turned his intense blue stare back to her. "What are your feelings about it?"

*Shaken, but not deterred.* With a boldness she didn't feel, she stared back at him. "I still want the job."

Just for an instant a smile slipped across his lips. "Very well." He inclined his head and pointed to the hallway leading to his office. "That way, please."

She preceded him inside. It wasn't a large room. Jonathan's desk took up the bulk of the space in the middle. In one corner was a brown leather couch, easily six feet long, with a colorful striped blanket spread across the back. A mini-fridge sat next to it, doubling as a lamp stand. For a moment Sharon speculated as to what kind of drinks her future boss kept cold. Little plastic bags from the local blood bank, perhaps?

Heart pounding, she eyed the couch and waited. Jonathan followed her gaze, hesitated and apparently decided against the intimacy that would afford. He directed her toward the top of the desk with an elegant wave of his hand. "If you will sit there, Ms. Colson?"

She did as he instructed, facing him as he approached. For the first time since that brief caress in the bar, he touched her, placed his hands on her shoulders. She'd thought they'd be cold, clammy, but there was perceptible warmth to them. She felt it through the thin material of her blouse. Not warm enough to be human, but there.

For a moment he studied her face. "You're sure about this?"

Sharon closed her eyes and steeled herself for the sensation of his mouth on her throat, the prick of his teeth piercing the skin. She hated pain. She was the kind to insist on local anesthesia before allowing a splinter to be removed.

"Just do it," she whispered.

He did nothing. She opened her eyes and his blue stare bore into her. "You must look into my eyes and let me into your mind, Ms. Colson. I'll take the fear from you and make it easy."

*He wanted to link minds with her?* Panicked, Sharon shook her head. "No, not that. I won't let you do that."

He frowned. "You don't understand. I can block what you feel and make it pleasurable for you. Without a mind link there will be pain."

"I do understand. I expect the pain. I can deal with it."

He shook his head, displeasure infusing his expression. "I'm not in the habit of causing discomfort. I enjoy feeding..." One long finger traced the vein in her neck. "I'd rather you enjoyed it too."

"It isn't important I enjoy it," she said, her voice desperate. How could she make him understand? Sharon took a deep and ragged breath. "There was a man I met who did a mind link to me once." She shuddered at the memory.

It had been...awful. She'd felt like she'd been ripped apart and afterward...no, she couldn't think about the "afterward".

"It was months before I could think straight. I'm willing to let you feed off me but I can't let you into my mind."

He let go of her and stepped back, disappointment in his face. "I'm very sorry, Ms. Colson. I would have enjoyed having you here...but the role of a companion requires my being able to touch your mind."

Moving to the door, he gestured to her. "Come with me to the bar and I'll pay you for this evening."

"No!" Nervously, she licked her lips. "Please...can't you make an exception? I really need this job."

Frustration showed in his face. "Exception to what? To the mark, no, it's too dangerous for me to have unmarked humans here."

Desperation made her bold. "What about the link, then? Just this once? Maybe when I know you better, can trust you more...I promise I'll let you into my mind."

For a moment she thought he was going to give up and send her on her way. Then she caught the hungry look in his eyes and the way he studied her neck with a possessive stare. She could tell he wanted this, to taste her, to mark her as his own. He might not ever take her blood again, but he wanted it this time.

The way he licked his lips told her that he wanted it badly enough to forego his principles and bleed her without the mind link.

"As you wish then." The vampire returned to her and took a different hold with his hands. One moved to the back of her head, the other to just below her shoulder blades. It was a more intimate embrace than the one he'd taken before—and more secure. His hand caressed her hair, pulling it back, baring her neck. It might have been the prelude to a kiss.

Piercing blue eyes stared into hers. "I will hold you to that promise," he whispered.

His arms tightened and he moved so fast that she didn't have a chance to say anything, couldn't have pulled away if she wanted to. Held in his vise-like grip, sharp pain stabbed through her as his fangs plunged into her neck, unerringly locating the artery. A burning sensation followed as strong lips drew the blood through the tiny holes.

*Pain.* It was worse than she'd imagined. Sharon wanted to cry out but couldn't. He held her so close she was crushed into his chest. His throat rippled as he swallowed and she felt his heartbeat stutter then pick up pace, growing faster, almost matching the furious pounding of hers.

She hadn't expected him to take so much, just a few swallows, a taste. This was more like a banquet for him as he guzzled her life's blood. Fear grew inside her...fear of what she'd promised, of what she would become at his hands.

A vampire and companion linked minds—it was "required". How was she ever going to deal with that?

As her body chilled, his grew warmer. A rushing noise sounded in her ears and dizziness encompassed her. She grew weak and faint and still he took from her until she began to wonder if he intended to stop feeding at all, or if her life would end in his arms.

*Was she going to die?*

A gasp of fear and pain escaped her. Abruptly his mouth stopped moving and simply rested. He breathed heavily, the heat of his breath scorching her throat. The worst of the pain ended at the same time but the relief from it put tears into her eyes.

His grip eased, and he allowed her to pull back, but only briefly. "A moment," he whispered. "I must stop the flow." He pressed down, covering the aching places where his teeth had pierced the skin.

She felt the touch of his tongue move across the holes, sealing them but not healing. He gently licked the rest of her neck, cleaning the remaining blood and soothing her skin. The throbbing abated under his tender ministrations.

The vampire drew back, a warm possessive glow in his eyes. An odd thought slid into her mind. *He was a neat eater.* Only the smallest amount of blood lingered at the corners of his mouth, and as she watched his flitting tongue removed even that evidence.

Deep amusement laced his voice when he spoke. "Congratulations, Ms. Colson. You have the job."

She tried to stand, but her legs wouldn't hold. Instantly Jonathan caught her up in his arms and carried her to the couch. He laid her down gently, pulling the blanket from the back to cover her as a shudder passed through her body. Pulling her into his arms, he stroked her cheek with a gentle hand. "I took too much, I think. Without the mind link it's hard to know when to stop and your taste was…unique."

He left her side and opened the mini-fridge. Moments later he pressed an open bottle of sweet juice into her hands. With odd gentleness he forced her to drink it in slow sips. When she finished, he continued to hold her until the shaking ended and her breathing became regular again.

It was so disturbing. He'd hurt her, fed off of her to the point of danger. Yet now he was protective. For the first time in as long as she could remember, she felt safe, almost cherished.

"Ms. Colson…"

His feeding from her had been more intimate than the most romantic encounter she'd known. "D-d-don't you think you should be using my f-f-first name?"

Amusement tugged at the corners of his mouth. "Very well, Sharon. And you should call me Jonathan." He pressed two fingers against the marks on her neck then shifted his hand to lift her chin so her gaze met his. His eyes glowed with ice blue intensity.

"I take you as my companion, to serve me as long as you bear my mark. In return you have my protection and support, from this time on." His deep voice intoned the words carefully. It sounded like an oath.

Unexpectedly she felt tears slip from her eyes. "Do I say something?" Her voice trembled.

His was calm and soothing. "It isn't necessary." One finger pulled a tear from her cheek and he raised it to his eyes, studied it. "It's been a long time since I've hurt anyone, much less someone like you. I'll not do it again nor will I risk losing you to my hunger. Next time we'll do this with the mind link."

Horror at reliving the last few moments gripped her, and she felt faint again. "Next time? Does there have to be a next time?"

Jonathan actually did smile, brief, enigmatic, then it was gone. "Not until you are ready to accept my mental touch, Sharon. That I promise."

For a moment Jonathan paused, cocked his head as if he heard a cock crow, or sensed the movement of the earth, the approach of dawn. "I must seek my rest. You can stay here until you feel well enough to return to your home. I'll send Marcus in to take care of you." He released her, rose and moved to the door, every movement as graceful as a dancer's. Pausing, he regarded her once more with his intense blue eyes. "I'll see you this evening."

After he'd gone, Sharon touched the twin pinprick scars he'd left in her neck, marking her as his. His what, she wondered. Time would tell.

\* \* \* \* \*

Jonathan rushed about his underground lair and prepared for his daytime rest. He'd stayed too long upstairs…only a few minutes were left until dawn. Once the sun had risen, the lethargy pulling at his limbs and mind would be complete and he'd be unable to stay awake no matter where he was.

All things considered, he'd rather be in bed. The last time he'd slept on the floor, his back had ached for hours the next night, until Marcus had taken pity on him and allowed him a quick nip from a vein.

Companion blood was the best cure-all for his kind. It was the main reason a nightwalker kept human companions, for their rich, nourishing and plentiful blood with its curative powers.

Jonathan smiled. Now he had a second companion, and a woman at that. Before too long he'd be able to feed from her as he did Marcus, at least once a week, maybe more. Do more than feed, if things worked out as they should.

*She was pretty, too.* At that thought his smile morphed into a grin. Fangs digging into his lower lip, Jonathan pulled off his clothes and tugged on a pair of loose-fitting sweatpants. Tightening the elastic waistband to fit snugly at his trim waist, he reveled again in the wonderful inventions of this age.

Kind of silly, really. Three hundred years of life and it was the practical improvements in clothing that he found the most interesting—zippers, snaps and elastic. And Velcro! Jonathan shook his head at that marvel, the invention of the space age. It was nearly as wonderful as commercially available blood products, refrigeration and electric lamps that made the night as bright as day.

Or the invention of the stereo, glorious sound at the push of a button, music stored on tiny thin discs, movies, where he could see the world bathed in daylight, and glorious sunsets... In spite of his rush, Jonathan paused to consider how lucky he was to live in this time. Truthfully, there wasn't much about this age he didn't appreciate.

Paying heed to long-engrained habits in spite of his haste, Jonathan put away his clothes, checking carefully for blood spots and thankfully finding none. Marcus was efficient at getting out stains but always gave Jonathan a hard time if he didn't soak them in cold water.

Sometimes his male companion was as fussy as...well, best not to complete that thought. Marcus couldn't always read his mind, but the last time the big man had overheard an undiplomatic comment, Jonathan had wound up doing his own laundry for weeks.

He grimaced. Sometimes even a nightwalker had to keep quiet to keep the peace.

Slipping into bed, Jonathan pulled up the blanket to cover his bare chest then leaned over to turn out the bedside lamp. He paused and stared at the colorful birds on the cut-glass lampshade, his smile fading for an instant. The shade bore images of the birds of sunlight, hummingbirds and wrens, birds belonging to a daytime he hadn't seen in centuries. When he turned off the lamp, they faded into the blackness of his lair.

*Dawn was coming.* He could feel it, the inexorable turn of the earth—the inevitable rising of the sun, bringing with it an irresistible lassitude that took dominion over his body. But before he gave into it—before he closed his eyes for his daylight sleep—there was one last thing he wanted to do.

He reached out with his mind, pushed it to his office, where he'd left Sharon. Using his mental powers he checked on her, seeing how she fared in the aftermath of his taking her first blood and leaving his mark.

*First blood.* No one else had ever fed from her before.

Jonathan grinned. They always said a person never forgot their first nightwalker—if they were permitted to keep the memory. Sharon would never forget this night.

The way she made him feel, he wondered if he would.

She had a strong mental shield. He couldn't see her thoughts but could read her body. The initial shock from the blood loss and pain had faded. She was weak, but he could tell that she'd recover. Jonathan could feel traces of Marcus in the room, but not his presence. The man must have just left, leaving her a bottle of water to rehydrate her.

Her heart still pounded, as frantic as that of the small bird he'd once held in his hand as a child. She lay on the couch and he could feel her exhaustion from the strain of the night. He could also feel her worry over what she'd agreed to. There was a story there, why she'd been so determined to become his companion, not knowing what it would mean.

Perhaps he should have told her everything up front, but if he had she might've changed her mind. All evening he'd watched her, knowing he'd taste her by morning and enjoying the anticipation. He'd deliberately skipped supper this evening in his eagerness, and had gone to her hungry.

In retrospect, that hadn't been the best idea. He'd taken far too much for first blood. Jonathan sighed. Even after three hundred years he still couldn't reliably control his thirst. The only good thing was that the large blood loss would speed up the process and, physically, Sharon would be a full companion in a couple of weeks.

Mentally...that was going to take longer. Her strong aversion to mind linking wasn't going to make it easy for her to fit into his life. Again he regretted the pain he'd caused her. If she'd allowed him to show her pleasure she'd be eager to feed him again—as it was she'd be wary of him for some time.

But she would come around, eventually. He'd noticed the sidelong glances she'd thrown his way and the pretty blush that crept across her cheeks at times. Both had led him to think she'd liked what she saw of him.

It was quite possible Sharon found him as attractive as he found her and that happy thought sent thrills to regions of his body long dormant.

He sighed. It really had been a long time since he'd had a woman companion.

As he listened with his mental touch, Sharon's body quieted, her heart slowing and breath evening. She was falling asleep. For a moment he toyed with slipping upstairs and collecting her, bringing her down to his lair to share his bed. She needed warmth and comfort, and he'd be happy to provide both.

*More than happy*, his body told him in no uncertain terms.

No, better not. Dawn was too close and besides, she needed time to get used to him, to learn to trust him. If there was one thing he had plenty of, it was time. A few days more sleeping alone wouldn't be so bad. After all, he'd been sleeping alone for many, many years, since the death of...

Some of Jonathan's euphoria faded. No, he wouldn't think of her now. Better that his last thoughts tonight be of Sharon, not another woman, long dead, long mourned. The time of mourning was over—the time of morning, almost here.

Jonathan buried his head into his pillow and waited the sun's rise. *Sharon*. Sweet Sharon. Her blood still flavored the inside of his mouth—her taste lingered on his tongue, warm, rich. Sweetness. In German, *Süsse. Meine Süsse, my sweetness.*

In his last moments of consciousness he lapsed into his native language, learned growing up in the farmlands near Vienna. *Willkommen, meine Süsse. Willkommen zu meiner Welt.*

Outside, the sun slipped over the eastern mountains, and safe in his lair Jonathan fell asleep, fangs still exposed by his smile.

## Chapter Two

*Glasses, ice, limes, lemon twists, olives.* Going though her pre-opening checklist, Sharon took inventory behind the bar. The bottles along the back shelf—bourbon, gin, scotch, vodka, vermouth, and various liqueurs. A rack under the counter held a nice collection of red wines and in the cooler were cream, juices, white wine and sparkling water.

Jonathan might quench his thirst from a body instead of a bottle, but he kept a well-stocked bar. Sharon leaned back on her heels in satisfaction. She hadn't found anything missing.

It was early evening. She'd awakened an hour ago, having spent the day napping on the big leather couch in Jonathan's office. Marcus had wanted to drive her home, but she'd insisted she felt more comfortable where she was. She was certainly more comfortable than she had been the day before, sleeping on the beach. Since she was up, she'd decided to get to work even though the inn wasn't open yet.

The slightest exhale of breath alerted her that she was no longer alone. Still crouched before the mini-fridge, she looked up. Jonathan stared at her from over the dark wood counter. "Good evening, Sharon."

Awkwardly she made it to her feet, fighting the dizziness that had plagued her all day. She clutched the bar for stability. "Good evening, Jonathan."

His watchful face told her that he'd noticed. He said nothing, but a look of dark concern crossed his handsome features. The bar wasn't as dimly lit as it had been last night—she could see his face more clearly. He looked older than she'd thought, maybe all of thirty-something. Of course she knew that was an illusion, he was far older.

In addition to the striking blue eyes, his nose was long and straight, cheekbones high in his thin face. It was the kind of face that would look good with a tan. Too bad sunbathing was out of the question.

He was dressed more formally than the night before, a navy blazer over a turtleneck two shades darker than his light blue eyes. She leaned further over the bar to check out the rest. Navy slacks and black loafers completed the picture. For a dead guy, he sure wore clothes well. He could be a model, could have stepped from the pages of *GQ*. Or maybe she should've said Nosferatu Quarterly.

She glanced back up to see him finishing a similar examination of her own clothing. He raised a quizzical eyebrow.

*Uh, oh.*

"It seems that I've seen this before." He indicated her maroon skirt and flowered blouse, which not only constituted her best job-hunting outfit, but at the moment was her only choice of clothing. "Is your wardrobe so restricted you must wear the same things two days in a row?"

Sharon flushed. She was going to have to explain eventually. "I didn't go home today to change."

A look of concern crossed his face. "Were you feeling that bad? Marcus would've driven you."

*It wasn't going to get any easier, out with it.* "I couldn't go home. I'm locked out." In the silence, she inhaled deeply. "I owe too much rent, the landlord padlocked me out of my room. All my stuff is in there...he's threatened to sell it if I didn't get a job." She glanced down at her wrinkled blouse. There were still a couple of telltale bloodstains near the collar that she hadn't been able to wash out in the sink of the ladies room. "This is all I have at the moment."

Her vampire boss' face cleared. "No wonder you were desperate enough to allow my mark." Humor laced his voice. "How much do you owe?" She told him and he whistled softly. "Good thing you have me. Let's go."

"Where?"

"To pay off your landlord and get your belongings, of course. We have an hour before opening." Jonathan reached across the bar, seized her elbow and led her forth to stand in front of him.

"I can't ask you to do that…"

He touched the marks on her neck and the gentleness of the gesture surprised her. "That's what these are about, Sharon. You, your debts, everything about you, are my business now. I take care of what is mine."

His hand on her arm, still warm as it had been last night, gave her an odd sense of security. Jonathan led the way to the kitchen and grabbed a set of keys out of a drawer near the back door. "Marcus, Sharon and I are taking the van. You keep an eye on things here and have Amber open up if we aren't back in time."

The big man nodded and returned to the pots on the stove. Sharon's stomach gurgled happily in anticipation. Something smelled wonderful.

Once in the attached garage, she eyed the late-model minivan. The back windows were blacked out and heavy dark curtains hung just behind the front seats. It looked like the entire back part of the van could be made as lightproof as a coffin.

Fangs flashing, Jonathan grinned at her observant look. "It comes in handy for long trips."

*All Night Inn*

Like the bar, the garage had double doors that opened to the outside. Between the two, the interior could be kept totally free from unwanted sunlight. He punched in a code near the kitchen door. First the inner door to the garage went up, then the outer one, revealing the early evening twilight. At his gesture, Sharon climbed into the passenger side of the van while Jonathan strapped himself into the driver's seat.

Her amusement at his fastening his seat belt must have been obvious. "I believe in safety!" he responded with an injured air.

Jonathan started the van and pulled out of the garage with a practiced manner.

Sharon watched him, surprised at his expertise. "I didn't think that vampires could drive," she said.

Jonathan shot her a disapproving look. "I'd prefer that you didn't use the 'v' word. If you must use a name for my kind, we prefer 'nightwalker' to anything else. To call me a vampire is the same as calling a shapeshifter a 'werewolf' or a spellcaster a 'witch' or 'warlock'. You wouldn't want to do that, would you?"

Amused, Sharon wondered at how political correctness seemed to have reached the supernatural community. Possibly things weren't going to be that different in Jonathan's world, after all.

Meanwhile, the "nightwalker" continued to speak. "And of course I can drive. I live in this century, every bit as much as I did in the ones before. Living in California, I have to be able to get around. I even have a license."

A license. She had a comical vision of Jonathan in line at the DMV—assuming he could find one that took nighttime appointments. "What did you put down for your birth date?"

Before making the next curve, he pulled a wallet from his pants and tossed it to her. "See for yourself."

Inside was an appallingly thick sheaf of money, a collection of gold cards, an ATM card from the local bank and his license. Sharon stared at the image. It just wasn't fair—even his driver's license picture looked good. The year of birth made him thirty-five. "Thirty-five?" she asked in disbelief.

He shrugged. "Give or take a few hundred years."

"How did you…" she indicated the contents of the wallet, the proof of identity cards.

"I live a modest and legal life. Mostly. But given who I am, it pays to know those who aren't completely legitimate."

"You mean these are fake."

A low sound that might have been a chuckle emerged from him. "They're as real as they need to be."

They lapsed into silence. From the inn, they drove through the woods down the narrow way leading to the three-mile stretch of highway into Los Niños.

Sharon's feet ached in remembrance as the van whipped down the steep hill. With no car and no money for a taxi, she'd walked this way yesterday to apply for the job she now had. Unconsciously she ran her fingers along the telltale scars on her neck.

Within minutes they were on the main highway. On one side was the coastal forest, redwood trees mixed with lesser giants, brush, grass—a hodge-podge of vegetation. She'd heard stories in town about loose assemblages of folks who lived in that forest, individuals who weren't quite people. She'd been warned that you didn't stroll the woods at night around Los Niños if you wanted to avoid meeting the were— that is, the "shapeshifter" crowd.

It had taken most of her courage to hike along the road to the bar last night and even now she watched the deep and spooky woods with a quiet worry.

On the other side of the road was a short drop to the shoreline. Sandy beaches alternated with scrub and rock. She rolled down the window, heard the distant breaking waves on the shore and smelled the ocean, the scent of saltwater and drying seaweed on the cool evening breeze. This was one of the things she'd liked about the town, its proximity to the sea.

Odd. Today the air smelled even sweeter than usual. Perhaps her near-death experience from Jonathan's bite made everything more poignant.

She directed him through town until they pulled up to the rooming house that two days ago she'd called home, until she'd returned from job hunting to find a padlock on the door to her room. Together they stared at the ramshackle exterior, the peeling paint and warped steps leading to the front door.

A look of disgust crossed the nightwalker's face. "You really live here?" he muttered.

Sharon shrugged. "After my car broke down, I couldn't find anyplace less expensive and I didn't have much money."

After climbing out of the van, Jonathan took Sharon's shoulders and turned her toward him. "Let me do the talking."

The door opened and instinctively Sharon stepped closer to her companion. Isaac Jones, generally called Jonesy, was short, fat, balding and owner of the worst flophouse on the California coast. He also wasn't happy to see them. Or, to be precise, he wasn't happy to see Jonathan. The proprietor of the All Night Inn was well known around town and the man broke out in a profound sweat on discovering a real bloodsucker at his doorstep.

Jonathan gave Jonesy his best glare. "I understand you have this woman's possessions?"

The portly gentleman waved his hands about, as if to chase away some flying insect. "Hey, she was a week behind in her rent. I gave her a chance to catch up. Even offered to let her do chores around here to make up."

Sharon swallowed her sudden nausea. Jonesy's idea of "chores" hadn't appealed to her at all. She took a quick glance at her tall, silent companion. There were a lot of things worse than getting nibbled on.

Jonathan must have guessed what the landlord had in mind—and he didn't like it. Sharon watched him examine the man the way he might a mosquito he'd caught horning in on his territory. His voice turned dark and deadly. "I assume if we pay what she owes, you will give her access to her room?"

"Sure, sure." Jonesy glanced at Sharon and she self-consciously put her hand to the scars on her neck. "Since she's working for you now, it might be good if she paid up until the end of the month." He eyed the thick wallet now in Jonathan's hand and licked his lips. "In advance."

Jonathan pulled out the exact amount Sharon owed and held it up. "Let us into the room. Now." The tone in his voice was all the threat needed. Jonesy grabbed the money and fled the doorway to get the key.

\* \* \* \* \*

Jonathan watched as she inventoried her possessions, clearly happy to see them all there. Apparently the odious creature who'd allowed them entry hadn't yet walked off with any of her pathetically few valuables. He observed her closely, noticed how carefully she moved, how weak she still was and an unaccustomed feeling of regret struck him.

He'd taken too much, far too much for first blood. If only she'd allowed the link, he would've known when she'd first begun to feel faint and could have stopped before she'd been so drained.

Maybe. Maybe he would've stopped. As he'd known, her possession of mental powers had flavored what he'd taken. Pleasure mixed with his shame at the recalled taste. Liquid nectar her blood had been, far too precious in flavor and strength for the brutish feeding he'd done. It had been many years since he'd forced a human to his lips.

Wryly, he considered that Sebastian would be amused that he'd resorted to an unlinked feeding. His prince had always said he was soft for a nightwalker.

Still, no point in recriminations, it was over with. She was marked, his now. It might be some time until he could savor Sharon's blood again but he had time to squander.

*Time.* Plenty of time. More time than anyone should have. Time to bring her to his side, convince her of her role as his companion and establish a proper link. Time, so that the next feeding he took from her would be as he preferred, gentle, pleasurable — possibly even more than that.

He smiled at that sweet thought. It really had been a long time since he'd had a female companion. Marcus was a good friend, but Jonathan didn't desire sex with a man and he never made love to clients.

But Sharon was a woman, and a beautiful one at that. Jonathan contemplated her form with pleasure.

The room lights were brighter than he preferred, but it allowed him to admire her appearance. Medium height she was, a little on the thin side, and even weakened her movements were graceful for an ordinary human. The skin of her face and arms was smooth and freckled, sun-kissed, an interesting contrast to his own paleness.

Her eyes were an odd shade, not blue or green, but somewhere in between, changeable. When she was frightened or angry, they were green, but as she'd calmed in his arms last night they'd appeared the deepest blue.

Jonathan smiled, remembering her eyes and the warmth of her in his arms, the satisfaction of feeling her acceptance of the mark. Only her tears had marred that moment, tears from the pain he'd caused, and he made a quick vow to never cause her pain again.

Sharon finished her inventory and picked up her hairbrush, applying it vigorously to the unruly waves that cascaded down her back. The color was a yellow he hadn't seen in a long time, the color of…of what? Not deep as gold or pale as corn silk, the color of…

He felt his eyes widen and his heart speed up. He had it—the color of the sun in the sky at midday, on his father's farm when he was a boy.

Her hair brought sunlight back into his life.

That was a thought too disturbing for the moment. Jonathan looked away from her and turned his attention to the room about them, her "home". Walking around, he regarded the interior with mounting revulsion.

The faded and peeling wallpaper wasn't bad enough, nor the shredded curtains that barely hid a cracked windowpane. There were also the patched bedspread and stained sheets, and the dingy bathroom with its fractured sink and rusty faucets.

But it was the bowed ceiling over the bed—that was the final straw! He examined it closely and decided how much force it would take before the ceiling would collapse on the bed's occupant. A 3.2 earthquake would do it. Or maybe just a heavy truck rumbling down the street outside.

*That creature is charging how much for this place—and they call me a monster!*

Jonathan cleared his throat to get her attention. "There's a room at the inn, where Marcus lived when we first moved here. It isn't elaborate, just a bed and small bath. I wasn't going to suggest it before…" he indicated the condition of the room, "…but it doesn't appear you're terribly spoiled."

Sharon paused, a fresh outfit from the closet in her hand. "You're saying I can stay there?" He had to suppress a smile—she could barely keep the excitement from her voice.

Jonathan watched an unidentifiable insect crawl along the bedspread and disappear between the sheets. "I think I may insist. Pack your stuff."

\* \* \* \* \*

The inn was busy when they returned. Marcus was dashing around the kitchen as they entered, one of his helpers washing dishes in the corner. Jonathan sped Sharon through, into the main room and to the bar, where a woman stood in her place.

Jonathan performed the introductions. "Amber, this is Sharon, our new bartender. Sharon, Amber's our waitress."

Both women sized each other up, neither apparently liking what they saw. Sharon eyed Amber's neck. "I thought you said no one could work here without your mark?"

Amber smiled, her teeth showing, pointed and sharp. Not a pleased expression. "Why did you bother with a norm, Jonathan? I told you Ralph wanted the job."

Suppressing his amusement over their instant animosity, Jonathan regarded them both. "First of all, Amber, it is my decision who I hire to work here. Ms. Colson had the necessary experience and was willing to take my mark. She works here. *Permanently*."

He'd emphasized that last and noticed Sharon startled. Well, she'd understand soon enough.

He turned his attention to Sharon. "As for why Amber works here without my mark, I said 'normal' humans couldn't work here without it. Amber isn't exactly normal."

Amber reached out one hand, which elongated and grew fearsome claws. She pointed them at Sharon's face, just beyond reach. Again with the unpleasant smile. "I'm what you'd call a 'werewolf', human."

Sharon stared at the claws and the woman bearing them, her eyes wide. This was what he'd meant about 'similar types' frequenting his bar and why she needed to be marked. Jonathan watched, ready to intercede but waiting to see how his new companion dealt with Amber's threat.

Apparently remembering her lesson from earlier, she quickly interjected. "I think you mean a 'shapeshifter', don't you?" Jonathan had to resist the urge to laugh as she tried to look innocent, while Amber snarled a suggestion that would have been physically impossible for even him to accomplish.

"Enough!" Jonathan exerted control, still suppressing his amusement. "Amber, Sharon. Both of you work here—both of you learn to work together." He grabbed Amber's arm, the one with the elongated claws, held it tight as the hand returned to normal shape. Pulling her from behind the bar, he left it to Sharon's dominion. "Sharon carries my mark, belongs to me. Remember that!"

Startled, Amber stared at him and then back at Sharon, who immediately picked up the orders the waitress had left unfilled. A speculative expression came over her face. "So, mighty Jon has found someone he cares about?"

Jonathan's amusement fled. His hold on her arm became tighter, and as strong as she was, Amber looked uncomfortable in his grip. "Behave yourself, furry one. I haven't selected a new companion in many, many years. Yes, I like her and I want to keep her." He watched Sharon effortlessly pass the newly filled glasses to the customers waiting at the bar. "Besides, she's good at her job."

Pulling away, Amber glanced at Sharon then back at him. "So am I, Jon. Don't forget that."

She paused before going to wait on the tables. "Oh, speaking of jobs, your prince called."

*Oh, no.* The last thing he wanted tonight was to deal with Sebastian. Jonathan suppressed a groan. "Did he leave a message?"

"He wants you to call him back. Something about Los Angeles." Amber smiled greedily. "You know, Jon, Ralph and I are interested in the inn. If you needed to sell it, or just wanted a manager…"

"The inn is not for sale, Amber, nor do I intend to leave it in hands other than mine. I'll deal with Sebastian as I always do." He paused beside Sharon, who was now making light conversation with one of the inn regulars. She glanced at him and her smile lightened his mood again.

"I'll be back," he told her. "I just need to make a phone call in the office."

\* \* \* \* \*

In the quiet moments at the bar, Sharon watched her employer as he circled the room, greeted the regulars and welcomed the newcomers. He spent time with each of them, his movements graceful, his quiet, sensual voice with its odd European accent easy to pick out over the crowd. She wondered why she felt so oddly drawn to him, why her body thrummed at his every ice blue look. It couldn't be just because he was handsome or because he'd rescued her from that awful boarding house. He wasn't alive, not really. How could she think of him that way — as a man?

After a while he finished his rounds and disappeared toward the office and she found it easier to keep her mind on her work. An hour passed, and a young woman came in. Blonde with a capital B, bright, perky and very pleased with herself, she first approached Amber. The shapeshifter sent her over to Sharon with a gleeful grin.

"Hi, there! I'm Kimberly." Her bright pink lipstick-colored mouth looked like it should be cracking gum. "I'm here to see Jon."

Sharon wondered what to do, but before she could respond, Marcus came out of the kitchen, carrying a plate with her dinner, an open-faced roast-beef sandwich with gravy and mashed potatoes. Sharon's mouth watered at the sight, her stomach growling in happy anticipation.

Marcus greeted the newcomer with a fond smile. "Hi, Kim, how are you?"

"Fine! Is Jon around? I was supposed to meet him last night, but he called and cancelled." Her bright pink lips pursed into a delightful pout and for a moment Sharon lost her appetite.

Marcus chuckled, nodded toward the hallway to the office. "He's waiting for you. Go on back." They watched her progress through the room.

"What's all that about?" Sharon asked.

"Dinner," was Marcus's short reply.

"He asked her to dinner?" The girl was a complete nitwit, what would Jonathan have in common with someone like her?

Marcus slid her a knowing look. "Not dinner with her—from her. Jon has a whole stable of people like Kim. He calls them clients. One of them will come in every evening, just about this time, except when he's feeding from one of us." He shook his head. "Didn't Jonathan tell you anything?"

Sharon suppressed a wave of queasiness. Jonathan fed from that bimbo? It made her feel…icky. "No." Her voice was hesitant. "I guess there wasn't time."

He patted her shoulder in a brotherly fashion. "Don't worry, Shari, you'll get used to it. Remember, you and I, we're special to him. The others, they're just nutrition." With that he returned to the kitchen.

Somehow she didn't feel better, and the knowing smirk on Amber's face didn't help either. She dug into her dinner but her appetite for it was gone.

An hour passed before she saw any further sign of "Kimberly". The hallway door opened and the tall, enigmatic Jonathan escorted the young lady through the door. If Kim had looked giddy before, she was positively loopy now. The little tart was leaning all over him, all but undressing the man with her hands.

Jonathan was in an exceptionally good mood, smiling as he led her over to the bar. "Some orange juice for the lady, Sharon, on the house." After placing Kim on a stool, he took her hand and kissed it gently. "In a couple of weeks," he told her before gliding through the kitchen door.

The little blonde gazed after him, rapture in her eyes. Sharon placed the tall glass in front of her and had to tap the girl's shoulder to get her attention.

Now that the object of her distraction was gone, Kimberly seemed able to focus on other things. The blonde took in Sharon behind the bar, and her eyes grew wide as she noticed the marks. "Oh, you're one of his people." A heartfelt sigh escaped her. "You're so lucky. He's just the dreamiest, isn't he?"

Dreamy wasn't the word Sharon would have used. Tall, dark and dangerous was more like it. Sharon indicated the glass. "Drink up, you need to replace those fluids."

Obediently Kimberly lifted the glass and sipped, her eyes still unfocused, mind completely somewhere else. She swallowed and a vacant smile crossed her lips.

If this was the result of allowing Jonathan to control her mind, Sharon wanted no part of it. She wasn't going to let anyone turn her into a blood-filled vegetable.

* * * * *

Sharon was finishing the cleanup when Jonathan reappeared. He checked through the receipts and turned to her. "A good night, particularly for a Sunday."

Still bothered by his dietary habits, she nodded briefly.

Jonathan waited a moment then lifted one elegant eyebrow. "Don't you want to see your room?"

Now he had her attention. Sharon put her hand to her forehead and groaned. "Oh no, I forgot. My stuff's still in the van…" She was so tired. The last thing she wanted to do was haul boxes and unpack.

A hint of a smile enlivened Jonathan's face. One hand grabbed her elbow and he pulled her from behind the bar until she stood next to him. "Come."

She let him lead her through the kitchen into a long, narrow hallway. Halfway down the hall he stopped outside a closed door, turned the knob and thrust it open, then reached inside for the wall switch, flipping it to bathe the interior with a soft, warm light.

"Oh!" Delighted, Sharon stepped inside. It wasn't large, but the multitude of furnishings made it seem cozy rather than crowded. A large armchair filled one corner, a comfortable-looking double bed, the other. Warm colors, reds and burgundy, dominated the bedspread, pillows and the shades of the lamps. Through a doorway at the end of the room she could see a small but serviceable bathroom, a sink and the edge of a large tub.

The whole place was clean and smelled of lemon furniture polish and bathroom cleaner. Dazed by the sight of comfort and unexpected luxury, Sharon wandered further in and, with surprise, noticed her favorite books placed on the top shelf of the small bookcase near the armchair. She looked in the bathroom and saw her toothbrush in a cup next to the sink, toothpaste beside it. Her hairbrush had found a home on the dresser under a small hanging mirror, and when she looked in the freestanding wardrobe, her clothes were hung and a hook held her nightgown.

Astonished, she turned back to Jonathan. "You cleaned this place up and unpacked my things."

"You were busy at the bar. I knew you'd be tired." He threw out his hands, a rueful expression on his handsome face. "And I didn't want you to see the place as it was. It needed fixing up."

The thoughtfulness of the gesture made her forget everything, including her resentment over "Kimberly". Without another thought she threw her arms around him and hugged him close, burying her face in his chest.

"Thank you, Jonathan."

For an instant he stood still then his own hands slipped around her back, caressing it gently. She raised her head to smile into his face. He hesitated then dipped to meet her lips in a gentle kiss.

It started gentle but didn't stay that way. The way his mouth moved elicited similar action on the part of hers and soon they were tightly clenched together. For an instant she forgot who he was and instead reveled in the feel of him, a warm man with arms hard as steel and lips soft as a dream. The usual thrill he gave her evolved into a full-grown passion and she warmed clear to the core.

Jonathan pulled her closer and she could feel all of him, his well-built chest, narrow waist and powerful erection.

*Erection?* Shock freezing her arousal, Sharon opened her eyes and took in his blue ones, molten, alive with passion.

She dropped her half of the embrace, pushed at him and he let her go, allowed her to back away from him. With a shaky voice she pointed to the unexpected bulge below his waist. "What is that?"

For a moment he seemed torn between anger and amusement. Hints of both emotions flitted across his face. He glanced down at his crotch and then at her. "'That' is a very reasonable reaction to my kissing a lovely and desirable woman. Surely this isn't the first time you've encountered a man in this condition."

She felt the blush as if it were a living thing, creeping over her face, leaving her hot and flushed. "Yes, of course I have. But you're, you're a vam...I mean a nightwalker."

Amusement won and his lips twitched into a smile. "I see. You have some misconceptions about my kind. Let me see if I can clear this one up at least." His voice became melodramatic, his unusual European accent more distinct — a very bad imitation of Bela Lugosi.

"I am not, as they say in the movies 'an animated corpse, an undead creature of the night'. I am indeed different, but I'm not dead." He gave a rueful glance at his still impressive arousal and chuckled. "It might be easier if I was. But you needn't fear. I may be a monster, but I'm one with principles. As far as 'that' is concerned, it's not something you need to worry about. Nothing will happen without your explicit permission."

He indicated the welcome-looking bed. "Dawn is coming. There is your resting place, *meine Süsse*. I must seek mine." He headed for the door. "Sweet dreams, Sharon."

She was still shaking as she sat down. Sure, she'd entertained erotic thoughts about Jonathan when she'd thought it wasn't possible, but now... He'd made it clear he wasn't going to force her into a bed, but he was ready, willing and able to go there.

*All Night Inn*

From the way he kissed, it could even be an interesting place to be.

# Chapter Three

It was late afternoon when Jonathan rose from his daytime sleep. Odd dreams had disturbed his slumber, dreams of sunshine hair across his chest and warm lips on his neck. Irritated at his interrupted sleep, he splashed water on his face at the sink in his bathroom before going upstairs to the main floor.

It was time for his usual wake-up drink, an icy glass of serum from the refrigerator in the kitchen, just the thing to take the edge off his hunger. It would be some time before one of his clients would come by to furnish him with nourishment.

Too bad he didn't have a companion he could snack on when he woke up. His old friend, Natasha, didn't have to satisfy her thirst with commercial blood products. But then Natasha had a bloodmate while he had…well, now he had Sharon.

Who knew, maybe someday… Jonathan shook his head at that pleasant but very unlikely scenario. He might be able to coax Sharon into his bed, but he couldn't expect her to ever be his bloodmate. Reluctantly, he pushed aside that appealing thought.

When he was a normal man, he used to have sweetened mead with breakfast, but he couldn't drink it now, one of the few things he regretted since his changeover, his intolerance for certain foods. Serum just wasn't as tasty as mead.

But the blood of his sunshine-haired Sharon tasted as good.

His route to the kitchen took him past his companion's new home. Jonathan stopped outside her room, intending only a brief check on her. Heightening his senses, he smelled her special aroma and heard the gentle sounds of her movements through the door.

Deep satisfaction filled him. Last night she'd been so pleased with the space he'd created for her she'd even forgotten her fear of him. He remembered her warmth within his arms, the press of her lips on his. Delicately, he let his tongue slide along his lips, picking up a little of her lingering taste, and his body tightened again. It really had been a long time since he'd had a woman companion, someone he could release his sensual side with.

Pushing his mind out, he tested the barrier around hers, a glancing stroke like a caress. So far she'd shown no awareness of his exploring mental touch. Someday he hoped not to feel the barrier at all, to instead find her mind open to his, welcoming. Soon, maybe.

*But not yet.* The mental wall was still there, solid as ever. Regretfully, Jonathan let the mind touch recede, allowed his other senses to tell him about her. He looked within her body, judging the volume and flow of the precious fluid within her veins. Her blood pressure felt normal, her body having already replaced the volume he'd taken just two days before.

It was still too soon to take more from her unless he really needed it, particularly since she would refuse his mind link at the same time. But she was no longer weak. That was good. As his companion her self-healing had improved already, and before too long she'd be creating more blood than she needed, blood he could take whenever he desired.

Music imposed on his ears from the radio he'd placed near her bed and over it rose the sound of water running into a deep basin. *Ah, she was taking advantage of the tub.* Without warning the image of a nude Sharon came to him, her sunshine hair piled on top of her head. A gentle splashing sound was followed by a low, feminine groan of contentment.

Jonathan imagined her lithe body immersed in the tub, the warm water lapping at the full breasts he'd felt pressed to him last night, and without warning his body quickened in response. For a brief moment he imagined slipping into the tub behind her, feeling her water-slicked skin beneath his hands, lips and tongue, his hard length sliding along her backside.

Jonathan shook his head in dismay. *This was a really bad idea.* No telling what he was going to do if he didn't stop eavesdropping. He started to turn from the door when a new song began on the radio, an old love ballad and one of his favorites. Unable to drag himself away, he lingered by the door and heightened his hearing to catch the sultry sound of the singer's voice, speaking of true love lost and found again.

But a second voice joined the recorded one, singing in unison. Jonathan listened in amazement as Sharon sang along with the radio, the combined sound pure liquid melody, twin voices soaring together through the first verse.

At the chorus the second voice broke away from the melody and switched into a descant a third higher, crystalline pure notes floating effortlessly above the main line of the song. It was as if heaven itself spoke, an angelic solo. Jonathan closed his eyes and allowed the paired voices to feed his soul.

The chorus ended and the second verse began. Now Sharon didn't sing with the singer but in harmony, the new notes flowing around the melody, filling holes in the composition he'd never noticed before. With the addition of her voice the song became whole, perfection. For a moment he wondered if the composer could've imagined this particular song sung as a duet, if it hadn't been originally written for two voices, so perfect was the result.

Moreover, there was a quality difference in her voice. In the descant, with the high notes, there'd been an immaculate property, pure and unsullied, but in her lower register Sharon had another sound—not innocent but warmer, all fur and fire. Sexy—that was the word for it and it made his arousal even harder to ignore.

The song ended, Sharon's voice finishing in a low trill that left him shaking, and Jonathan leaned against the door. His new companion had a *voice*. When he'd hired her, Sharon had mentioned she could sing. She sounded pleasant enough when she spoke, but nothing had prepared him for her impromptu bathtime concert.

He'd always loved the sensual arts, music, dance and theater, and had explored them fully in his long, long life. One of the advantages of immortality was the opportunity to enjoy such things to his heart's content.

Sharon said she could play the guitar but had sold hers sometime ago. If she could play anywhere as well as she could sing... Jonathan didn't own a guitar at the moment— he'd gotten rid of most of his instruments years ago, when he'd left Los Angeles.

But the music shop in town should still be open and he could get there before they closed if he hurried. Sporting a happy grin, Jonathan sped down the hallway.

\* \* \* \* \*

Sharon paused in the inn's kitchen doorway. Long metal countertops alternated with wooden cutting boards, cabinets below stocked with pans and bowls, the ones above with dishes and food staples. A refrigerator with clear glass doors took up one corner. Like the rest of the inn, no windows broke the long outside walls. All light came from the overhead fixtures.

Marcus stood beside the polished steel industrial-sized cook top, the sizzle of frying meat emanating from the copper skillet in front of him. Amber sat on a stool at the counter nearby, apparently having an early dinner. Her hand held a partially consumed hamburger bun.

The cook grinned a welcome. "You must have slept well, Sharon. Jon get you settled in last night?"

She nodded, subduing the thought of how unsettling her boss' goodnight kiss had been. The aroma from the pan made her mouth water and she pointed to it. "Is that breakfast?"

Marcus applied a spatula to the patties sizzling in the pan. "Sure is. I'm under strict orders to feed you up, get a little fat on those bones of yours."

Amber broke her silence. "Yeah. 'All the better to eat you with.' Can't have Jon's favorite dish fading away, can we?" She took another bite of her burger and juice dripped onto her plate. Bright red juice.

"Like your burger rare, Amber?" Sharon slid onto the stool near her.

In response, the shapeshifter pulled back on the bun revealing the raw ground beef tucked inside. "Yeah, real rare." She took another bite and juice dribbled down her chin. "Cooking spoils the taste," she muttered, her mouth stuffed.

Sharon's stomach twisted and she indicated the pan. "If one of those is for me, I prefer it well-done."

At the stove, Marcus snorted and lifted one of the cooked patties onto another bun. "Not to worry, Shari. Well-done it is."

Sharon took her first bite, and warm, rich meat flavor filled her mouth. She nodded her thanks at Marcus. "Just the way I like it." The next bite was even better. "Well, I'm not going to starve."

Chuckling, Marcus finished preparing his own breakfast and sat beside her. "Nope, we'll feed you right. Jon takes good care of his people." He gave Amber a long hard look. "All of his people."

She grimaced. "Yeah, yeah, I know. He's already given me the lecture, 'play nice or else'." Finishing her burger tartar, she jumped up and went to the refrigerator. Mischief blossomed in her golden eyes as she pulled out a closed pitcher from the top shelf. Sharon could see a straw-colored liquid sloshing about inside. "Want some juice, Shari?"

The look on Amber's face was far too innocent. Leaning over to Marcus, Sharon asked, "I don't know—do I?"

He shot a disgusted look at the shapeshifter. "Put that back, Amber. Jon's told you and now I'm going to say it. Stop teasing Shari or I'll not allow you to eat in this kitchen again. If you want to be helpful, get the real juice." Her eyes wide with surprise, Amber did as he asked and soon Sharon had a glass of orange juice in front of her. The shapeshifter pulled her stool further away and settled on it, glowering over the rebuke.

Sharon's curiosity got the better of her. "So what was in the other container?"

Marcus chewed well on the bite in his mouth and swallowed. "Blood serum—the clear liquid left after the red blood cells have been removed. Jon discovered that his kind tolerates it well and it makes a nice change from whole blood. Thirst quenching without being too filling."

Admiration crossed his face. "Jon has a whole set of recipes that use blood products. He's a genius when it comes to this sort of thing. Drinking the pre-packaged stuff can get boring, so he jazzes it up. That's one of the reasons this place is so popular—nightwalkers come from all over for Jon's concoctions."

Sharon couldn't resist. "You mean he's a gourmet blood-drinker."

Somehow Marcus didn't realize she was kidding and the look he gave her was frankly admiring. "That's a very good way to put it. 'A gourmet.' Jon enjoys taking blood straight from the source, but he likes a bit of variety now and then as well."

"Yeah, variety. That's why he doesn't just stick to his companion's blood but takes from the norms around here." Sarcasm colored Amber's voice. "Most of his kind either keep a stable of companions or hunt for their supper. Jon is the only nightwalker I know who keeps only one or two companions and never hunts."

"He doesn't hunt, not at all?" Somehow that made Sharon like him better, to know her boss wasn't a predator. "Why doesn't he have more companions?"

Marcus shrugged. "He's funny that way. I think Jon likes being what he is to a point, but all things being equal, he just wants to live a normal life."

Sharon glanced at the pitcher of serum in the refrigerator and Marcus chuckled. "Well, as normal as he can get," he amended. "Jon is picky about the folks he lives with."

Amber's snort earned her a glare from the cook. "Listen, just because he doesn't like shapeshifter blood..." Marcus began.

That caught Sharon's attention. "He doesn't? Why?"

"He says it makes him jumpy, like drinking too much caffeine."

Now it was Sharon's turn to giggle. With a disgusted look Amber left the kitchen. After she was gone, Marcus patted Sharon's hand. "Don't let her get you riled, Sharon.

She's just upset that Jon didn't give her boyfriend your position. She was hoping that if Ralph got a steady job he'd start thinking seriously of settling down." He ate some of his own burger. "I think she wants to get married and start a family."

Sharon shook her head. Amber wanted to marry her shapeshifter boyfriend and have baby shapeshifters? What did you call a baby shapeshifter anyway—a cub or a kitten?

Amused, she stared at the cook. "So what about you? Do you mind my being here?"

"Are you kidding?" Marcus's grin took over his face. "I couldn't be happier! With you around we might actually be able to go places. Having an extra companion means Jon can take more trips since he can draw on both of us when he gets hungry."

The man sat back with a satisfied smile. "Plus he won't be so reliant on me. I may even be able to take a vacation and I've been dying to go to Las Vegas. I've heard there's this Star Trek thing that is just terrific."

\* \* \* \* \*

On weeknights the inn closed early, at three a.m. It had been fairly uneventful, a few regulars in addition to Jon's special guest, another young woman just as giggly as last night's. Sharon told herself she didn't care. Why should she mind whom he fed off of?

The rich dark wood of the bar took on a new sheen under her rubbing. Sharon took her time with the cleanup, no need to hurry. Her room would be waiting for her when she was done.

Her room, her own private sanctuary—almost comfortable to a fault. She still couldn't believe how Jonathan had gone to all that trouble to fix it up for her. The bed had felt like heaven after the lumpy mattress at Jonesy's flophouse, and the linens smelled of clean soap and flowers. And that tub!

Sharon closed her eyes at the luxury of it, a bathtub big enough to soak in. A thrill of anticipation shot through her. She'd bathed when she'd awakened, but repeating the experience was high on her list of activities for the rest of the night.

"Sharon."

With a start she jerked up, stared into Jonathan's unblinking blue eyes. He certainly could move quietly — she never seemed to hear his approach! A small smile flitted across his lips. "My apologies. I startled you."

She nodded, her heart still pounding. "Do you have to sneak up on me?"

His smile returned and stayed, the corners of his lips lifting upward, almost revealing his fangs. "An occupational habit. It comes in handy sometimes to not have someone know you're approaching."

"Why? You don't hunt, at least that's what Marcus tells me."

Jonathan shrugged, a graceful, elegant gesture. "I don't need to hunt these days. That doesn't mean that I haven't or that I won't have to again. All things are subject to change with time." His eyes bored into her and she felt something push at her mind, not a probe like before but more like a brushing caress from the back of a hand.

Shaken, she stepped back. "What are you doing?"

He cocked his head to one side. "Saying 'hello' in my own way. Don't worry, Sharon, it won't hurt you. I'll never hurt you."

Without thinking, she lifted her hand to the scars on her neck. Those had certainly hurt.

His smile disappeared at the gesture and bleakness grew in his eyes. "I should never have taken you without the mind link, it was selfish and stupid. You'll never forgive me." Bitterness laced his words.

She took her hand from the small scars, letting it rest on the bar. "No, it's all right. I didn't give you any choice. I made you mark me that way."

Jonathan leaned forward and grabbed her hand, eyes blazing, face intense. Again she felt the brush against her mental shield, much stronger this time. She felt his strength, the force of his mind as it wrapped around hers. Inside, her shield felt as fragile as a soap bubble and abruptly she realized he was holding back and could pop through with the slightest bit more pressure.

"It was your desire to avoid linking with me, but my choice to give into it. I didn't need your cooperation, Sharon."

Then the pressure was gone. Her heart raced as he leaned back, his eyes bleak again. A sardonic smile settled across his mouth. "And now I've given you another good reason to fear me. You thought you could keep me out and now realize you cannot." He dropped her hand and crossed his arms, glaring down at the counter.

"I'm usually much better behaved than this — somehow you make me forget myself. Or you make me remember myself, I can't decide which."

Confused, she shook her head. "I don't understand."

"Usually I don't have a problem controlling my actions. But somehow when I'm with you, I can't resist...I guess you'd call it showing off. You could say you bring out the monster in me."

Sharon hesitated. "And yet, even though you could have forced the link, you didn't. You left it my choice." She looked up at him. "I don't see you as a monster, Jon."

He stared at her, eyebrows raised. "You don't?" Again his face held that fleeting smile. "I'm glad to hear that." Her hand still lay on the counter and with a swift grab he recaptured it. "Come with me."

"Where?" she asked as he pulled her to the end of the counter to stand beside him.

Mischief blossomed in his eyes. "To my lair, of course." One finger traced the marks on her neck. "I have something to show you."

"But I'm not done cleaning up."

His swift glance took in the almost nonexistent clutter behind the bar. "Nothing here that can't wait until tomorrow."

"But…" One arm was around her now, guiding her to the hallway door at the back of the room.

The possessiveness of Jon's arm reminded her of his kiss the night before and the way he'd responded. *Oh no, no way she was going to bed with a vamp…er, nightwalker!* "No, Jon, stop." Sharon dug in her heels and grabbed a chair.

She was no match for his strength, but still he halted, eyes narrowed in concern. "What is it, Sharon? Surely you don't think I'm going to hurt you."

"Hurt me, no. But…" Again she tried to pull away from the arm around her waist and this time he released her, allowed her to move beyond his reach.

"But what?"

"Jon, that kiss last night…you don't think I want to…" Her voice trailed off as his expression of concern faded into an offended glare.

"I said last night I had principles, Sharon. Believe that if nothing else about me." Again Jonathan moved faster than she could expect, one hand on her shoulder, the other on her neck, two fingers covering the marks. The warmth of his hands contrasted with the icy blue of his stare. "You have trusted me with your life. Please trust that I'll not compromise your virtue."

Her virtue had been compromised long ago, but this didn't seem the right time to bring that up. Shame heated her cheeks. "I...I do trust you."

The hand on her neck fell away. For a moment he just stared into her face. Perhaps reading her soul? Something glittered in his eyes, a hint of the desire she'd seen there the night before. Then it was gone and all she saw was amusement. The hand on her shoulder moved to grab her own. "So come, my trusting companion, and see what I have for you downstairs."

\* \* \* \* \*

Sharon gaped at Jonathan's self-described "lair". The entire basement of the inn had been transformed for his personal use. Engrossed, she wandered around the large open room, examining it carefully, her host's wave giving her explicit permission to snoop.

The place reminded her of a stage set for *1001 Arabian Nights*. Thick oriental carpets hid the floor, with large pillows in rich red, purple and blue scattered on top. Several divans and cushioned chairs were upholstered in the same richly colored fabric. Heavy drapes covered the walls, absorbing all sound. Even the ceiling had been covered in some sort of acoustical tile.

A separate bathroom was in one corner and when she looked inside she found it held a toilet, a sink without a mirror, a separate shower and a huge sunken tub.

Did nightwalkers really need a toilet? Perhaps he kept it for visitors.

Unable to resist poking about more, she brushed aside one set of curtains. Behind them dwelled a big screen TV, with VCR, laserdisc and DVD players. Sharon smiled at the sight. *Arabian Nights meets Western Civilization.* Movie titles in the shelves sprang at her: *Dracula, Nosferatu, Interview with a Vampire, Waterworld.*

She turned to see Jonathan watching her, an amused look in his eyes. "*Waterworld?*"

His lips twitched. "Great movie sunsets."

"Oh…" She let the curtain drop. A curtained alcove drew her eye and under the nightwalker's steady gaze she moved to it, glancing back with a questioning look. Again his gesture gave her permission to pull the curtain back. For a moment, her breath caught in her throat. *This must be where he hides his coffin.* She screwed up her courage and pulled the sheer draperies aside.

Revealed was a king-sized cherrywood four-poster bed made up with white satin sheets, huge fluffy pillows, and a heavy down comforter. She turned to him. "You sleep in a bed?"

The amusement threatening to burst finally did and Jonathan's loud peals of laughter filled the room to be absorbed by the surrounding draperies. Helpless with mirth, he collapsed on one of the divans. "You really expected I used a coffin?" he got out between guffaws.

Embarrassed, she turned back to the alcove. Matching tables flanked the bed. One held a charming stained glass lamp, the shade decorated with the images of small, brightly colored birds. The lamp was a twin to the one by her own bed.

She pointed to it. "You decorated my room with stuff from yours."

His merriment died away and he sat back up, leaning on one hand. "I wanted you to be comfortable and it was a little late for shopping. If you like, we can order new things for you."

He really was a sweetheart for a vam…for a nightwalker. Touched, she shook her head. "I'm fine with what you've done," and his smile rewarded her.

She wasn't sure why she was there. "Thanks for showing me around, but I should go." Sharon made for the door.

Instantly his humor disappeared. Before she could take a step he stood beside her, holding her elbow. "I haven't shown you my gift, yet," he said softly. With a single push she was compelled to sit on the divan. Once she was seated, he released her and disappeared behind the draperies of the bed. When he returned he carried a bulky object, which he gently placed in her lap.

Astonished, she recognized it as a guitar case and excitement filled her as she unlatched it and lifted the lid. Inside was a six-string acoustic guitar, its wood gleaming in the soft lighting. Reverently she pulled it from the case, examined the label inside the body. It read "Martin". Her mouth dried in wonder. "A Martin? You have a Martin guitar?"

It was a beautiful instrument, top-of-the-line and in perfect condition. With trembling fingers she plucked the strings, testing the sound. One string gave her trouble and she adjusted the key at the top of the neck to bring it into tune. Satisfied, she strummed one gentle chord, then another. The rich mellow tone filled the room, warming her clear to her soul.

Jonathan sat near her on the divan, watching. When she raised her head to gaze into his eyes, she had tears in her own. "It's beautiful, Jonathan."

His smile lit his face like the sun on the sea. "It's yours, Sharon. A gift. All I ask is your promise to play for me and sing like you did today."

"Today? You heard me?" She could almost swear that a blush sped across his face, then she remembered where she'd been at the time and it was her turn to blush.

"Yes. I heard. Please, sing something for me."

She worked through a few chords, trying to find the ones she wanted. A song came to mind, not her favorite but it would do. At first tentatively, then with more and more confidence, she strummed the opening bars.

*"In the morning when I wake up*
*With my lover's arms around me*
*And the warmth that is surrounding*
*Causes both of us to stay,*

*Abed with my own darling*
*The love between us lingers*
*And between us passion flickers*
*As we greet the brand new day.*

*Loving in the morning*
*With the dawning sun around us*
*And the gentle light revealing*
*Deepening passion in our eyes.*

*Loving in the morning*
*As the warmth of day approaches*
*As the sun climbs ever higher*
*In the ever blueing sky."*

Silence greeted her as the last chord faded. Jonathan's expression was enigmatic. He leaned forward, hands steepled together. "An interesting choice. Does it mean that much to you, to have a man who can make love during the day?"

Her cheeks burned at his implication. "It's only a song."

Jonathan leaned back, one eyebrow raised. "Of course it is. I'd not heard it before."

She rested her fingers against the smooth body of the guitar. "I wrote it a long time ago."

"A songwriter as well as a performer. You are very talented. Still, I prefer 'Subterranean Homesick Blues'."

That made her laugh. "The Dylan song? Do you know it?"

"Know it?" Jon's mouth twitched. "I met him in the sixties and helped him write it." One hand reached for the guitar. "Let me show you."

For an hour they took turns playing the guitar and singing. Jon's voice was a non-descript baritone, but he had plenty of breath control and perfect pitch. In addition, his guitar playing was excellent. He could hit every progression without hesitation, make difficult bar chords without breaking a sweat.

Sharon watched in admiration. "You really know how to play!"

"You do something for long enough and you get pretty good at it." Jon strummed a few chords. "I've been playing one of these for over a hundred years."

He hit a final chord and handed her the guitar. "It's getting close to dawn."

She replaced it in the case. "I guess I should get back to my room."

"You don't have to." He indicated the corner where the bed lay hidden. "I wouldn't mind if you stayed."

Sharon's latent awareness of him blossomed for a moment, but she ruthlessly stamped it down. She'd told herself she wasn't interested in going to bed with him, and she was going to stick with that. "No, Jon. I don't think so."

For a moment he watched her, and she wondered if he knew how attracted to him she was. "It's all right, Sharon. You don't have to do anything you don't want to do. I do want one thing, though."

Apprehension filled her. Maybe he did know. "What's that?"

"Would you mind calling me 'Jonathan' and not 'Jon'? I know everyone else uses the nickname, but somehow I'd rather you didn't."

Relieved, she managed a smile and headed to the door that led upstairs. "All right. Good night, Jonathan."

His return smile was small. "You mean 'good morning'. Rest well, Sharon."

## Chapter Four

Sharon sat at the kitchen counter, nursing a cup of coffee. Three weeks had passed since she'd come here, taken Jonathan's mark, become his companion/bartender. She stretched out her arms, relieving a nagging cramp in her back.

Three weeks. Three weeks of sleeping the morning away, waking in the early to late afternoon. Staying up all night with Jonathan meant her sleeping hours were the same as his. She hadn't seen the sunrise since the morning before she took his mark.

Three weeks free from worry about money or where her next meal was coming from. Jonathan paid all the bills and Marcus did all the cooking. Sharon helped Marcus and Amber with the shopping and helped keep the inn clean. She worked the bar at night until closing and after that spent the rest of the time until dawn in Jonathan's room, playing guitar, singing or watching movies.

In the past few weeks Jonathan and Marcus had run her through the special drink book kept in a drawer under the bar until she was familiar with the kinds of beverages and snacks that the All Night Inn's more unusual customers demanded.

Shapeshifters fell into two categories. The down-to-earth variety liked beer and tequila, same as most motorcycle-riding toughs. But instead of putting out pretzels or nuts for them to nibble on, they preferred liver-flavored snacks. The first time she'd come across the bag in the kitchen, she'd asked if Jonathan had a dog.

More sophisticated shapeshifters liked martinis made with just a hint of wolfsbane in the vermouth, which gave a new meaning to the expression "one man's poison". They wouldn't eat the liver-flavored snacks but preferred fish nibbles instead. Sharon kept a box of kitty crunchies behind the bar.

Spellcasters preferred rich red wine spiced with garlic powder. They tended to lead lonely lives.

So far no nightwalkers had come to call, but she'd learned to make a mean variant on the humble screwdriver, with serum instead of orange juice.

She'd seen for herself why her boss wouldn't let a normal human work at the Inn without his mark. It was two weeks ago, after midnight, when the "norms", as Amber insisted on calling them, had cleared out and several small groups of "specials" had come in. As was predictable, they kept Amber busy with orders for beer, raw hamburgers and puppy chow.

Another group, from San Francisco, were clearly spellcasters, for once traveling together. Sharon figured the reek from that corner would keep Jonathan away, but it turned out that the supposed garlic aversion was another one of those myths, at least as far as this nightwalker was concerned. He spent a long time with them, joking and laughing. She avoided them. Their random mental casting felt like fingernails on a chalkboard against her mental shield.

One shapeshifter, a young male, his light-brown hair in a ponytail and eyes like golden pools, made the barstool in front of Sharon his home for the evening. Swigging his beer directly from the bottle, he nibbled the puppy chow and grinned his pointed teeth at her whenever she passed by. It wasn't the first time a customer had developed a "crush" on her. Sharon simply ignored him.

But the young man wasn't to be deterred. On one of her passes, he grabbed her elbow in a vise-like grip and dragged her so close she could smell his dog-like breath. One fingernail elongated and traced the outline of her cheek. "Come on, sweet thing. You're too pretty to be stuck back there all alone. Why don't you come keep Chucky company?"

Sharon tried to break his hold on her to no effect. She knew shapeshifters were strong. Amber routinely lifted close to two hundred pounds when they were moving cases of beverages in the walk-in cooler. This man's hand might as well have been welded to her arm.

"Is there a problem here?" Having approached from behind with his usual silent skill, Jonathan's voice could have cut glass. Chucky's head swiveled to meet the nightwalker's steady gaze. Sharon glanced up at her boss, saw his eyes emitting a deep ice blue glow.

Full of life and beer, Chucky apparently felt up to the challenge. "Just inviting the lady for a drink, Jon. What's it to you?" His voice was defiant.

Without a word, the nightwalker reached over to Sharon's neck and pulled back the hair she'd decided to wear down for the evening, revealing the marks on her neck. He'd then snarled, for once baring his upper canines, the sharp fangs a clear threat. Heart pounding, Sharon stared at the furious nightwalker.

Chucky's grasp fell away immediately and his hands went up, placating. "Okay, Jon, sorry for the misunderstanding. I didn't know she was yours."

For a moment, the nightwalker continued to glare at the shapeshifter, tensed to spring. Then just as quickly, the threat was gone, and the genial innkeeper was back. Jonathan gestured to Chucky's beer. "Perhaps you'd be more comfortable at a table." His voice was solicitous, as if all he had in mind was the well-being of his guest.

Chuck took the hint, grabbed his bottle and moved to join his friends. Jonathan turned to regard Sharon, a hint of humor in his eyes. He reached over to pull up the lock of hair that had covered her neck and firmly placed it behind her ear, leaving the marks visible. "On nights like tonight, you might want to consider your hairstyle more carefully, *meine Süsse*."

After that there were no further issues. No one messed with her, not even normal people, once they saw the marks. Sharon made a point to put up her hair when on duty behind the bar.

Now it was late afternoon. She took another sip of her coffee. Warm, rich, delicious, par for the course for the All Night Inn.

The rest of the crew wandered in—Marcus with sacks of food, followed by Amber. Sharon went to help them, pulled the heavy boxes of bottled drinks into the walk-in cooler, plus a box marked "medical supplies"—blood—"keep refrigerated". She stored it on the shelf with the other mixers.

Once they were done, they sat down together. Oddly enough, in spite of their differences, Amber and Marcus had begun to feel like family to Sharon. The shapeshifter had overcome the worse of her resentment at Sharon's taking the bartender job and while her fellow companion hadn't shared many details of his life, he took a big brother attitude Sharon found comforting. It had been years since her own brother had shown interest in anything but his own pleasure, leaving just her father as family. She'd never felt that comfortable around other people.

In this group of equally unlikely souls, she felt at home.

The kitchen phone rang. Marcus went for it then stopped and stared at the buttons at the base. "It's Jon's private line, the one downstairs." Abruptly the ring silenced in mid-cadence. The light stayed on for a moment then blinked out.

The worried look on Marcus's face intensified. The idle chatter he and Amber were indulging in continued, but it was subdued. An odd disquiet began to build in Sharon as she watched them. Something was wrong and they knew it.

After a moment, Jonathan entered the kitchen, holding one of the bar glasses, an amber liquid sloshing around in the bottom. His other hand held a tall thin bottle. These he placed on the countertop near Sharon. Without a word he went to the refrigerator, pulled the serum container and returned to the rest of his paraphernalia.

A disapproving scowl turned down the corners of Marcus's mouth. "It's a little early in the evening for this, isn't it?"

Jonathan ignored him. "Come, Sharon. I have a recipe for you." His voice sounded strained, as if the vocal cords had been tightened with a tuning key.

Apprehensive, she moved to his side. "What's in the glass?"

He spared her a humorless smile. "We start with tequila, Cuervo Gold, of course." He held up the glass and eyed it, swirled the contents. "About two ounces, I think. Next we add the serum." He poured the straw-colored fluid into the glass, stopping about an inch from the top. "Then just a little grenadine. You want to pour it down the inside…" He dribbled the heavy liquid into the glass and a deep rosy blush spread through the contents.

Sharon interrupted. "I know how to make a Tequila Sunrise, Jonathan. And you used far too much tequila. The customer will be drunk before he knows it."

A totally mirthless laugh escaped him. "This isn't a Sunrise, Sharon, this is new. I call it a Los Niños Sunset." He took a sip, closed his eyes in a satisfied grimace. "Yes, perfect."

Marcus looked guarded. "What's up, Jon?"

Another deep sip took a quarter of the beverage out of the glass. Jonathan's eyes became mellow, the blue softer under the alcoholic influence. "What's up? Oh, not much. We have company coming."

"Company?" The guarded look of her fellow companion deepened to one of worry.

"Yes. Family." He drew the word out and gazed into the sunset hue of the drink as if certain an answer dwelled there.

He blinked as if another thought had occurred to him. Jonathan turned his steady gaze to Sharon, eyed her simple shirt and jeans. "I'm thinking, perhaps you could perform tonight rather than tend bar. You have a dress, I believe, red, simple..." His attention shifted to her bosom with something resembling a leer. "...low-necked. I'd appreciate it if you would wear it."

Sharon felt her cheeks redden. Jonathan returned to his drink, sipped it again. "We must all be prepared to make a good impression on my...siblings."

The odd note in his voice surprised her. Obviously he had mixed feelings for these family members. "Your siblings—brothers and sisters? They're still alive?" Were they also vampires?

"Siblings—those who were made by my maker. One was once my best friend, a brother to me. The other..." He took another deep sip. His lips twisted ironically. "I guess she's more of a niece than a sister."

He didn't explain further. Rising to his feet, a death grip on the glass holding his 'sunset', Jonathan moved to the hallway door. A smile moved his lips, a smile that went nowhere near his eyes, which remained aloof, untouched by emotion. Dead eyes.

"I'll be in my office if you need me."

In the silence he left behind, Sharon stared at the others, the pale quiet of both Amber and Marcus. Finally Marcus gave a great sigh. "We'll need a bartender. Amber, why don't you see if Ralph is free?"

A brief smile brightened the shapeshifter's face. She moved to the telephone and they listened as she spoke to her boyfriend.

Sharon almost smiled. At least someone was happy.

When she returned, Marcus rapped on the table, demanding their attention. "It's going to be an interesting evening. Amber, you remember them from before. With Ralph here, no one will bother you and they don't ever mess with me." He turned to Sharon. "Sebastian will be, well, Sebastian, but the 'niece' Jon mentioned will likely want to play games. Don't let her. Just be yourself, but keep her and whatever character she has with her at arm's length. Jon won't let them hurt you, but he can't control how they behave around you."

"What do you mean 'play games'?"

He grimaced. "You'll see when the time comes."

\* \* \* \* \*

The red dress was actually a little large on her. Nervously, Sharon smoothed the fabric over her thighs. Worry over her father and the lack of good eating had taken its toll on her since last she'd worn it. She'd lost weight in the past few months and Marcus' cooking hadn't put it back on yet. The looseness of the dress showed how at risk she'd been before Jonathan had taken her in. Still, the deep red color looked good on her, and the low neckline really did show off her breasts.

*I owe it to him* was her thought. Jonathan wanted her to impress his "family". Therefore, that's what she would do.

In trepidation, she put up her hair, keeping the mark on her neck fully visible. A touch of makeup overcame her anxious pallor. Finally she felt ready to face—whatever it was she was going to face this evening.

She picked up the Martin's case and left her room.

\* \* \* \* \*

The crowd was light. About half a dozen tables held some of the furry crowd, and a couple of spellcasters held court in their usual corner. Two very pretty young women, a blonde and a brunette—norms no doubt out for a daring adventure—had decided to sit at the bar.

Ralph held Sharon's normal position. Tall, broad-shouldered and heavily muscled, the male shapeshifter was the sexiest guy Sharon had ever met—outside of her boss, that is. The only symptom he showed of his kind was a significant furriness around the time of the full moon.

She'd never seen him in full change. Right now the worst was a heaviness to his eyebrows and some dark black hair on the back of his hands. Sharon was grateful for the black long-sleeved turtleneck he wore. No telling how much hair he had on his arms and neck.

The cute young things at the bar cast admiring glances at him and giggled to each other.

Sharon tucked the guitar case behind the bar and moved to the other end of the long counter, near Ralph. The once-over he gave her as she took possession of one of the empty bar stools did nothing to relieve her worries about the evening. His wolfish grin made her feel like a juicy steak in a red dress.

He drew her a diet cola and set it on the polished wooden surface in front of her. "Wow! Darlin', you look good enough to eat."

Amber wandered over and swatted him on the head with her order pad. Hard—Sharon heard the force of it. Turning, Ralph rubbed his scalp with an injured air. "What did I say, lamb chop? I was just complimenting the lady."

Both hands went on Amber's hips and her eyes narrowed dangerously. "Don't 'lamb chop' me. I could hear that mating cry a mile away. Sharon is Jon's meat."

His lips twitched. "Don't tell me you're jealous, lamb chop?" He glanced at Sharon, a mischievous look in his eyes. "Given his liquid diet isn't she more his 'cup of tea' than meat? Anyway, you're the dish I'm most partial to."

Amber spared a glance at the girls at the other end of the bar, still openly admiring the bartender, and sniffed loudly. "See to it you remember that. The moon's full tomorrow night and it could be feast—or famine if you aren't careful. I need two garlic specials for the pair in the corner."

He obliged her and watched as she carried the drinks away, his eyes firmly on her backside as she swayed under the drink tray. "Woof," was his under-the-breath comment.

A young man came through the front door, blinking a little at the dimness inside the tavern. He was slightly built, thin, cute in a non-Charles Atlas kind of way, with a shock of light blond hair, and doe-like brown eyes. His face lit up when he spied Ralph. "Is he in?" he asked eagerly.

With a grin Ralph nodded and jerked his head toward the back door. "Sure thing, Kevin. Go on back. He's expecting you."

Must be Jonathan's dinner date. It was the first time Sharon had seen a male on the menu, but she supposed the nightwalker was an equal-opportunity nibbler.

The young man blushed as he made his way across the room and disappeared into the hallway leading to Jonathan's office.

Ralph smirked. "Marcus will be in for some fun tonight."

"Marcus?" Sharon was confused. "Why?"

His grin widened. "You don't know? Kevin is Marcus' main squeeze. After feeding Jonathan, he'll be a little lightheaded but totally in the mood, if you know what I mean."

Sharon's jaw dropped. "Marcus is gay?" Come to think of it, he never did have any lady friends come by…

"Yeah, sure." Ralph gazed into her face. "That doesn't bother you, does it?"

After being around shapeshifters, nightwalkers and spellcasters, why would something as normal as homosexuality bother her? "No, of course not. I'm just surprised he didn't tell me."

"Marcus is a kinda private guy. Keeps his affairs to himself. Plus, he's old-fashioned, comes from a time when you didn't shout out your sexual preference to all of the world."

"Comes from a time?" Sharon scoffed. Marcus wasn't much older than she was. "He's only about thirty."

Now Ralph's wolfish grin really took hold. "Don't judge by appearances, especially with parafolk. He's older than you think. You should have a talk with him, Shari. Or talk to Jonathan. There's a lot you don't know about being a companion."

The norms at the end of the bar called for his attention and dutifully Ralph went to answer them, leaving Sharon with a deep-seated unease. As she watched Ralph flirt lightly with the girls, she thought about what he'd said.

For the first time she wondered if Marcus wasn't a lot older than he appeared. When they'd talked about music, he'd gone on and on about the music of the Beatles and the Beach Boys. She'd thought he was just a fan of the oldies, but maybe there was another explanation.

An explanation having to do with Jonathan and what it meant to be a companion.

\* \* \* \* \*

She felt them before she saw them. The edge of her mind detected tendrils of awareness, exploring, sensing out the room before they came through the door. Two of them out there, the signature on the mental probes reflecting their gender, one male, one extremely female. Not like spellcaster magic, more like what she felt... Sharon turned her gaze to the door.

It was more like what she felt when Jonathan tried to merge with her. Nightwalkers — Jonathan's family was here. Surprised panic rose within her.

"They're here." She wasn't aware she'd spoken aloud but Ralph's attention was caught. He shot a glance at her and then stared at the door. His habitual grin faded as he returned his gaze to Sharon. Her face must have showed some of her fear.

He cleared his throat, made a small growling noise. Amber's head swiveled around, instantly alert. She moved towards them, stopping at a couple of tables to mutter to the occupants, a low whisper that sounded much like the growling noise Ralph had made. Shapeshifter heads nodded and they put aside their beer for the moment.

Suddenly Sharon realized why so much of the crowd tonight was from the furry set. Amber and Ralph must have stacked the house in Jonathan's favor. For a moment, she wondered just how much serious trouble they were in if Jonathan's family required her formidable boss to retain a personal guard.

Another probe came through the door, powerful, demanding. It hit at her shield and slid around it, just as intense as Jonathan's could be. The male nightwalker was clearly curious about her. She shuddered as she remembered that anyone as powerful as Jonathan would be able to crush her shield. Only his forbearance had left her alone and who knew what this other male would want.

Ralph leaned against the countertop in front of Sharon. "Why don't you go get Jon? He should be here to greet them."

"He's with someone..." She'd never been to his office when one of his 'clients' was with him.

The shapeshifter glanced at the clock. "It's been a half hour, he should be done by now."

Reluctantly, she pulled herself off the stool. Another insistent probe from outside drove away the last of her hesitancy and hurried her into the direction of the office.

The knob was cool in her hand. She listened at the door but there wasn't anything to hear through the wood. A passing thought urged her to head for her room, pack her things and make a run for it.

Make a run for it? In the middle of the woods outside Los Niños, without a car, without anywhere to go?

Besides, this was her home now. Her place, and she wasn't going to be driven away from it. Resolutely she turned the handle and stepped inside, closing the door behind her.

The office interior was dimly lit. The desk lamp was off, the one on the table next to the couch turned to its lowest setting. It gently illuminated the scene there.

Kevin lay supine on the couch, stretched out fully. Jonathan knelt on the floor next to him, his head buried in the young man's neck. The light fell across Kevin's face, revealing his mouth open, eyes shut. His long eyelashes fluttered and a sweet moan emerged from his lips. Whatever he was feeling, it wasn't the pain Sharon had experienced.

One of Kevin's hands rested in Jonathan's—the other played with his quite evident hard-on.

*Oh, my god...* Frozen in shock, Sharon stared at the pair. No wonder Jonathan's clients were so happy to see him.

Jonathan raised his head and twisted to stare at her. His eyes glowed with an inner light, ice blue and piercing. Blood stained his mouth, bright against the pallor of his skin. His tongue flicked out and licked his lips, cleaning them, moving gingerly around the razor-sharp fangs.

Blood dribbled from the narrow pinpricks in Kevin's neck. His eyes flickered open, "Jon?" His voice was soft, confused.

It broke the spell. Sharon reached for the doorknob behind her. Instantly Jonathan bent his head and closed the holes, sealing them. One hand rested on Kevin's head. "Sleep," he whispered, his voice a deep, hypnotic compulsion.

Before she could open the door more than a crack he was there, slamming it shut. He rested his hands on either side of her, forcing her back against the door, trapping her in the room—and inside his arms.

His spotless white shirt was open, revealing the hard planes of his chest. Freshly fed, he radiated warmth, all six feet of sexy male that he was. His breathing was rapid, his breath hot against her face. He moved closer. There couldn't have been more than an inch between them.

Sharon could have melted from the heat he gave off.

His ice blue stare bore into her. "You came to watch me feed, *meine Süsse*? I didn't think you were interested. I would have invited you otherwise." His voice was breathy, deep with meaning, desire. An odd smile crossed his lips.

"I didn't…I'm not…" Her protests sounded feeble, even to her ears. He bent his head to rub his cheek against hers, the caress igniting a flame within her skin.

Her breath caught in her throat. His mouth stopped inches from her, his lips parted, fangs gleaming.

*He's going to kiss me.*

Then he did. His mouth closed on hers, intense, passionate. Without thinking, she opened to him and his tongue swept across hers. The copper taste of Kevin's blood was a shock, both because it was there—and because it didn't repulse her as she'd expected. Jonathan leaned in closer, pressing against her, hands planted against the door. Through his clothes she could feel the rock-hard evidence of his arousal.

Her lower lip encountered one of his fangs and was nicked. With a groan he drew on the slight cut, pulled some of her blood into his mouth, tasted it with his tongue. The wound was so slight it barely registered in the midst of the other sensations she was feeling.

Deep within her rose the desire to return his kiss then to force his mouth further down her body. For a moment she imagined his lips and teeth on the sensitive skin of her neck, the sting of his fangs there, the draw of her blood into his mouth. Her hands went to his waist to pull him closer.

Kevin moaned in his sleep from the couch. The sound forced awareness back into Sharon, caused her to put her hands instead on the nightwalker's chest and push him back. He allowed it, withdrew from her, amusement replacing the passion in his face.

With a dramatic sigh he shook his head. "So difficult, *meine Süsse*. I never know how to please you."

She had to focus on something besides his sexy mouth. "*Süsse*...what's that? You've called me that before."

He pushed back from the door and returned to lean one shoulder against it, allowing her freedom from his embrace. Sharon moved further into the room and watched his expression, his difficulty in remaining standing, and recognized finally what was wrong. He was drunk!

A wayward chuckle escaped him. "A word from the language of my youth. Something you remind me of. It means 'sweetness' in German. As to the why..." He ran his tongue across his lips, seemingly still tasting the miniscule amount of blood he'd taken from her. He closed his eyes and smiled appreciatively. "Your blood is sweet, Sharon. Sweet like honey, or the finest mead. Like chocolate was when I last sampled it."

For an instant he eyed her neck. "You interrupted my dinner but I don't mind. I could use some dessert..." He took a step forward.

Alarmed, she put up her hands. "No!" Desperate, she remembered her mission. "Your guests are here."

He halted in mid-stride. The smile on his face faltered then fled. "Already?" One hand rubbed his face, ran through his hair. He glanced down at his disheveled clothing and began to button his shirt. Once done, he took a hairbrush from a drawer in the desk and used long strokes to put it back to rights. The feral, passion-driven creature she'd discovered at Kevin's side disappeared, became the sophisticated tavern owner she was most used to.

*Which is the real Jonathan?* She couldn't help but wonder as he turned to her.

A sardonic smile graced his lips, doing little to warm his eyes. "Do I look all right?"

More at ease, she nodded.

He took a moment and examined her outfit, ran his gaze appreciatively from the red high heels to the bottom of the skirt that started at mid-thigh, then paused for effect at the deep vee of the plunging neckline.

A true smile blossomed in his face. "Sharon, you look good enough to—"

Holding up one hand, she groaned. "No more. I've already heard that one tonight."

## Chapter Five

He preceded her into the main room of the tavern. Sharon could feel the newcomers' minds long before she actually passed through the door. Reluctant, she hung back, waiting by the door as Jonathan moved to meet the others standing by the bar.

There had been three additions to the room since she'd left — a tall, thin man and woman, and another man, blond and tall, whose muscular physique startled her after seeing the sparer frames of the nightwalkers. The body-builder stood at the far end of the bar, apparently entertaining the normal women still ensconced there. Abandoned by Ralph at Amber's displeasure, the pair were now making friendly overtures to the new man who'd appeared in their midst.

He didn't seem to be fighting it much.

The female nightwalker moved in first. "Jonathan," she said in a deep sultry voice, greeting Sharon's boss with obvious pleasure. The silky tone made Sharon bristle with its implied intimacy. Whoever this woman was, she'd been most likely far more than friends with Jon. A smooth movement brought the woman within inches and her elongated hand brushed Jon's white shirt in a suggestive gesture.

Tall, slender — elegant. Rich chestnut brown hair that fell in a rippling cascade down her back. Eyes like liquid chocolate, thick with regard and intent, set in a face so pale it could have been made of fine porcelain. Her deep red lips parted in a feral smile that revealed even white teeth — and a pair of delicate fangs.

"Vanessa." Jonathan's voice was equally warm, but was there a note of regret in it? He allowed the female nightwalker's graceful embrace but then stepped out from her arms just as smoothly.

A thin shadow detached itself from the bar, the second nightwalker Sharon had detected. As he moved into the light Sharon caught herself staring. Like Jonathan, he wore his hair long, but it was gold in color, rather than Jon's rich black. Grey eyes with a sardonic arch to the brows topped a face like that of an angel.

She'd thought Jonathan was handsome — this man was actually beautiful. Only the soulless expression in his eyes detracted from his looks. She found herself preferring her boss' appearance. His imperfections provided a humanity the golden nightwalker didn't possess.

The man strode to Jonathan, a slight smile on his perfect lips. "My brother." His voice was soft, but it rang, clear as a bell and audible to all. All in the room seemed to take a single breath at once and held it, waiting for the outcome of this meeting.

Jonathan bowed deeply. "Sebastian. My prince. We are honored to serve you." He raised his arm and turned it, offering the wrist. The smile on the other nightwalker's face deepened. He grabbed the proffered hand, pulling it to his lips.

To Sharon's horror, he bit deeply and drank, eyes ever on Jonathan's face. Her boss' reaction was a tightening of his lips, not quite a grimace. Still, she could feel no mind link between the pair. It must have been painful.

The exchange lasted less than a minute. Sebastian broke contact and with a delicate swipe of his tongue closed the holes he'd torn in Jonathan's wrist. He continued to hold it and the smile on his face was more genuine now. "I thank you, brother. As always, your hospitality is beyond reproach."

With a genial wave, Jonathan indicated the bar. "Can I offer you another indulgence? Something more—mundane?"

A genuine smile now displayed itself on Sebastian's face. "You seem to have already indulged yourself." His tongue played across his lips and he laughed. "And now me as well. Still, perhaps Vanessa wishes something…"

"Oh, I'm always interested in Jon's concoctions." The woman returned to slip a possessive arm around his waist. "What was it you were drinking?"

Pulling her arm away, Jonathan led her to the bar. "Get the lady a 'Los Niños Sunset', Ralph."

Confusion filled the shapeshifter's face. "What's that, Jon?"

Without thinking, Sharon sprang to Ralph's rescue. Smoothly she slid behind the bar and grabbed the serum pitcher from the mini-fridge. "Here, I'll show you." As he watched, she carefully measured out the ingredients, although she was careful to use a normal amount of tequila rather than the larger amount Jonathan had indulged in. She placed the finished drink on the bar.

Vanessa stared, a piercing glance taking in the twin marks on Sharon's neck. "So, what's this, Jon? A new companion?" An icy flash of anger flitted through her eyes and instinctively Sharon took a step back. A skittering of mental touch scattered against her shield, the feel of it malevolent.

As quickly as it had appeared, the touch disappeared. A slow sardonic smile slid across her lips as the female nightwalker settled onto the stool in front of her drink. She took a slow sip then leaned back. "Very good. She has talent." Her voice dripped insincerity.

Jonathan took hold of Sharon's arm and guided her from behind the bar. "My apologies, I should have introduced you before. This is Sharon Colson, my new companion, and, of course, our regular bartender. Sharon, these are two of my oldest friends, Vanessa Hind and Sebastian Moret." He indicated the paired nightwalkers, now arrayed before her. Vanessa still glared daggers, but Sebastian had a watchful look, as if he hadn't quite made up his mind about her yet.

Again Sharon felt a mental touch, but this one was pure curiosity. A touch like Jonathan's, but not...Sebastian did feel like his brother in kind if not in flesh. It glanced against her shield then fled, as if that one encounter had been enough.

Oblivious, Jonathan continued. "I asked Ralph to tend the bar because I wanted Sharon to sing for us. She's quite a performer." The warm pride in his voice strengthened her.

The speculative look on Sebastian's face lifted. "A musician. How appropriate, Jonathan. I can see your interest."

A wicked little smile filled Vanessa's face. "Of course." With a sinuous gesture she beckoned at Sharon. "By all means, let's hear her."

Sharon fetched her guitar from its case and took it to the makeshift stage Jonathan set up. He'd pulled a barstool to the far corner of the bar, moving an empty table to create space and flicking a wall switch to activate a spotlight over the corner. Apparently this area had been used for such a purpose before.

Under the glare of the lamp, Sharon carefully tuned her instrument. After a few moments she realized she was delaying the start—she looked up to see everyone's gaze upon her, impatience in their faces. Jonathan was sitting with Sebastian and Vanessa, careful to keep the golden nightwalker between him and the female. He raised one eyebrow as if to say, "What are you waiting for?"

Enough delaying…it was time to begin. She thought for a moment about the crowd and what to sing, picking one of her recent songwriting efforts, one likely to make an impression. Strumming the opening bars she launched into it.

*"Full moon rising,*
*Over the woodside,*
*Over the mountain,*
*Over the sea*

*Full moon rising*
*Makes the blood burn*
*Makes the world turn*
*For my love and me.*

*Moonlight makes my feet run faster*
*Faster than the quickest river*
*Makes the woodland my dominion*
*Makes me part of all of nature.*

*When the moon is full above me*
*All around is simply magic*
*Then I seek my lover's side*
*And she becomes part of me."*

As the final chords died down, the shapeshifter crowd applauded enthusiastically. Sharon nodded her head at them. The nightwalkers by the bar had a more mixed reaction. Vanessa and Sebastian looked annoyed, while Jonathan appeared to be suppressing a chuckle. He pulled himself away from his stool and wandered over to her.

"Well, I suppose you could have sung the morning lover song instead. Do you think you could find something to suit everyone's interest?"

Sharon fingered the neck of the guitar. Her smile turned mischievous. "How about 'On Moonlight Bay'? Or perhaps 'Blue Moon'? Maybe 'After Midnight'?"

The chuckle he'd tried to suppress erupted. When he finally retrieved control, he ran a possessive hand along her neck, lingering on the scars. "Those will be fine." He grinned and returned to his seat.

She started with "After Midnight" then continued into the rest of her "moonlight madness" repertoire. By the end of the set, most of her audience was trying to sing along with her, and it was clear she was a hit. Even Amber was grinning from her place at Ralph's side.

Then she looked at the bar where the nightwalkers had been sitting, and her heart took an unexpected tumble. Vanessa was there, but Jonathan and Sebastian were gone.

\* \* \* \* \*

*My god, but she was beautiful.* The thought filled Jonathan's head as he watched Sharon perform. Her voice was, as always, perfect, her playing appropriate to the place and song. And as for how she looked... His gaze threaded along the length of her dress, lingered on the décolleté that revealed her breasts so lovingly. Wouldn't he love to run his hands along the tops of them, sink his teeth into the creamy flesh...

Enough of that. He shook his head, tried to clear the lingering tequila-induced cobwebs. It was bad enough that he'd mistook her entrance into his office as an invitation to pounce on her. He'd scared her, probably undoing weeks of careful planning. Still... He ran the tip of his tongue over his lips, which still held the taste of hers. Memory provided the flavor of that single drop of blood he'd taken. Need…for more of the same, for the feel of her body, for the sweetness of her essence, need for that, and more, raged through him.

How could he really regret kissing her when all he wanted was to do it again? The last couple of weeks had been wonderful, keeping her by his side, allowing their friendship to develop, to flourish. It was nice to have someone to talk to.

But talking wasn't enough…not now.

"She is very talented." Sebastian's voice broke in. Reluctantly, Jonathan subdued his aching body and turned his attention to his oldest friend…and now, his prince, the one to whom he was subservient.

He watched how Sebastian kept his dark gaze on Sharon as she sang. Her choice was another old song and again a favorite of the shapeshifter clan that had taken over the inn for the evening. A measure of amusement slipped through Jonathan. Clearly Ralph and Amber had been concerned that some issue would rise from having Vanessa and Sebastian here, and they had "stacked the deck" to see to it "their vampire" would win.

And they would win too. A physical fight, that is. Few nightwalkers could outfight a shapeshifter…but there was more than one way to win a battle. By offering his blood to Sebastian, Jonathan had forgone any immediate difficulties. He'd acknowledged Sebastian as his prince and with any luck that would hold things for now.

Sharon began another song, again a shapeshifter favorite. As the crowd sang along, Sebastian chuckled then leaned over to whisper, "As much as I'm enjoying this, I have things to discuss with you."

Inwardly Jonathan cringed, but he nodded his assent. He followed his prince to the back of the tavern and the hallway leading to his office. In the doorway he gave one last look at

Sharon, sitting golden in the spotlight, then reluctantly closed the door behind him, silencing the sound of her voice.

Sebastian's gaze took in the remains of Jonathan's dinner—Kevin, still unconscious on the couch. "Still taking nutrition in your own special way, I see."

Ignoring him, Jonathan picked up the phone and buzzed the kitchen. "Marcus, I'd like you to get Kevin and take him back to the kitchen." After hanging up, he touched the young man's forehead. "Wake," he whispered.

Kevin was still blinking sleepily when the cook arrived. His face lit up as the big man came in the room. "Am I glad to see you. This time was the best ever." He gave a warm, somewhat sultry look at Jonathan. "I must have dozed off," he said with a sleepy grin.

Inwardly, Jonathan cringed. Kevin was an excellent client, but he did tend to misinterpret Jonathan's interest. Male blood was tasty, but their bodies held no attraction for him. Then there was the hard look Marcus gave him as he helped the younger man to his feet. Mentally he made a note to avoid using Kevin for a while. Much as the young man enjoyed the experience, he didn't need his oldest companion upset with him.

Marcus put a possessive arm around his lover and led him away. "Come on, Kev, I'll get you something to eat in the kitchen."

Sebastian watched the interaction with interest. When the door closed behind the pair, he turned a sardonic eye on Jonathan. "So, trouble there as well. How do you do it? One companion worried you give better satisfaction than he does, the other you're too much in love with to touch."

He felt himself pale. "I don't know what you are talking about."

"Oh, yes, you do. That woman out there…you haven't drawn on her in weeks. I'm surprised her blood pressure isn't through the roof."

With a groan, Jonathan collapsed on the couch. "It hasn't been that long, she'll be fine. I'm going to take from her soon."

Sebastian settled next to him. "How soon? Tonight? No, I saw the young man you fed on, you don't need more. Tomorrow then? Why are you waiting…she's ready."

"She isn't. She won't let me link minds with her."

"Then how'd you get her to take your mark in the first place?"

Jonathan simply looked at him. Sebastian read his expression accurately and stared in astonishment. "You took without the link?" He shook his head. "Why did she let you?"

"She wanted a job bad enough to become my companion. I wanted her…" His voice trailed off.

Sebastian threw back his head and laughed. "Jonathan, you are the only vampire I know who can develop domestic trouble. I'd never let one of my companions tell me what to do. Not that I've had one recently. Your experiences have been enough to put me off."

Jonathan arched an eyebrow. "Oh? Vanessa isn't causing trouble?"

Sebastian grimaced. "Vanessa is nothing but trouble. But you knew that already."

"Of course I knew it. She was my companion in the first place. You took her from me."

"And I've regretted it ever since." His prince gave a deep sigh and both men exchanged long-suffering looks.

Jonathan shook his head. "I'll never understand why you brought her over, Sebastian. She was trouble enough when she had a limited life span. Now..."

Unaccustomed agitation took over Sebastian's face. "Don't remind me—it seemed like a good idea at the time. She was lying in a pool of her own blood. If I hadn't taken her over, she'd have died."

"And she counted on that. It was no accident her wrist was cut—Vanessa opened her own vein, knowing that you would save her life."

"You would have preferred her death?"

"No, of course not." Jonathan decided to change the subject. "I'm sure you aren't here to discuss my domestic woes. What is it you wanted of me?"

Sebastian took a deep breath. "I need you in Los Angeles. Will you go?"

The question wasn't really unexpected. Neither was the answer. "No."

Sebastian grabbed his arm. "Don't answer so fast. You haven't heard the offer."

"Not interested in the offer. I like it here, domestic problems and all. I've had enough of life in the fast lane, Sebastian. Two hundred years and I'm finally feeling at home."

"This isn't home, Jonathan. It's a cocoon and it isn't good for you. You've built a nice quiet place here where you can control everyone and everything. You're afraid to leave it. So afraid you'll do almost anything to avoid doing so. I bet you guessed what I wanted and made a point of getting drunk tonight, just to try and convince me you weren't fit for the job."

His guilty silence made Sebastian snort in disgust. "Not that it would do any good. I know you far too well, my brother. Anything you drink wears off in no more than an hour, anyway."

"Listen, Sebastian, I can't help you…"

"You listen, my friend, I need you in LA. Things are getting out of control—too many accidents. The Watchers have grown stronger."

Jonathan couldn't help laughing. "You see them as a threat? They bumble more than they accomplish anything." The Paranormal Watchers had been around for decades but hadn't even been able to prove the existence of the parafolk, much less do anything to hinder them.

"Their bumbling has gotten more effective. Deaths have occurred. Unexplained happenings, and it's getting worse. I spend too much time up north to control things there. I want you to be city chief. The young nightwalkers and other parafolk need someone they can look up to."

"What about Estaban? He's nearly as much an elder as I am."

"Estaban is dead," Sebastian said grimly. "By his own hand. Laura too."

"What?" Shock then sadness shook Jonathan to the core. The Hispanic nightwalker and his companion had been two of his oldest friends. "What happened?"

Sebastian stood and paced, clearly agitated. "We still don't know. There was a note written by him that claimed responsibility for her death. She seemed to have died from blood loss, although how Estaban could have killed her that way, I can't understand. It is just too hard to bleed out a companion. One of his other people said he hadn't been feeling well and she'd given him extra blood to help him recover. Maybe his illness had affected him and he simply took too much."

His face showing his weariness, Sebastian leaned against the edge of the desk. "Anyway, you know how close they were. He apparently carried her outside, held her in his arms and waited for the sun."

Jonathan shuddered. Suicide after killing the woman you loved. He understood what Estaban had felt probably better than most could. If it hadn't been for Sebastian he might have taken that route himself once. Sudden guilt rose. If he'd been there, he might have been able to talk Estaban out of it, the way Sebastian had him when Angela had died.

"It's gotten everyone down there upset. You can see why I need someone strong as City Chief."

Dismissing his lingering guilt, Jonathan got off the couch and paced. "And you think that's me? I haven't held a chief position in a century."

"But you were very good at it when you did."

He folded his arms and shook his head. "I don't want that kind of life, Sebastian."

The other man's voice softened. "I know you don't. But if you don't do it, you know who I'll have to choose instead."

He stared. "You can't be serious. She's…"

A shrug of his broad shoulders. "Yes, but she's got seniority. The others will listen to her, and I can control her. At least somewhat," he amended quickly as Jonathan snorted his disbelief. "Plus, she wants the job. I'm sure it's why she's been so attentive to me lately."

*Vanessa, Parafolk Chief of Los Angeles.* That was a frightening thought. Jonathan's concern deepened. He still didn't want the job but… "You'll have to give me some time to think about it. I can't leave here right now."

"I can give you time. Not much, but enough to get your house in order." A slight grin crossed the prince's lips. "I can see that you need some time with this new companion of yours. Just don't wait too long."

\* \* \* \* \*

Sharon shut off the spotlight and returned her guitar to its case. At loose ends since Jonathan and Sebastian had disappeared, she went to sit at the bar, well away from the remaining nightwalker. Her effort was in vain...the woman promptly moved to the stool at her side.

"So, you are Jon's new companion. I must admit, I'm surprised. You aren't exactly his type."

Sharon took in the other woman's long cool elegance and for the first time since dressing that evening felt dumpy. "Oh, and you are?"

"I was..." Vanessa turned to her, pulled her own hair off her neck. Twin scars were there, identical to the ones she bore. For a moment, Sharon found it hard to breathe.

Unconsciously she fingered her own marks. "You were Jonathan's companion?"

"I was. Until I converted over." Vanessa sipped at her drink and shot Sharon a mischievous glance. "I was his companion for many, many years."

Sharon couldn't resist the question. "How many years?"

Vanessa gave a ladylike snort. "Oh, twenty at least." She sipped again, waved a nonchalant hand. "Maybe more. His companion...as well as other things. At the time, he was quite a man." Her self-satisfied grin said more than her words had.

Sharon stared. *Twenty years?* It wasn't possible. Vanessa didn't look more than thirty. How could she be...no, she must have misheard. But "converted over"? "He made you a vampire?"

"Jon? Heavens, no. He'd never do that...doesn't believe in sharing the gift. No, I was sired by Sebastian." Satisfaction laced the nightwalker's voice. Apparently she enjoyed having a special bond with the prince of vampires...that is, nightwalkers.

Vanessa eyed her with a speculative gaze. "You haven't been with Jonathan long."

"No. A few weeks."

"I wonder how long you'll stay with him. He's not the same as he was when I was with him. Then he had charm, taste. Back then he wouldn't have kept company with low-lifes like shapeshifters, or people of unusual—sexual appetites." Her amused sidelong glance spoke volumes. "By comparison, you seem normal."

A probe hit her shield, leaving a nasty tang behind. "Except for this resistance you seem to have to letting others speak mentally to you. Jonathan has always enjoyed being close to his people."

Sharon resisted the urge to rip the woman's dark hair out.

Oblivious to, or simply ignoring, Sharon's ire, Vanessa went on. "He's become weak for an ancient. The weakest of them. Doesn't hunt, won't kill. An embarrassment to the rest of us. Sebastian's here to tell him so."

The falsity of that statement struck home. From what she'd seen Sebastian hadn't been upset with Jonathan at all. Overall, he'd seemed pleased.

Ralph placed a fresh glass in front of the nightwalker. Sharon watched his bland expression and wondered if he'd heard the woman's insults. If so, he didn't seem too upset.

"Vanessa." An irritating whine in his voice, the bodybuilder appeared at her elbow. Apparently he'd grown weary of the adoring norms at the bar. "Were we going to do something tonight?" Sharon examined his neck and saw the twin scars. They were smaller, closer together than hers...made by a smaller mouth.

Vanessa's companion?

She looked uninterested, sipping deeply at her fresh drink. "We are here at Sebastian's pleasure, Alex. Don't you understand how important that is?"

"Yeah, but I'm bored. This place doesn't even have any video games, and the jukebox has nothing but old stuff in it. Nothing to do here at all." He gave an appreciative glance at Sharon. "Not that the scenery is bad."

His admiration wasn't lost on Vanessa. She snarled at him. "Don't even think about it, Alex."

Standing, she wavered a little. Sharon checked her partially empty glass. The smell of tequila was overpowering. Ralph must have made the refill stronger. Plus there was another smell. Not the scent of serum.

The wobbling got worse, and Alex caught her up in his arms. "Hey, it's okay, sweetheart. I've got you."

Vanessa paled and clutched at his arm. "I think—I'm going to be sick." Alex took charge, leading her to the door of the tavern and into the night beyond. Before the door closed, Sharon heard the unmistakable sound of retching.

Sharon held up the glass and stared pointedly at Ralph. "What do you suppose could have made her sick?"

A concerned look crossed his face. "Oh, was that HER glass? Gee. I guess I could have used OJ instead of serum in it."

*Orange juice?* Great, now they were trying to poison the guests. Of course, given that it was Vanessa... She handed the glass to him. "Why don't you wash it before they come back in." Around her, quiet laughter filled the room. Apparently no one else liked Vanessa any better than she did.

From the back hallway, Sebastian returned, looking coolly in control. To her relief, Jonathan was right behind him, neither of them the worse for wear. If Vanessa's predictions of what Sebastian wanted to discuss had been correct, it hadn't bothered Jonathan any.

Jonathan's mental touch slid along her shield, a peculiar habit of his she'd come to expect. She found the caress reassuring.

The golden nightwalker examined the room, noting the amused — and deceptively innocent — looks on the faces of those near the bar. "Did I miss something?"

Ralph broke the sudden silence. "Vanessa isn't feeling well. Alex took her outside."

"Oh?" Sebastian glanced at the glass still in the shapeshifter's hand and arched an eyebrow. "Something she drank, perhaps?" A genial hand waved off any further explanation. "We must be going, anyway."

Abruptly he took Sharon's hand, turned it wrist up. For an instant, she wondered if he was going to feed from her, as he had Jonathan, and she stiffened and closed her eyes as he bent his head. Instead of the rending fangs, she felt a gentle kiss. Opening her eyes, she met his amused stare. "Not to worry, little companion. Your master is the only one to do otherwise to you."

"My master?" Her voice quavered.

The amusement deepened. "You and Jonathan need to talk. He has been most lax in your training. The gift of companionship is not to be taken lightly." Another glancing touch to her shield and then he withdrew, both mentally and physically. Sharon pulled back her shaking hand, clutching it to her chest.

"Prince Sebastian..." Alex's whine came from the doorway. The nightwalker raised his head to glance heavenward then turned his steely gaze to Vanessa's companion.

"What is it?"

"Vanessa doesn't feel so good. She wants to go home."

"So I hear. Tell her I'll be there momentarily." He returned his attention to Jonathan. Suddenly Sharon could envision Sebastian as a prince, strong, handsome. In control. "You will think about what I said?"

Jonathan nodded, obviously sobered. "I will."

That seemed to satisfy him. Sebastian nodded his farewells to the rest and exited after the others.

# Chapter Six

The tavern had emptied for the night and everyone had gone home, leaving Sharon alone to close up. Amber, whispering something that left Ralph's eyes gleaming in anticipation, had led the temporary bartender out the door. Apparently she'd been thrilled at the trick he'd played on Vanessa and some reward was coming his way.

Sharon made a mental note to find out just what Vanessa had done to earn so many people's antipathy. Whatever it was, she didn't want to make the same mistake as the former companion.

After changing into jeans and a T-shirt, she cleaned up the bar, finishing by polishing the countertop. Suddenly an image of dark hair and pale skin moved across the reflective surface, and startled, Sharon dropped her rag and looked up to see Jonathan's contemplative stare.

She pointed to the bar. "Your reflection—I saw it!"

A smile scooted along his lips. "I'm solid, light bounces off me. Of course I cast a reflection. *Meine Süsse*, you really have seen too many horror movies."

"Then why don't you have any mirrors?"

He stilled, examined the wavy likeness of himself on the bar. When his head lifted, there was an intense sadness in his eyes. "Perhaps I simply do not like what I see in them." He ran a hand along the side of his face, pulled it back to stare at it. "It has been a long time since I've seen what I look like. I am not what I was before my conversion."

"What were you?" Her voice emerged, barely over a whisper. "Why did you become…what you are?"

Some of the sadness parted. "The answer to that is long, and not one I wish to broach tonight. There are other things we should discuss…as my prince has reminded me."

His prince. One question came immediately. "Should I call you 'master'?"

Jonathan grimaced. One hand clenched and lightly pounded the bar top. "I'd rather you didn't. Sebastian may be my brother, but he is far too much of a traditionalist. Someday that's going to cause him trouble in dealing with the people of this century, particularly women. I only hope I can be around to see it," he said with a light laugh. "I notice you call me 'boss' sometimes. If you must think of me as holding power over you, I prefer that label. You work for me, and I take care of you."

Sharon pressed on. "But there are duties I'm not taking care of, right? Things you're supposed to have explained to me." Too many questions had been raised tonight for her to ignore them any longer. Better to get them out into the open, even if she didn't like the answers.

He was so handsome, so…sexy. Just looking at him brought heat to her face. But she didn't want to have an affair with him without knowing more. Vanessa had been his companion, and clearly a lot more, probably his lover. And now she was a vampire.

"Yes. 'The time has come to talk of many things', *meine Süsse*. Like Alice in the looking glass, you need to know more about this world you are in." He tugged her away from the bar and toward the back.

"Your lair?" Sharon didn't want to be that alone with him. A room with a bed was definitely out. "Why can't we talk here?"

He considered the question. "Perhaps you are right. A neutral location might be more appropriate." A sudden inspiration struck him. "My office. Much less intimate."

*Oh, yeah, just the last place he'd kissed her.* But still, better the office than his bedroom. "All right."

Sharon watched as he turned on the lamp by the couch then crouched by the mini-fridge underneath it. "Could I offer you something? Wine, perhaps?"

The thought of alcohol sent a wave of queasiness through her. Never much of a drinker in spite of her profession, Sharon realized that she'd become even more resistant to drink than usual. Since Jonathan didn't drink—or at least, she'd never seen him drink until this evening—she hadn't noticed how little beer or wine appealed to her until now. Still, she was thirsty. "Do you have any juice in there?"

With a twitch of his lips, he fetched a small bottle and opened it. After handing it to her, he indicated she should sit and then took his own position at the opposite end of the couch. In spite of the space between them, she felt the warmth of his gaze. For a moment she toyed with the idea of scooting closer to him.

No, bad idea.

He tilted his head. "You are probably thirstier than you were. Plus, you don't want to have liquor of any sort."

Uneasy at how he'd guessed all this, Sharon stared at him. "You know this…"

"I know this because you are a companion. You are not the same as you were."

"How am I different? Why?"

He shrugged. "The 'why' I'll answer first. You carry my mark and the unhealed scars contain a part of me. The scientists of your people have a fancy name for it, but it's enough to say that it acts in your body as it does in mine…to a lesser extent."

Sharon's mouth dropped open. "You mean I'm going to become as you are…a vam…I mean, a nightwalker?"

"Do you feel the need to drink blood? No. Can you go into the daylight without burning? Yes." He shook his head. "No, you remain human. Mostly. But there are some changes. You can see better at night than you used to, are more sensitive to bright light, enough so that you will want to wear sunglasses when you are outside. You have a tendency to be sleepy during the day." A minor hesitation. "And not just because you stay up with me all night.

"You are stronger than you were. Healthier. You tend to heal faster. Your metabolism is different. Part of it is speeded up to better create new blood, more than you need for yourself. The rest is decelerated. You age at a slower rate." He stared at his hands, folded in front of him.

A fresh wave of confusion filled her. "I'm aging slower? How much slower?"

"It depends on the companion, but the average is about one year for every ten."

She remembered what Vanessa had said about being Jonathan's companion for twenty years. If that were true, then she'd only aged two years in that entire time. The enormity of what he was telling her sank in. "I could live ten times longer." It wasn't the same as being immortal but…

His eyes were watchful. "True enough. You will live longer, stay young longer. You won't get sick, injuries will heal very quickly."

She listened, awestruck. "No wonder your prince called it a 'gift'. It sounds too good to be true." She eyed him. "What's the catch?"

A humorless chuckle escaped him. "The 'catch' is that you supply me with blood."

*Oh.* "I see." Sharon swallowed, her mouth dry with anxiety. He'd said she was producing more blood, more than she needed. "How much blood?"

"Not much. Younger nightwalkers require more blood at a time, but I've been around for over three hundred years. I can make do with as little as a cup if I'm feeding from a companion. A companion's blood is unusually rich. It's made for me. I could draw up to three, four times a week for an extended time. With some companions it can be as much as daily although that's unusual."

Sharon stared at him. He made it sound like it was as simple as milking a cow. "What about me? Am I healthy?"

"From what I can determine. You're producing at a very good rate now." He looked pleased. "Your blood pressure is very high."

"I have high blood pressure?" That wasn't good, people died from that, from strokes and heart attacks.

The panic in her voice must have been obvious. He reached over to lay a comforting hand on her arm. "It's all right, *meine Süsse*. It is normal for a companion…the pressure will go down when I feed."

*Oh, great!* That's what he'd meant when he'd said he would be taking from her again. He had to, it was part of all this. The memory of the pain she'd suffered from his bite returned to haunt her. There was no help for it. She'd have to let him feed again.

Otherwise she could die.

Convulsively, she wrung her hands together. He'd said the pain would be avoided if he linked minds with her. He could even make it pleasurable. The writhing image of Kevin interrupted her thoughts. He'd certainly enjoyed being

Jonathan's dinner. The thought of experiencing such passion made her almost as uncomfortable as allowing his bite.

It wasn't like Sharon was completely inexperienced. She'd had plenty of lovers…well, two anyway. And one had been quite fulfilling—at least a couple of times. She was sure she'd felt something like the ecstasy everyone talked about when they spoke of sex. Really, she'd had an orgasm. Probably.

Jonathan's mental touch slid over her shield, a gentle caress. Without meaning to, she shied away from it. So intimate. Without physically touching her, he could make her feel so much.

There was more, of course. Jonathan had been so good to her. The idea of being able to provide for him held an appeal she hadn't expected. Part of her wanted his mouth on her neck.

Jonathan watched the emotions flitting across her face. Even with her mind shielded, he could read her clearly. His words had frightened her. Her body was changed, in some ways for the better, but in others… Now she knew he would need to feed from her to keep her health. And his too, the truth be known.

The pain wasn't something she wanted, but she couldn't bear the thought of linking minds. She was still too unsure of him to let him past her shield.

He could break it—no, that wasn't an answer. She'd never trust him if he overcame her reluctance by force. On the other hand…maybe… "Sharon, perhaps there is a way we could do this without the mind link, exactly, but so that I don't hurt you."

That caught her attention. "How?"

A thrill of hope infused him. *She was interested – this was the answer!* "You could learn how to use your mental powers. Rather than have a shield to block all entry, you can use something more flexible. It would allow me to keep a small entry without a complete mind link."

She looked dubious. "That would work?"

"Yes. It would also be more protective for you. Allow you to keep strangers out, let others in, but on your own terms. You'd control the link."

Now she looked hopeful. "You could teach me? How long would it take?"

"Just a few minutes, most likely. We can start tomorrow, if you like. The moon is full, so we're closed."

"Closed?" Sharon showed surprise. As he thought about it, it had only been about three weeks since she'd been with them. It was her first full moon holiday.

Goodness, it seemed longer.

Jonathan shrugged. "A full moon means most of my usual guests are out having a good time in the woods. I'd have to work short-staffed anyway...might as well shut down. We aren't closed that often."

She seemed to mull that over. "So, we can start when you wake up?" She fingered the scars on her neck. "And once you teach me then..." a small shudder shook her fragile frame. "Then you'll be able to drink from me without it hurting."

It was all he could do to curb his enthusiastic grin. "Absolutely. No pain, Sharon, I promise. We'll start as soon as I'm awake."

\* \* \* \* \*

He found her in the kitchen the next evening, the rest of the place deserted. The Inn's closure during the full moon was well known, and Marcus had already announced to Jonathan his intention of spending some "quality" time with

Kevin. No one would be around this evening to disturb them and that idea brightened his night.

Sharon was reading the newspaper, the evening edition, a bowl of stew in front of her, an opened can on the counter near the microwave explaining its origin. The dying steam from the surface told him she'd been ignoring her dinner in favor of reading.

He leaned over her to see what had so taken her fancy that she'd forget to eat. To his amusement, she was reading the comic page. "Good evening," he whispered into her ear.

She gave her characteristic yelp and turned to glare at him. "You snuck up on me again!"

He fetched a glass of serum from the glass-fronted refrigerator and settled onto a stool opposite her. "You were so deeply involved, it didn't take much this time. Really, *meine Süsse*, what do you see in those little boxes?"

With a snap of the paper, she pointed to one of the cartoons. "This one is funny."

He examined it closely. A very thin character with prominent fangs lay on a towel, wearing a tiny swimsuit, apparently under some sort of sun lamp, and talking to another vampire character wearing a black cape. He read the caption aloud. "And then she says she misses seeing a tan line, so here I am." Chuckling, he handed the paper back to her. "Some of us will do anything to get our lady's attention."

Sharon laughed and took back the comics, folding the paper onto the countertop. "Wouldn't a sun lamp cause problems?"

"I wouldn't know. I've never been that fond of having tanned skin anyway. It wasn't respectable when I was mortal." He frowned at her bowl. "Aren't you going to eat that?"

She glided her spoon around a few of the vegetables and chunks of meat, reluctance all over her face. "I suppose I should. I'm not really hungry."

With a gulp he drained half of his glass. "Maybe you aren't, but I am. And I can't feed unless you take good care of yourself. So…" He tried an intimidating glare at her. "So, my companion—eat!"

It didn't work. Sharon dissolved into giggles then struck a melodramatic pose. "Oh, yes, oh lord and master. I hear and obey." Still shaking with merriment, she began to shovel the cooled stew into her mouth.

He took another swig of his serum. It barely diminished his appetite, but he had work to do before he could get access to this evening's main course. At least his dinner was in a good mood.

Sharon finished and put the bowl and spoon in the dishwasher then returned to sit next to him. Nervously folding her hands, she watched him consume the last of his drink. "So what do we do now?"

Jonathan twisted the glass in his hand then put it down. "Now I teach you how to filter your mind rather than shield it."

Glancing around the sterile kitchen, he decided another venue was in order. He grabbed her hand. "Come with me."

* * * * *

*Her bedroom?* Not good, not good at all. Sharon allowed herself to be led to the bed and seated herself at his intense look. Swallowing nervously, she watched as Jonathan turned off the light and went to stand by the window. Her room held one of the Inn's few windows, a simple thing with a louvered blind. He played with the strings on the blind, moving it up to reveal the moonlit woods beyond. While not completely past twilight, the moon had risen and its fullness lent a soft illumination, an ethereal glow.

The pale light played across the nightwalker's features, softening the hard planes of his face. He was so handsome. He smiled at the scene beyond and Sharon suddenly pictured those perfect lips on her skin, taking from her the nourishment he needed. A warmth that had nothing to do with the idea of feeding him filled her and pooled deep within her.

His deep voice interrupted her wayward thoughts. "See the window, how all the light comes through with the blind raised?"

Blinking, she nodded.

He lowered the blind, and opened the slats to their most horizontal position. "Now the light is filtered a little, but we can still see outside."

Unsure of his direction, Sharon nodded again then watched as he adjusted the blinds so the slats were vertical. The light dimmed, leaving a soft glow that outlined the slats and the gap between the blind and the window.

"Now most of the light is blocked, so we can't see through the window, but the light comes through anyway. That's what I want you to imagine, *meine Süsse*, a blind rather than a shield across your mind. You can open it, adjust it, allow light to filter through but not block it entirely." He glanced over at her. "Do you understand?"

She gave a hesitant nod. "I think so. A blind, not a shield."

His beaming smile felt like a reward for her quickness. Jonathan moved to sit on the bed next to her, his weight shifting the mattress beneath her so that she nearly toppled into him. He steadied her then moved his hand down to her arm to grasp her fingers.

His gliding touch left a trail of sensation in its wake and where it clasped hers, his hand was cool, strong in its gentleness. Sharon fought the urge to pull away.

"Close your eyes. Imagine a blind before you, blocking your mind from the outside world. Leave it open for now." His voice was soft, hypnotic, but she didn't think he was trying anything with it. It was just his usual way of speaking, gilded with the intensity of his need. Jonathan was hungry.

She did as he asked. Slowly she built up the image of a wall containing a window, with an open blind, gradually filling in the details. "I have it," she said when it was finally fixed in her mind.

"Good. Now close the blind. Imagine how that space is darker now."

In her thoughts, the cord pulled shut and the flat slats took their vertical position. The light dimmed and it became dark. She nodded to show she was ready.

*The outside world is filtered now. But you can see light, meine Süsse. You can hear. You can hear me in your mind.*

Startled, her eyes flew open, her mental window slamming shut. She pulled on her hand, held fast in his grip. "What are you doing?"

Jonathan released her, held up his other hand in a placating gesture. "Easy. I didn't mean to frighten you. I was only trying to prove a point. You were protected but could still sense me." Anxiety filled the ice blue eyes drilling into her. "Are you all right?"

She swallowed, her fear dissipating under his concern. "I'll be fine." She returned her hand into his keeping. "Let's try again."

This time it was easier to build the wall with the window. When her imaginary blind was once again shut, she told him.

Again she heard his mental 'voice'. *You will see a light approaching, glowing through the blinds. It will be like the moonlight outside and just like that light, it will not harm you.* She heard a hesitation. *That light is my essence, meine Süsse. What you would call my soul.*

Just as he'd said, a glow began to form around the edges of the closed blinds, lighting her internal room. It grew more intense, until it appeared to be just outside the blinds. *But this wasn't like moonlight.* It wasn't a pale light at all, but yellow, golden. There was warmth in it, the warmth of the sun. Why, if she were to open those blinds, she'd bet it wouldn't be a moonlit forest and black sky she'd see, but a blue sky and green, sun-kissed meadow.

"It's beautiful," she whispered, hardly realizing she spoke aloud.

There was amusement in his 'voice'. *Is it? If you say so. Now just relax.*

She barely noticed as he raised her arm, or the feeling of warmth on her wrist, his lips in a gentle kiss at the pulse point.

From him came another mental touch. *No pain.*

Deep warmth flooded her, a sense of well-being. Not desire, but satisfaction. Pleasure. She felt caressed, cherished. Cared for. Owned.

Owned? No, not owned, but belonging to. She was Jonathan's, his companion. Warm blood flowed through her veins, his for the asking. All was as it should be.

From her wrist there came a drawing sensation, a pulling on the skin. It didn't hurt, but it tugged at her thoughts, drew her attention. Slowly she opened her eyes, still caught in the golden glow.

Jonathan held her wrist to his mouth, his eyes shut, lips pursed, throat rippling as he swallowed. Bemused, she watched him feed. The same intent look was on his face as the night before, with Kevin, but in addition there was something else. He looked...happier?

A moment passed and a deep lassitude overcame her. The golden glow waiting within her mind beckoned to her and she closed her eyes to see it better.

The pulling sensation stopped. A pause, and then more warmth on her wrist and the glow outside her "blind" grew faint. Sharon opened her eyes again to see Jonathan carefully licking clean her wrist. When he released her hand, she pulled it back, examined it for herself. Outside of a little dampness, it was perfectly fine. No scars, no evidence of his feeding.

At her questioning stare, his eyes met hers and his hand traced her neck to linger on his mark. "These alone are enough. I will leave no others on you."

This had not at all been what she'd expected after seeing the way he'd fed from the others. No passion, no intensity. Just a feeling of well-being and pleasure in feeding. She found her voice. "Is that it? Are we done?"

A deep chuckle erupted from him. "Yes. That's it."

"You've had enough."

A pleased smile crossed his lips. "Enough. I took less than I might have, but I didn't need more. How was it for you? No pain, yes?"

"No pain. I felt..." She struggled for the words. "It wasn't what I expected. It felt good but not...not like the others..."

He put an arm around her. "You are talking about Kevin? In his mind he saw what he wanted, a man making love to him, but it wasn't real." Jonathan hesitated. "I will not do that with you. You are my companion. I won't fill you with false passion. I want you to feel what I feel, Sharon. I told you I enjoy feeding. There is a satisfaction to it. A rightness."

Eagerly she snatched at that image. "Yes. That's what I felt, satisfaction. It felt—right."

He hugged her into his chest. "That's what you were supposed to feel. So many people have such odd notions about my kind. Because we feed on living blood, we must be evil. But we aren't. At least, not any more so than our human brethren can be."

Gently he stroked her face. "I feed because I must. As my companion, you provide for me. It feels right because it is." He planted a soft kiss on her forehead. "Nothing could be more natural, Sharon."

It was so wonderful to be in his embrace, but not just because he was an attractive man. They belonged together, nightwalker and companion. She'd fulfilled her role, she'd provided for him, just as she was supposed to. Elation filled her and a huge smile broke out over her face. She was his companion in truth now!

Jonathan watched her face and guessed the meaning of her smile. She was happy. He ran his hand down her arm, measured her innate response. Not quite ready, but almost. A feeding as innocuous as this one had been satisfying, but he could hardly wait for their next. No false passion between them.

Only the real thing would do.

For a moment he toyed with what that would mean. Her body writhing under his, his mouth drawing the blood from her neck, her breast, as he thrust into her. It had been a long time since he'd had a female companion, a long time since he last indulged in physical pleasure. Her warm body, so complacent within his arms, fed other hungers and he felt his body tighten with unexpected quickness. One hand toyed with a lock of her soft, sunshine-colored hair and he eyed her lips with longing.

"So what shall we do now?" Sharon turned her trusting face to his.

At her innocent question, he ruthlessly suppressed his fantasy to deal with her reality. At long last she was comfortable with him. So be it. That would be enough for now.

He returned her shy smile. "Now, my sweetness, I think we should go out. The moon is full and our friends are intently celebrating. This night truly belongs to its children and I, for one, intend to join the party."

# Chapter Seven

"So where are we going?" Sharon asked when she met Jonathan by the back door. After he'd left her in her room, she'd taken his advice and dressed for the early spring weather outside, heavy black jeans and a black sweater, for warmth as well as concealment.

Jonathan was dressed similarly. His form-fitting black leather pants clung to his thighs, a black T-shirt and leather jacket completed the ensemble. With his dark hair and piercing blue eyes, he'd never looked more dangerous—or sexy. Sharon felt her mouth go dry just looking at him. The chaste way he'd fed from her hadn't prepared her for the way his gaze slid down her frame, a glance that seemed to promise a much more intimate experience to come.

Suddenly his dark expression changed into a grin and he handed her a bottle of water, fresh from the refrigerator, and the outside of the plastic damp with dew. "You're probably thirsty again."

Taking it, she opened the bottle and drained the first third, eliminating at least one reason for her mouth being dry. Now if there was only something she could do about the other. The man was simply too good looking!

He leaned against the door. "I'd thought we start by finding the werewolf party."

What happened to Jonathan's political correctness? "Don't you mean shapeshifters?"

"Not tonight. During the full moon they take on their alternative forms, wolves and panthers, and keep to their own packs. The wolves will be in the forest, where the best game is, the panthers near the streams that feed into the ocean. They prefer fish to rabbit." He shook his head in mock sympathy. "Tonight is not a good time to be either a bunny or a trout."

The image of fangs rending meat filled her mind, and Sharon's stomach lurched in response. "Just so long as it's only game they are killing."

Jonathan slid an arm around her, directing her into the garage. "Not to worry, my soft-skinned companion. You'll be safe with me."

Instead of heading for the van, he led her to the garage door leading outside.

"Aren't we taking the car?" she asked.

"Nope, where we're going, there aren't roads."

For a moment Sharon wondered if she shouldn't have worn her hiking boots instead of the less functional canvas shoes she'd selected. "Are we going to have to walk very far?" Her voice must have revealed her apprehension.

A deep chuckle answered her. "I don't walk much if I can help it. Certainly not when I can fly."

"Fly? You aren't going to turn into a bat, are you?" An image of a bat wearing a leather jacket flitted through her mind.

"A bat!" Jonathan could barely contain his laughter. "I can't change form, at least not that far. And even if I could, I can't change my mass. That's why shapeshifters are normally about the same size as their alternative forms." He grinned at her. "Can you imagine a hundred-and-seventy-pound bat?"

The image he created was even worse than the one she'd conjured. Now he was a really big bat in a leather jacket, eyes glowing blue. She shuddered. Shaking her head to clear it, she tried to understand. "So if you aren't going to change form, what are you going to do? How can you fly?"

"I can't, normally. Only during the full moon." A perplexed look crossed his face. "I'm not sure how to describe it. You'll just have to take my word for it."

Well, it wasn't like just being a vampire—um, nightwalker—wasn't odd enough. Now he could act like a bird too. "Okay, I believe you. You can fly. So how am I supposed to go with you?"

He smiled and pulled her outside, into the waiting moonlight. "Stand behind me and put your arms around my neck," he instructed.

Tentatively, she obeyed, trying to ignore the deep smell of him that permeated the jacket, an earthy smell with a hint of cinnamon, warm and sweet. It must have been very old to have picked up so much of his scent. She breathed it in as she clutched him tight.

"Ready?"

Throat suddenly frozen with apprehension, she nodded. "Ready," she said in a voice that sounded anything but certain.

He bent his knees then straightened, pushing upward. To Sharon's astonishment, he rose, not a little, but a lot, and continuously. Within a few seconds, they were the height of the inn, hovering over the roofline.

Sharon looked over his shoulder and yelped. "Are you sure this is safe?"

A deep rumble moved through him and she realized he was laughing. "Just hold on, *meine Süsse*. We'll be there in a little while." He moved forward, away from the inn and into the woods.

Effortlessly, they floated over the surrounding forest, taking a course leading directly for the distant mountains.

Once Sharon realized that Jonathan really was able to perform this magic carpet trick of his, she tried to relax, but every time she looked down, she saw how high they were and ended up clutching him tighter and tighter. Suddenly he grabbed her clenched hands and pulled them away from his neck, lifting her higher on his back. Settling her into this new position, he said, "I know I don't breathe very much, but I do need some air."

Chastised, she whispered into his ear, "Sorry." He just patted her hands comfortingly then changed direction, following a thin trail she could now see stretching through the trees before them. Every once in a while, she spotted a shadowed figure running on all fours beneath them.

Eventually they came to an open area filled with well over twenty jumping, leaping bodies. Jonathan tilted his head and they slowly lowered to the ground. He bent his knees again as he landed, and Sharon found the ground beneath her feet. Reluctantly she released her hold on him and took a step back.

The wolves came to sniff at the newcomers, not quite friendly but not aggressive either. Some weren't quite full grown while others had the whitened muzzles of old age. At the edge of the clearing stood a female, big and gray, who had two cubs with her, cavorting about like the youngsters they were. She watched Jonathan and Sharon with suspicious green eyes and kept her offspring away from them.

Jonathan nodded to the young ones and smiled. "Twins, Peter and Casper, four years old. I remember when they were born. This is their first full moon ceremony, first time for the change, so they're a little excited. Shapeshifter children don't change for their first few years. They remain human."

He called out to the female, using her name. "Anna! I've someone for you to meet."

At his voice, the female lowered her guard and moved toward them. "Stay very still, Sharon. Let her smell you. She will know my scent and know you are part of me."

It was as he'd predicted. The gray wolf came toward them, her tail at first stiff, then wagging, picking up speed as she recognized the nightwalker's scent. In a moment she was pressing her nose into Sharon's hands, begging for attention, the cubs on either side doing their best to edge their mother out of the competition. A snarl and a snap, and the pair tumbled away, whimpering mournfully. Immediately the female gave Sharon a last nudge, and with the long-suffering air peculiar to motherhood, turned away to comfort her wayward cubs.

Sharon laughed. "They act just like people."

Jonathan threw an arm around her and turned her to face him, his face deeply serious. "That's because they are people. All of the parafolk are, deep inside. We may be what norms would call monsters in some ways, but in others we are just like anyone else. That includes the shapeshifters, like these folks, the spellcasters—and me. Nightwalkers are normal people in most ways." He ran a gentle hand down her cheek. "In the most important ways. Sleeping and dietary habits aside, I'm just a man."

She felt the truth of that, right down to her tingling toes. It was hard to think of Jonathan as anything but a man when he caressed her.

A short bark came from the bushes, and the general rough and tumble of the assembled wolves ceased. Everyone seemed to come to attention as two new animals entered the clearing. One was a massive wolf with a rich black pelt and deep green eyes. Majestic, in his glorious prime, he strode into the midst of the others, allowing their gentle brushes against his fur, the greeting of the pack to its leader.

Behind him trotted a smaller wolf, with reddish brown fur and golden eyes. The female stayed behind the male, also allowing the others to brush against her but occasionally giving brief warning snarls to the females who'd displayed a little too much eagerness in making their greetings to the leader.

"Is that Amber?" Sharon whispered to Jonathan who was standing behind her, his hands on her shoulders.

Her answer was a low chuckle. "Yes. And still trying to keep Ralph's attention."

The pair halted in front of Sharon and Jonathan. The wolf, Ralph, turned a questioning gaze on Sharon then returned to stare at the nightwalker. Jonathan merely pulled Sharon back into his chest, putting possessive arms around her.

The animal's jaw dropped into a wolfish grin. Like the others had before, he butted his head against Sharon and Jonathan both, marking them with his scent, then returned to the pack.

Amber continued to stare at Sharon in Jonathan's embrace, apparently still not convinced. Jonathan spoke to the she-wolf in a low whisper. "Look at it this way…if Ralph sees me with a female, maybe he'll seek a mate as well."

Her head swiveled back to stare at the black wolf, now back in the midst of the pack. With an almost human shrug, she performed a perfunctory head rub on Sharon and Jonathan then trotted back to Ralph's side. He pulled her closer with his jaw and greeted her with an affectionate caress of his tongue. With an expression that bordered on surprise, she allowed it then snuck another look back at the nightwalker and his companion. A brief nod of her head and she returned Ralph's lick.

Jonathan chuckled softly in Sharon's ear and wrapped his arms more securely around her. "See what I mean? I bet Amber is much nicer to you come tomorrow."

His firm chest pressed into her back and she felt solid warmth flowing from him, only part of which was his body heat. Something was happening between them, something far more akin to a man-woman relationship than that of a companion to her nightwalker boss, and for once Sharon was comfortable with that difference.

The black wolf gave a short bark that sounded like a command, and the rest of the pack stopped milling about. The animals took positions around the clearing, moving so that they filled the entire space, even the twins taking positions on either side of their mother. Outside of a few minor yips and yelps and the sound of brushing fur, the clearing became very quiet. Many of them sat or stood, completely still, heads directed to the sky above.

Overhead, the moon cleared the treetops, filling the clearing with light. It became so bright Sharon raised a hand to shield her eyes.

Then the music started. Ralph began it, a single howl, at first very quiet, but it grew in volume until it filled Sharon's ears. A higher-pitched voice joined in, Amber, sitting beside him, her muzzle raised to the moon. One by one the rest of the pack came in, adding their own howls to the song, the wolf voices blending and soaring like the most exquisite music. Even the cubs joined in, their howls shorter, lacking the staying power of the adults.

It was a natural music, like water over a rocky streambed, or the breeze through the early spring leaves. An ethereal concert in homage to the full moon.

Her breath caught in her throat and tears welled in the corners of her eyes. Behind her, Jonathan stood firm, his soft, rare breath a whisper on the back of her neck. When the song finally ended and the echoes from the mountain behind them died away, he leaned forward. "That was one thing that old movie got right—'Children of the night—what music they make'." Overwhelmed, she found herself unable to do more than nod silent agreement with him.

No doubt, down in the town of Los Niños, the normal inhabitants who were uncomfortable with their paranormal neighbors were left fearful by what they heard of the wolf-song. Sharon could imagine her former landlord, Jonesy, rushing around his rat-trap of a boarding house, closing the windows and locking the doors, all the time quaking with fear. Here she was in the midst of the festivities and all she felt was wonder and joy.

Of course, some of that might have been due to the tall, dark, bloodthirsty gentleman still holding her close. In Jonathan's arms she'd always felt safe, even the first time he'd bitten her. Somehow she doubted that would ever change.

Now that the concert was over, the participants began to peel off, to hunt or—whatever the werewolves did on their night in their alternative selves. Ralph began to slip off by himself, then stopped and looked over his shoulder at Amber, still seated in the center of the clearing. He yelped, a questioning tone, and she cocked her head in answer.

Walking slowly back to her, he stopped and bent his head to gently lay it on top of hers, rubbing it. She responded by seizing his throat in her teeth, and he allowed that indignity without so much as a whimper. She released her hold then licked his throat, and he nuzzled her back.

Finally, he turned to leave, and this time she trotted behind him, neither of the pair casting a backward glance. Jonathan and Sharon were left alone in the clearing.

\* \* \* \* \*

Pulling Sharon up onto his shoulders, Jonathan took off again, pushing up out of the clearing above the treetops. Through a slight shift of his weight, he changed direction and headed toward the ocean. The burden of her slim form was only a minor issue to him. After all, he could have easily carried Marcus, who weighed over a hundred pounds more.

Of course, carrying Marcus wouldn't have been nearly as much fun.

Her breasts pressed firmly into his back, giving him a particular thrill. It made him long to be alone with her. But not quite yet. The moon was still high in the sky, and he loved how, under its bright light, he could float so effortlessly into the sky.

Flying was one of the advantages of his race that he enjoyed most. When he'd first discovered his new ability, he'd spent hours in the air over Vienna, taking in the sights of the city, lit with a thousand candles. How glorious that had been, well worth the sacrifice of his daylight hours and the taste of solid food.

As the dark forest passed beneath them, he experienced that same thrill. Sharon shifted, moving higher on his back, looking over his shoulder as they swooped along. Her joyous laughter reminded him of another night, another full moon, another woman with soft breasts on his back, her gentle arms around his neck.

Some of his pleasure faded away. No, best not think of that now, how that relationship had ended. What had happened to Angela would never happen again.

Below them was another clearing. In the middle stood a knot of dancers twisting within a circle marked by smoking candles, their naked bodies pale in the moonlight. The spellcasters had their own rituals to celebrate the full moon. On this night, only normal folks stayed home and out of sight.

He took a couple of passes overhead, allowing Sharon to look her fill, but didn't stop. Best not to disturb their rites. There was an uneasy peace between the supernatural folks of fur and fang, and those who made their own magic. Rarely was he invited to join with the other groups, the werewolves being the one exception. Ralph and Amber accepted his presence at their concerts as a matter of course, some of which was due to his great love of their music.

Of course, the fact that he signed their paychecks didn't hurt.

Continuing on, he carried Sharon closer to the shoreline. Again dark shapes appeared through the trees, this time along the streams that led to the ocean. More independent than the werewolf pack, the werepanthers collected in small groups of mostly twos and threes. He found one family unit, a mated pair and set of cubs, and landed on a high branch of a tree overlooking their position.

A hand over her mouth muffled Sharon's inadvertent squeal when he pulled her off his back as he sat down, placing her onto the branch next to him. "Shush, *meine Süsse*. We don't want to disturb them."

Eyes flashing, she shut her mouth, refraining from further comment. His arm steadied her as she wriggled around on the branch, finding a comfortable seat. Inwardly he groaned at the way her curves settled into his side. For a moment he considered ending their evening early.

Sharon pointed to the cubs along the stream and whispered, "Look! They're so cute!" The pair took turns splashing about in the water, ignoring the growls of their parents. Finally each adult grabbed a cub by the neck and hauled it up on shore. Leaving the chastised cubs with a not-entirely-playful cuff to their foreheads, the adults then went back to the water and waited by the now quieted stream.

"Why did they do that? The cubs were only having fun." Sharon's soft heart showed in her eyes.

"There is more than fun to be had tonight. The cubs were muddying the stream, and that wasn't good for the rest of the night's entertainment. Watch what the parents do now."

In a few minutes, the big male raked a paw through the water and a long silvery fish was thrown onto the shore, directly in front of the larger of the waiting cubs. Immediately the playful cub pounced on the wriggling form and tore into it with eager yips. The smaller cub eyed her brother's treat and whimpered mournfully until the adult female performed the same feat, landing a second fish directly into the cub's face. Snorting, she shook the water out of her eyes then pounced on her dinner with cries of happiness.

The adults took turns fishing the stream until all four animals were happily munching away. When the cubs were done eating, they crept up on the stream and tried to mimic the way the adults had caught the fish. Sharon clapped quietly when the small female cub managed to land a tiny fish of her own.

There had been nights when Jonathan had spent the entire evening watching the werepanthers, but tonight he had further plans. He checked the late evening sky, his internal clock telling him the sun's location on the other side of the world. They still had a few hours until dawn. Grabbing Sharon's hands, he pulled her into his arms, across her chest. Holding on to her tightly, he slid off the branch and into the open air beyond.

With her in front, he could speak directly into her ear. "I want to walk on the beach."

\* \* \* \* \*

The crashing waves greeted them as he landed lightly on the sand. The moonlit beach was empty of all evidence of anyone else, no midnight seagulls, no signs of life at all. They might have been the only two creatures in the world.

Sharon walked the sand side-by-side with Jonathan, moving slowly along the shore.

It was getting harder and harder to ignore Jonathan's innate maleness. He'd declared himself a man, if not precisely human. As his arm settled around her shoulders, pulling her close, she felt him as a man…and responded as a woman. Her head rested on his shoulder and she felt the slow rise of his chest as he breathed, once to every two of hers. His heart beat quietly beneath her fingers.

Not human. Not a real man. But did it matter?

Not to her body, it didn't. His handsome face turned to the ocean, the light glinting off the waves in the distance. She suppressed the urge to run her fingers along his jaw, turn his mouth towards hers.

Outside of her mental window the golden glow appeared around her imaginary blind. Like the mental caress she'd felt against her shield, the glow felt warm, accepting. Jonathan's mind, linking to hers, as much as she was allowing. For a moment she wondered what would happen if she opened the blinds and let the glow enter all the way.

*What are you thinking, Sharon?*

Fear, sudden and intense, stopped her breath, then her thoughts. *Nothing…*her mental voice replied.

She couldn't do it…to allow him entry would be a full link. A brief replay filled her mind, a memory from one time she'd allowed such a thing before.

Her shuddering caught his attention. "What is it, Sharon, are you cold?" Jonathan had to shout into her ear to be heard over the sounding waves. Her body shook as if with the flu and the mental shield he'd thought to never feel again was back in force. In her eyes was an intense fear, one he'd seen once before, when she'd refused his link the first time.

*What had happened to her?* He stopped on the shore and pulled her closer into his embrace, held her tight to his chest, soothing her with gentle words and gentler hands on her back. He made no further effort on her mind, simply let his body speak for him. She was safe now. She would always be safe, so long as he was there. That was the message he intended to convey.

She must have received it. Her shaking diminished then stopped completely, taking with it her silent tears, leaving her eyes bright with dampness. The fear left, replaced by…what? Did he see desire, feel it in her no longer trembling body?

Perhaps.

He lowered his head and kissed her mouth, a tentative and brief meeting of lips. Just a simple kiss to ease away her tears, and it could have been so innocent if it hadn't left him shaking, far too eager for more of the same.

The image came to him again, of her sweet body under him, his mouth on her neck, feeding again…perhaps where the sand was the softest, high above the reach of the tide.

There was another tick to his internal clock. Dawn was but two hours away, and they were far from home. Too far to indulge any further fantasies.

He drew a shaky breath. "Time to go home."

* * * * *

Barely an hour remained of the night when they landed back at the Inn. Jonathan had flown directly there, no detours or further exploring. He was unusually quiet too, and Sharon wondered what was on his mind.

He lingered only a little while outside the Inn, bathing in the last of the moonlight before it disappeared over the edge of the trees. While he'd clearly been in a hurry to get home, he couldn't go inside without one last look.

There was a smile on his face as he finally directed her through the door into the garage.

When they reached the kitchen, he handed her the bottle of water she'd left unfinished. Hardly realizing how thirsty she'd been, she finished it in a few gulps. He watched, an indecipherable expression on his face.

Where to begin. She'd never had a night like this one. Listening to a werewolf concert, watching werepanthers fishing from the top of a tree. The intricate dance of the spellcasters as they wove their magic spell. And flying with the moonlight in her hair in her dark companion's arms. It had been a night of enchantment from beginning to end.

"Thank you. I had a wonderful time." The words seemed completely inadequate. She played with the empty bottle in her hand. "I wish tonight didn't have to end."

His voice was very soft. "It doesn't have to."

Her attention flew away from the bottle. "What? What do you mean?"

Now he watched her face, a slight smile on his lips that did not show in his eyes. Electric blue eyes with a wanting look. "I'm told I'm a quiet sleeper. I don't hog the bed or the covers. Since I don't breathe when I'm resting, I don't snore."

An uncertain thrill rushed through her. "You want me to go to bed with you?"

"I want you to sleep with me," he corrected. "Just sleep. My bed is very comfortable."

"Why?"

He shrugged. "I like the humanness of it. The feel of you in my arms. I want to hold you while I rest. I want to wake to it."

After such a glorious night, it seemed a simple request to answer...and she trusted him, didn't she? She hesitated.

She hesitated too long. The hopeful look in his eyes faded. "It's all right. Another time, perhaps." At the door he stopped. "Rest well, *meine Süsse*."

The door swung shut behind him, leaving her alone in the kitchen.

In her room, she fingered the Tiffany shade of the bedside lamp. When she'd first moved into the Inn, he'd placed it there to make her room more comfortable, to give her a sense of home. He'd cleaned and decorated her space with his own belongings.

The lamp's twin rested beside Jonathan's bed, in his lair beneath the Inn. It was a reminder of how thoughtful he was, her nightwalker friend, how much she owed him for taking her in. How much he valued her.

How much she cared for him, ever since the first night he'd kissed her.

She pulled her nightgown from the wardrobe and changed into it, leaving her sweater and jeans on the chair, smoothing the heavy cotton fabric against her skin. The feel of Jonathan's arms was still in her mind, how he'd lifted her from the beach and cradled her next to his chest all the way back home.

For the first time since she'd moved in, her bed didn't seem welcoming. It looked...lonely.

Pulling on her slippers and robe, Sharon turned off the Tiffany lamp and left the room.

He answered the door on the second knock. Something like surprise flickered on his face, quickly replaced with understanding, then a quiet joy. Wearing only a pair of drawstring pajama bottoms, Jonathan stepped away and allowed her entry.

"You changed your mind?"

"I hadn't made it up when you left." Her voice sounded shaky, even to her. "I'm not as certain of things as you are, Jonathan, it takes me longer."

"I'm a patient man. I can wait a long time to get what I want."

She could see that. When a man lived as long as he did, he could afford patience.

His head cocked to one side and he looked like he was listening to something. An ethereal cockcrow? His attention returned to her, a gentle smile in place. "We don't have much time now, though." One hand reached out to her. "Come."

Clutching his hand, she followed him to the bed behind the curtains. The covers were pulled back, the sheet beneath rumpled. He must have been lying down when she'd disturbed him.

Expertly, he undid the tie to her robe, pulled it off her shoulders, tossing it onto the nearby chair. She removed her slippers and laid them next to the bed. He climbed in first, then opened his arms to her, an invitation she wasted no time in responding to.

For a moment, he held her next to him, her head on his shoulder, hand against his bare chest. But then he turned onto his side and pulled her back into his chest so they resembled a pair of spoons, nestled in a drawer.

"This is how I prefer to sleep," he whispered into the hair at her neck.

Intimate, warm and comfortable. Drowsiness began to claim her. "You sleep this way with all your companions?"

He chuckled. "No, not all of them. Not with Marcus."

The idea of him resting in bed with the big cook struck her as humorous. "And why not?" she teased. "Don't you believe in equal opportunity?"

His breaths were coming slower now. Dawn must be breaking and he was close to the deep rest of the nightwalker. "I do in some things. But there are two problems with sleeping with Marcus. One, he snores."

"Oh, poor Kevin."

"Kevin doesn't mind," Jonathan said. "He cares too much and so forgives everything."

A laugh escaped her. "And the other?"

"And the other..." He was definitely close to sleep. He tightened his grip on her, snuggled closer into her neck. His voice was little more than a whisper now.

"And the other is that I'm not in love with Marcus."

With her last conscious thought she felt his breath on her neck cease and he became very still. After that she knew nothing.

# Chapter Eight

She woke just before he did, and at first everything was fine. More than fine, she felt wonderful, from the best night's—that is day's—rest she'd ever had. Warm, comfortable...safe. One strong arm held her firmly against him, only the faintest whisper of breath against the back of her neck. The embrace bespoke cherishing. Love.

*Love — that's what he'd said last night.* Jonathan didn't wish to sleep with Marcus because he didn't love Marcus. He did, however, wish to sleep with her. Therefore, through the rules of logic...

Sharon's eyes popped open, just as she felt the nightwalker stir behind her. His gentle hold tightened and she felt the pinprick of fangs as his mouth nibbled the back of her neck in a nuzzling kiss. A deep, contented sigh followed. "Good evening, *meine Süsse*. I presume you slept well."

Of course, he knew she'd slept well. Somehow she'd fallen dead to the world as soon as he had and that couldn't be a coincidence. "Yes, I did. I don't suppose you know why I would just drop off that way."

A kitten purring couldn't sound more contented than he did. He nuzzled the skin just below her ear. "Perhaps I do. It wouldn't be right for me to sleep while you were unable to."

Turning in his arms, she examined his face. "So you played sandman and sent me off to sleep?"

His eyes grew cautious at her disturbed tone. Still keeping one arm around her, he moved further up in the bed, the covers falling away, revealing his chest, and some of

Sharon's irritation melted at the sight. It had been a long time since she'd been alone with a man this delectable.

All right, truth be known, she'd never been alone with a man like Jonathan, and it wasn't just because he was a nightwalker.

He stared at her with his unblinking, pale blue gaze. "Something is bothering you?"

She hesitated. "What you said, last night...this morning. About love."

Amusement lightened his eyes. "About love. What did I say about love?" he teased.

Her tongue might as well have been tied into knots. "You said you weren't in love with Marcus."

Jonathan nodded gravely. "I also said he snored." Mock concern crossed his face. "I'd rather you not mention that to him. It might hurt his feelings."

If he didn't quit being so clever, she was going to punch him. For a moment, Sharon eyed his washboard stomach and wondered if a blow there would hurt him anywhere near as much as it would her hand. Unlikely.

She took a deep breath. She had to know what he'd meant, and the only way he'd tell her was if she asked. "Jonathan, did you want to sleep with me because you're in love with me?" The words gushed forth like blood from an open artery. For a moment she wondered if she'd spoken too fast.

He cocked his head. "Yes."

It was an answer so direct it left her speechless. Gaze fixed on her face, he ran the edge of his hand along her cheek, ending with his fingers under her chin. His voice was a low murmur. "I seem to remember you once wrote a song about this situation."

Without waiting for a response, he moved to cover her mouth with his, effectively silencing any protest she'd had in mind. The instant his lips hit hers, all thoughts, plans, expectations and intentions departed her brain, drowned in a whirlpool of simple sensation.

He'd kissed her before. In her bedroom, the night she'd moved into the Inn, then in his office, with his dinner asleep on the couch. Finally there was last night, on the beach — a sweet kiss that had come close to knocking her to her knees.

Not one of those kisses held a candle to this one. Jonathan wasn't holding anything back, her lips burned under the assault of his. He was pure seduction with a pair of lips, and Sharon didn't stand a chance.

His fingers found her breast under the heavy flannel of her gown and she moaned as he stroked the hardened tip through the cloth. Not content with that, his hand moved back to the closure at the front of the gown. Sharon barely registered its activity. Only when his hand wriggled through the opening and seized her nipple as its prize did she realize that he'd effectively opened her gown to the waist.

By now resistance was a fairly moot point. His lips ruled hers, one hand held the tip of her breast hostage. His other hand sought the bottom of her gown, dragging it up to her knees. As his fingers slipped between her thighs, Sharon managed to regain some of her senses.

She planted a hand on the middle of his chest, but the smooth, solid expanse felt so good she had to stifle a groan. It was all she could do to push rather than run her fingers along his flat nipples, exploring him further. With an effort she pulled her mouth away from him. "Jonathan, wait…"

He blinked. So did she, in surprise. She'd rarely seen him close his eyelids for anything other than rest, and even then…he'd been behind her last night.

For the moment, he stopped his sensuous assault on her body, although neither hand retreated from its position. His left hand held fast onto its captured nipple, the right gently caressed the thigh beneath it.

He eyed her lips with longing. "I'm waiting." His breath was coming almost as fast as hers, and his heart pounded steadily under her palm. He dragged his gaze back to her eyes, staring with pale blue intentness. A gentle, ever-so-talented thumb slid around the edge of her nipple, sending a tremor through her.

His voice was ragged. "Did you wish to discuss something?"

Desire flowed from his eyes, flooding her, and again her wits went adrift. She swallowed hard and dragged a loose net through the whirlpool overwhelming her mind, fishing for any excuse to stop this before it went further.

One idea surfaced. "I have to go to the bathroom."

A rueful grin tugged on his lips. "Oh. I see. Human needs." The hand holding her nipple released it but not before giving it a tug that sent an electric shock to her core.

She pulled from his embrace, carefully avoiding his eyes. Clutching her gown together, Sharon headed for the bathroom, not even bothering to grab her robe. After closing the door, she quickly buttoned her gown then splashed water on her flushed face, attempting to calm her fears.

Once she'd covered herself by flushing the toilet, she hesitated at the door and listened, not hearing anything from the other side. Most likely Jonathan was still in bed, waiting for her return.

*What was she going to do?* She'd entertained fantasies about Jonathan…clearly he'd had some of his own. The man wanted to make love with her…and under any other circumstances she'd be thrilled by the idea. Her body still tingled from his touch, his kiss…

Oh, let's face it, girl…he's a hunk and a half, even if he is bloodthirsty. Any red-blooded American girl would gladly donate a pint or two to be in her position. Or any other position he might have in mind.

But was she prepared for something like this, an affair with a three-hundred-year-old nightwalker? It wasn't like she'd had that much experience. He'd probably been with hundreds of women over time, most of them far more sophisticated than she was. He was way out of her league and she'd probably disappoint him.

What did she even look like? Her hair was no doubt a mess. A futile glance around the bathroom revealed no mirror so she could check her appearance. He, on the other hand, had looked wonderful. She closed her eyes, gave an inward moan. Too wonderful.

She should simply walk out there and tell him "no", for their own good. She'd come to regard him as a friend. It was too much for them to become lovers now.

Yes. She should simply open the door, walk over to that bed and tell him that.

Full of resolve, she opened the door only to walk right into him standing right outside. Hair still mussed from sleep, pajama bottoms slung low across his hips, one hand on either side of the doorway, filling it. His eyes were narrowed, searching her face, only the hint of a smile on his lips.

"I was beginning to worry about you."

She regained the use of her tongue and indicated the room behind her. "Did you need to go too?"

He looked over her shoulder then returned his stare to her. "No, not today. I don't when I haven't overindulged."

The facts of his life were forever a surprise to her. "You mean you still…"

"Depends on how much I've fed." He eyed her neck. "You might say I'm on a diet at the moment."

One hand left the doorway to capture her shoulder, pulling her closer. Appreciation for his strength warred with her reluctance. "Jonathan, I don't know what you want—" she began.

Mischief bloomed in his eyes. "Why is it I find that hard to believe?" His other hand now reached for her waist and with a single tug she was in his arms, his mouth inches from hers. "I think I've made myself perfectly clear." He ran his tongue along her lower lip.

She put her hands on his chest and this time pushed hard. "Listen to me, you overgrown mosquito."

Surprise filled his face and he burst into laughter. "Mosquito? But among them only the females suck blood, *meine Süsse*!" He recovered, shook his head in mocking disapproval. "I am not female."

*Oh, like that was ever in doubt.* The erection pressing against her stomach made his maleness totally apparent. Feeling as weak as a kitten, she continued to struggle in his arms. "Jonathan, please."

"I intend to please you. Come back to the bed, I'll show you." He let her struggle a little longer then released his hold and let her slip away. For once he looked uncertain. "Sharon, I can feel your desire for me. Why are you so reluctant—do I really frighten you that much?"

"No." It wasn't fear…exactly. "I'm not very good at this, Jonathan." She shoved her hair out of her eyes. "I'll disappoint you."

Understanding filled his face. He reached out to her but didn't take hold of her this time. Instead he ran a gentle thumb along her cheek, down her neck. For once it stayed away from her marks, as if he wanted to avoid reminding her of the nature of their relationship. "I could disappoint you too. But I doubt it. We won't know unless we try, though."

"Man to woman?" The words jumped out of her. "We'd do it like normal people, not...whatever else we are."

He actually held his breath for a moment. Stillness filled him and with it came a look of disappointment on his handsome face. The playfulness was gone but he still wanted her, she could tell from the desire in his eyes.

What had she asked of him, that it would bother him so much?

He nodded. "Whatever you wish. Man to woman. Normal man," he emphasized. His ice blue eyes bore into hers. "I will be as normal as I can be, for you."

Once again he pulled her into his arms, bent his head into a soul-stealing kiss. The next thing she knew he'd carried her back to the bed and set her down next to it.

One finger traced the line of buttons on her nightgown. "Do you value this garment, Sharon?"

Startled, she glanced down. "Yes."

"Then remove it please. I've undone it once already and don't trust my patience to do it again."

His voice held a note of impatience. She fumbled with the buttons. "You're upset with me." Every movement toward this told her it was a bad idea to continue.

"No. Not upset." He sighed. "You don't trust me, and that is troublesome."

She had the buttons half undone. "I do trust you."

One hand grabbed hers, stopping her progress on the nightgown. "You don't, not if you want me to be human for you. My inhumanity is what I am and what I must be, even with you." He forced her to meet his steady gaze. "Whatever happens between us, for whatever purpose, I won't hurt you. I promise."

"I know that." And somehow she did know—Jonathan would never hurt her. "But today...I need to know the man a little better, before..."

A brief smile flitted across his face and it lost its stoniness. "...before you can trust the monster in me. Very well, let me earn that trust, Sharon."

He pulled her trembling fingers from the gown and worked the last of the buttons free, pulled it open to reveal her. As he gazed his fill, he shoved the gown so it fell off her shoulders and accumulated into a circle around her feet. The warmth returned to his eyes and appreciation filled them as he took in her uncovered form. A slight smile formed on his lips. "You are magnificent."

She felt a blush forming then decided to meet boldness with boldness. Why should she be the only one naked? She pulled on the drawstring to his pajama bottoms. "Okay, your turn."

His smile broadened into a grin. "Very well...but you have to promise not to faint." She rolled her eyes at his overwhelming self-confidence. Eyes twinkling he released the knot and let the pants slide to the floor.

"Oh, my." Sharon's eyes riveted to what the pants had hidden. Her experience wasn't extensive, and she'd seen bigger, at least in pictures, but Jonathan's had all the right proportions, length, width and circumference. It was, in a word, "magnificent".

He crossed his arms and stared at her, daring her to comment. "Well?"

Determined to be nonchalant, Sharon nodded her head. "Yes, well. Very nice."

He blinked again, and she made a note of it. Twice in one day, somehow she kept managing to surprise him.

"'Very nice.' Is that all you can say?" An anxious look entered his face. "You're not disappointed, are you?" He glanced down. "Size isn't everything, you know."

She was quick to reassure him. "I'm sure it isn't." He continued to look worried, so she patted him on the arm. "It's fine. Really. I'm not that picky."

Something in her voice must have given her away. "You're teasing me?" he asked, astonished.

Nerves and awkwardness combined to undo her and Sharon collapsed into a fit of giggles. "You should see your face."

Eyes blazing, he swept her up in his arms and deposited her on the bed, jumping in on top of her for good measure. Stretching out, he captured her hands and held them firmly on the pillow over her head, his body pressing her deep into the mattress. Her giggles disappeared under his fierceness. "Didn't anyone ever tell you it isn't smart to tease a monster?"

She swallowed and found her voice. "I told you before I don't see you as a monster, Jonathan."

He closed his eyes and breathed heavily for a moment. When he opened them again, there was a tenderness in them that took her breath away. "I hope you never do."

His mouth sought hers, and before she knew it, the world evolved into one of simple senses, cool sheets beneath her, warm man above. Hands roved everywhere, touching, stroking, leaving electric trails of sensation behind. His mouth moved too, tasting her, his tongue wet against her skin. When he pressed her head into his neck, she nibbled, digging her teeth in just a fraction, and he gave a gasp that left her agape.

His eyes bored into hers. "Be very careful of that, companion mine. You don't want to switch sides." She remembered what he'd told her, how a nightwalker was made, by drinking the blood of another of the kind.

Surely he hadn't thought… "I was just…I mean." Her voice faltered.

"I know." He spoke in a harsh whisper. "What we do now, is as normal humans do. Were I to do the same to you, I'd be doing more than that." He barely nicked her skin, the edge of his fangs mere pinpricks against her neck. A touch of his tongue and the sting was gone.

"You feed this way?"

He licked his lips, looked wanting but resigned. "Not without a full link." He managed a smile. "Far too dangerous. Sex is feral enough without adding feeding into it. I promised you, this would be man to woman and nothing more."

He rubbed himself against her core, the sensation nearly driving her out of her mind. Shaken, she stared into his eyes, saw humor slip into the desire there. "Somehow, I believe that will be enough for now," he told her.

He tested her readiness with his hand, one finger, then two, the gentle probing causing her to cry out. A grimace appeared on his face. "Too tight, Sweetness. I don't wish to hurt you."

Bending his head, he captured first one then the other of her nipples, sucking on them gingerly in succession. The tips of his fangs teased and tickled her until she almost wished he would sink them in. It couldn't be more mind-bending than this slow torture she was enduring. Meanwhile his hand worked the entry to her center until she wasn't sure where her mind was anymore.

A tension, like that of a coiled spring, began to make its presence known, filling her middle. Each stroke of his hand or touch of his mouth was like a key to the watch works controlling that spring. It wound tighter and tighter then, without warning, released, a wave of relief that swept through her. Her mouth flew open and a cry emerged, one she barely recognized as her own.

"Yes, like that." Jonathan's low voice spoke to her, encouraged her. His eyes were like blue flame when she gazed into them, helpless in the aftershock of her release.

Her first coherent thought was that she was wrong—she hadn't had an orgasm before and her second thought was that Jonathan was taking advantage of her new, relaxed state. Mounting her with sudden swiftness, she found herself pinned to the bed by his legs, his shaft deeply embedded within her.

For a moment he rested there, keeping his weight on his arms, face staring into hers. Wanting, needing, now having. He looked—happy. She felt full, warm. Possessed, and content with that possession. The feeling was sufficient.

Then he moved and nothing was sufficient any longer. Without thinking, Sharon grabbed his back, wrapped her legs around him, tying him to her. Enough now, he was hers, she his. Now they moved together as one. What part of her brain still functioned, worked to keep track of what he did, and to do it to him moments later. When his eyes glazed over and his breath speeded up past hers, she knew she'd learned how to please him.

The spring of sensual tension returned and this time they both worked to wind it, ever tighter, until it nearly killed her with anticipation. And now she could feel it in Jonathan as well, the need for release, basic, primitive. As he had said, feral. She could see it in his tortured face. He caught his breath, moved once more. It was all she could take as well, her throat felt raw from her scream.

He didn't cry out, but the shudders that ran through him were more eloquent than the loudest shout. As his breathing returned to normal, he whispered into her neck, gentle words, soft, not English. *"Meine Liebe, meine eigene Liebe. Meine Süsse sind Sie, überhaupt mehr."*

Once again she was reminded of his origin. She stroked his face and he turned to gaze into hers. "What was that?"

He smiled, a brief enigmatic smile. "I said: 'My love, my own love. Sweetness you are, ever more.'"

"Your love?"

He grabbed her hand and kissed it, his fangs a gentle touch across the back. "My love. We are lovers now."

Humor laced its way into his serious eyes, twinkled gently. He hoisted himself onto one arm, allowing the other to stroke her body. "And now, tell me. How was I, man to woman? Adequate? Size, it is not that important, yes?"

She grabbed his hand and kissed it, smiling into his face. "Size is the least important part. Love is what matters."

# Chapter Nine

Sharon needed to return to her room and dress for the evening. Jonathan watched from the bed as she pulled on her nightgown and buttoned it up, all thumbs, the result leaving one lone button undone at the top, an empty hole at the bottom. Too flustered to fix it, she hurried away and he had to remind her to take her robe and slippers as she glided out the door and up the stairs.

Once she was gone, the room fell into silence, into peace. Yes, peace, the peace of unburied dead. Jonathan groaned and reminded himself he wasn't dead. That was an untruth spread for years by narrow minds.

*Like a man to a woman.* That's what she'd wanted, that's what he'd given her, and it had been glorious, for all of the insult endured. She hadn't realized what she'd said, not really. Fear of the unknown had birthed that requirement. She'd been to bed with a man before, knew what it was, and so hadn't been afraid to let him love her.

In truth, he couldn't have done as he'd wished anyway, loved her in the proper manner. Not without a full link. That would come, eventually. He hoped.

Now she'd been to bed with him and had enjoyed herself immensely. More than that…she'd shown such surprise at her climax. It had been a new experience for her. He'd pleased her, as a man to a woman, shown her ecstasy, even felt his own, a welcome treat after so many years. He'd felt ecstasy as well.

And yet it still hurt.

Hunger tore at him. Making love without taking blood…it had been centuries since he'd tried that. It was one reason he never took physical pleasure with his meals, too dangerous with someone not prepared for it.

Too dangerous for someone who was not a companion.

And since he hadn't had a female companion since…since Angela. Jonathan closed his eyes. His sweet angel, ever pure of faith and of love. Hair the color of flame, eyes of bright emerald, skin thin as porcelain, blood like honey.

Never had he expected to find another like her, not in a hundred years.

So it had taken eighty instead. Eighty lonely years, living off humans seeking a thrill, or male companions with longevity in their thoughts.

Sharon was special—too much so. Sebastian was wrong, as always. Jonathan needed to coddle her, to teach her slowly what it was to be a companion. The knowledge could be too much for a woman like her. He had so much time to offer both of them. It was right to take it slow.

But Sebastian was also right—that Jonathan should have explained everything to Sharon from the beginning, how it would be between them. Should have explained about the feedings, how a mind link was essential for everything, particularly when it came to the most basic of interactions. For food, sex—and healing. To replenish the soul and the basic health of a vampire.

Vampire. It had been years since he'd thought of himself that way. But holding Sharon close, he wanted so much to taste her, had felt the blood lust in his mind and his heart. What he'd felt with her had been wonderful, but it was a mere trifle compared to what he hoped to have soon.

As soon as he could talk her into it.

In the meantime he needed more than he could take from his still-reluctant companion. He pulled himself from the bed and found clothes appropriate for the evening. Once dressed, he considered his options. After having sex, he needed a deeper than normal feeding. He'd fed from Marcus less than a week ago. It was too soon to draw from that well, nor could he take from Sharon.

Decision made, Jonathan reluctantly reached for the phone. It wouldn't be as satisfying as a companion feed, but he really didn't have any choice.

* * * * *

Sharon was halfway down the hallway when she ran into Marcus. His eyes lit up as he took in her mis-buttoned nightgown and the robe and slippers in her hands. Furiously blushing, Sharon slipped by him and fled to her room. She heard him chuckling as she reached the door.

Once inside, she took a quick shower then grabbed a pair of jeans and a T-shirt, suitable for dinner. She'd change later, before taking her position behind the bar. Making love had given her an appetite and she was too hungry to dress up now.

Marcus was in the kitchen when she arrived, tending a pair of good-sized steaks on the grill. He grinned as she came through the door and raised one knowing eyebrow. "Have a good time last night?"

How could she possibly explain to Marcus what happened last night—and this evening? It was all way too confusing, too private. For a moment she relived being in Jonathan's arms, the intense pleasure she'd felt there. She still could barely believe she'd made love with him. Instead of answering, she grabbed a mug and filled it from the coffee pot.

With a long fork, Marcus turned the steaks, the browned sides still sizzling. The smell was intoxicating. Famished, Sharon considered asking him to make her steak rare. Only the image of Amber, chewing on a piece of raw beef, kept her from doing just that.

"Here, you probably need this." Marcus held out a bottle of water to her.

"Thanks." Sharon opened it and sipped gingerly. She wasn't as thirsty as she'd expected. When she put the bottle down, she caught Marcus's expression, the surprise in his face. He'd expected her to drink more. Feeling self-conscious, she took a deeper gulp from the bottle.

Marcus finished one of the steaks and put it on a plate for her. Eagerly Sharon dug in, more hungry than she could remember. He prepared a second one for himself and sat opposite her, a thoughtful look on his face. He watched her down a good third of the meat before speaking. "Well, you're hungry at least."

"Yes."

"But not thirsty."

Something in his voice made her pause. She put down the fork and considered him. He definitely knew something he wasn't saying.

Jonathan entered and headed for the refrigerator without speaking. He poured himself a tall glass from the serum bottle, drank it quickly and refilled it. Marcus watched, his dark eyes speculative. When Jonathan finished his second glass, the cook pursed his lips for a moment. "Who should we expect this evening?"

Jonathan studied the empty glass for a moment, apparently reluctant to answer. He glanced over at Sharon and returned his attention to Marcus. "Kimberly," he said shortly.

Marcus nodded. "Okay. I'll stock the refrigerator in the office."

Kimberly? He'd invited that bimbo in to feed on? A feeling of outrage rose within her at the memory of the blonde nincompoop.

He moved and put the empty glass inside the sink, then headed for the back hallway. "I'll be in my office."

After he'd left, Sharon stared at her plate. What had happened, had she done something wrong? Marcus clearly knew what was going on. She studied the man. "Marcus…" Her voice trailed off into uncertainty.

The big man took another bite of his steak and chewed it slowly. When he'd swallowed, he followed up with a sip from his coffee mug. Meeting her eyes, he grimaced then laid down the mug. "Okay, Shari, what do you want to know?"

Unsure how to ask, she stalled, but Marcus must have figured it out. "You want to know why he's asked Kim in for dinner, right?" She nodded. "That one's easy—he's hungry and Kim is good for that. She's a regular and he knows he can take a lot from her at one time without hurting her. Also she hasn't been in for some time. As to why he's hungry…" Marcus looked meaningfully at the barely touched water bottle in front of her.

Sharon stared back, defensive. "He fed from me last night! He did it before we went out."

The big man shrugged. "Good, I'm glad to hear it. But I don't think he took enough. Then there's what else went on." He toyed with his coffee. "You went to bed with him."

Sharon's cheeks burned. "Not that it's any of your business…"

He waved an impatient hand. "Of course it's my business. I'm Jon's companion, same as you. More to the point, I've been here longer and know more about it. I've talked to others like us. What you and Jon did isn't unusual, but it can be dangerous if he hasn't fed properly. Usually that isn't a problem because a little nibbling happens during the act, but since you aren't thirsty…"

*Like a man to a woman* — her words came back to haunt her. Sharon was suddenly very glad she was seated since her legs felt like rubber. That's why her request had bothered him. Jonathan needed to feed when they'd made love. Her voice shook when she spoke. "He didn't tell me that."

Marcus shook his head. "No, I imagine not. Jon's like that, he wouldn't ask if he thought you weren't ready for it. He's been like that as long as I've known him."

Sharon had been reluctant to ask questions about Jonathan and Marcus. Now it became important to know everything, as much as she could find out. "How long has that been?"

The big man grinned at her. "You want to hear my story? Okay, sure. Might help." He leaned back, toyed with his mug. "It was 1968, and I was living in Venice."

Sharon leaned forward. Marcus met Jonathan in Europe? "You mean in Italy?"

He laughed. "No, nothing so romantic. Not Italy. Venice Beach, down in LA." He took a big sip of coffee, studied the steam coming out of the cup. "Actually, when he met me, I wasn't so much living on Venice Beach…I was dying."

Horror gripped her. "Dying?"

A soft grunt emerged. "Yeah, dying. I'd dropped out of school, lost my job, my latest lover had dumped me for someone else." He glanced up at her. "I'd told my folks what I was and they'd disowned me immediately. This was before the days where someone like me could even hope for acceptance." A thoughtful look passed over his face. "I wonder if they're still around, my folks. I haven't talked to them since the early eighties."

He shook himself and continued with his story. "In addition, I was totally strung out on methamphetamines—you know, speed? Life suddenly didn't seem worth living, so I walked to the beach with a razor blade and decided to make my way out." He grimaced. "I was so stoned, I didn't even feel the razor when I sliced my wrist."

It tore at her that this pleasant, confident man had felt so alone. "I'm sorry, Marcus."

Marcus shrugged. "It was a long time ago, Shari, but I appreciate the sympathy. Anyway, I was telling you about Jon. There I was, sitting on the sand, bleeding from a couple of cuts in my arm, when this tall, dark dude walks up and sits down next to me on the beach. He grabs my wrist and asks me, ever so politely, if I minded if he had some, since I clearly didn't want it. I was too strung out to argue, so he sucks for a while and seals the holes I'd made. He thanks me and suggests that he buy me a drink in return.

"Next thing I know, I'm in this basement apartment with him over in Santa Monica, with a cold beer in front of me, telling him my life story. Then he told me his and offered me a job as his companion. It seems I had just the right amount of mental power to permit the link needed, plus he liked the way I tasted—for a man, that is. He prefers women, you know."

Sharon blushed at that reminder while Marcus grinned. "Jonathan put me to work in his restaurant, The Nighthawk. It was a really hot place to be—there was a nightclub attached to it that attracted the trendiest entertainers in town. I met them all, the songwriters and bands that came in. Everyone knew Jon, although not everyone knew what he was. Only a very select few ever suspected he was anything but a guy who liked to party late and avoid solid food." Marcus leaned back, pleased with his memories. "Man, those were the days."

He glanced around the kitchen with possessive pride. "He sent me to culinary school so I could cook in his restaurant and gave me a place to stay. He's been my friend, Shari, ever since." A wry laugh escaped him. "If only the man were gay, he'd be perfect."

But Jonathan wasn't gay. He was very heterosexual, very sexy, and he very much desired her. Sharon leaned her head on her hands. "He told me he was in love with me."

Marcus's eyebrows beetled together into a single line. "Did he? Well, now, that's interesting. I've never heard him say as much to anyone else, and heaven knows he's had the opportunity." A hand as big as a dinner plate reached out to pat hers gently. "If he said it, Shari, I'd believe him."

"But to love him, I'm going to have to let him take blood when we're...we're..." Her voice trailed off. Somehow the words were hard to say. "When we're making love," she finally finished.

He squeezed her hand and stood up, grabbing their plates as he did. As he moved to the sink with them, he responded over his shoulder. "Somehow I suspect you'll figure out what to do, Shari. Love makes people do the right things."

\* \* \* \* \*

Heart in mouth, Sharon reached up to knock on the door and it opened before her hand hit the panel. With a smooth motion, Jonathan pulled her inside the room and closed the door behind her.

His face was pale, intent. Drops of sweat dotted his brow. Abruptly, he tilted her head and kissed her, his lips moving seductively over hers, his tongue lightly slipping within her mouth, a tentative visitor. But there was nothing else tentative about him as he pulled her to him with increasing force. Breathless, Sharon allowed it all, grateful for his intensity. She didn't need to talk to him if he was kissing her and she wasn't sure what she had to say.

Finally he broke off the kiss, still pinning her to the door behind. "Just in case you thought I'd changed my mind about us." He closed in for another round of kissing.

Sharon held him off, cupping his face in her hands. Laughing, she ran her mouth down his neck, finding the thin pulse point. Shocked, she realized she could feel its weakness, that she was aware of how slight it was and how drained he'd become. "You need to feed."

He rested his forehead against hers. "Yes, I do," he admitted. "It's being dealt with, I can wait until Kimberly gets here."

Sudden jealous fury filled her. Pricked, Sharon offered her wrist to him. "You could feed from me."

His eyes grew cautious. "Not now. It's too soon since the last time, Sharon. I won't risk it."

"You could," she insisted. "You didn't take that much last night, and you could have fed this evening, had you told me."

A bleak expression filled his face. "No, I couldn't, not without a full link. I won't, Sharon. I won't risk hurting you, not now, not ever." He cupped her face in his hands, his mouth a whisper away from hers. "Don't tempt me like this. I'm hungry and I can't feed from you tonight."

He pushed away, turned to the desk. "Perhaps you should go. We need to open up soon."

He'd dismissed her, just like that. Humiliated, Sharon stared at him, the graceful line of his back as he stood next to the desk. Arguing was useless and she did need to change clothes before the bar opened. She felt behind for the doorknob, turned it and slipped through the door without another word.

* * * * *

The crowd was a quiet one that night. Several of the shapeshifters came in, later than usual, looking somewhat the worse for wear. Some appeared to have been brawling under the full moon of the night before.

On the other hand, Amber looked like the cat who'd caught the canary and swallowed it whole. If Sharon hadn't known her to be a werewolf, she'd have predicted a more feline alternative self for the golden-eyed shapeshifter. The woman practically purred.

"Have a nice night?" Sharon asked when Amber smiled with all of her pointed teeth.

"Oh... Yes...you might say that." She grinned. "A very *productive* night, if you know what I mean."

Amber leaned against the bar, her pose relaxed and comfortable. She sniffed, startled, and took a deeper whiff in Sharon's direction. Her eyebrows lifted. A grin spread across her face. "Hmm, maybe I wasn't the only one. I think I smell a little eau de nightwalker on you, Shari."

Shocked, Sharon stared at the shapeshifter. "Well, I did spend the evening with him," she offered weakly.

Amber's grin widened. "Oh, you spent more than the evening—I'd say a good part of the day, right up to a few minutes ago. A few very intimate moments. Mighty Jon really has lost his heart, hasn't he?"

Was everyone going to know that she'd shared a bed with Jonathan? Sharon's face burned under Amber's amused scrutiny. The shapeshifter's eyes glimmered in the dim light of the bar. "Maybe he isn't the only one."

Sharon was in no mood to discuss the state of her heart. Right on schedule, the feeder blonde arrived, Kimberly, all five-foot-ten of her, happy as a lamb to the slaughter. She bounced over to the bar and headed for Sharon. "You're still here!" she exclaimed.

Where else would she be? She was Jonathan's companion, not this blonde bimbo. Sharon managed a smile. "He's waiting for you, Kim."

"Thanks!" She all but skipped across the room to the back doorway. Sharon watched her go, then turned to find Amber's gaze on her, the werewolf's expression one of unexpected understanding.

"He's hungry."

"Yeah. They always are. Too bad one woman can't be enough for them, right?"

A group of patrons at one of the tables hailed Amber, drawing her away from the bar. Sharon watched her go, and wondered if it was possible for one woman to be enough...one companion to be enough for a nightwalker.

Later that night she found the opportunity to quiz her fellow companion about it. "How many companions does a nightwalker need, Marcus?" Sharon cleaned the bar while the big man picked up the chairs, stacking them on the tables in preparation for sweeping the floor. At her question, he paused and a cautious smile crept across his face.

"That depends. Some, like Sebastian, don't have any, simply hunt or seduce what blood they need. Some live off supplies from local blood banks, although those folks aren't as healthy. Jon's gotten by with only one or two for centuries now. One isn't enough without supplements."

*Yeah,* she thought bitterly. *Bleach-blonde supplements.* Vitamin Kim had emerged from Jon's office with an expression of satisfaction that left Sharon's hands curled into knots. She went back to polishing the bar surface, trying to work out her latent fury at the self-satisfied look Jon's dinner had displayed while sipping her orange juice.

Marcus put down the broom and came over to the bar. "Does it really bother you that much, having him feed off of someone else? You're special, Sharon, you know that don't you? Someone like Kim..."

"I know...she's just nutrition." She stared up at him. "Yes, it bothers me. He gives them pleasure, like..."

"Like he did you?" The big man nodded with understanding. "Yeah, I don't much like sharing my lovers."

No, it wasn't like that. Jonathan hadn't shown her pleasure when he'd fed from her, just a warm glow. Was that it, that she'd felt cheated when Kim came out feeling like Jonathan had made love to her when he hadn't done the same to *her*? But he had, in bed just hours before, real pleasure that they'd both shared. They'd made love and it had been glorious. So why should she begrudge Kim's little bit of glow when she'd had the real thing from Jonathan?

Because it was *wrong*! Deep in her heart she knew that. Maybe to Jonathan it was just playacting when he was with someone like Kim, but that didn't make it right.

But what could she do about it? If she couldn't provide enough blood and Marcus couldn't either, Jon had to have others. That he used his ability to give pleasure to them to keep them coming back for more, that was just part of the process. Nothing Sharon could say or do was going to stop it and she might as well get used to it.

He hadn't appeared after Kim left and hadn't been in his office when Sharon had gone by to check after closing. For a moment she wondered if he'd gone out, but surely he would have said something. He'd kissed her in the office before, told her that he hadn't changed his mind. Just because he couldn't feed on her didn't mean he didn't still want her.

*Not to worry, meine Süsse, I still want you.*

At the intrusive thought, her head shot up. Jonathan's mental touch had sounded amused—and a little sad at the same time. *I didn't feel you in my head.* Closing her eyes, she saw it, the golden glow he'd labeled his "soul", hovering just out of reach.

*It's easier now, to speak with you this way. We are closer than we were.*

*Because we... because we made love?*

Now he was amused. *That's part of it. You don't fear me the way you did.* There was a moment's pause. *Come to me now. I'm downstairs.*

Sharon looked over at Marcus who apparently wasn't privy to their telepathic conversation. He'd finished stacking the chairs and was sweeping the floor. She didn't want to abandon him, but her work behind the bar was done. "Marcus, do you need me?"

The big man paused, leaned on the broom. He tilted his head for a moment, as if listening to something, then gave her a knowing smile. He shook his head, "Not as much as Jonathan does. Go on, Shari."

# Chapter Ten

Sharon hesitated outside the door to the lair until she began to feel silly. Why should she feel awkward? Jonathan had invited her. She reached up to knock.

*Come in.*

This time the mental touch didn't surprise her. He'd twice now known when she was near. She opened the door and the sound of music greeted her. Jonathan sat at a portable electronic keyboard, his fingers dancing over the keys. It sounded like a harpsichord and once again Sharon realized how brilliantly he played any instrument.

She tried to place the piece as he continued to play. When he finished and turned to her, she had it. "Mozart. One of the sonatas, isn't it?"

"Yes. Sonata in G." Jonathan restlessly tickled a pair of keys. "It's one of my favorites."

"You play it very well."

Old sadness and resignation filled his eyes. "He'd be pleased to hear you say that. He taught it to me."

Sharon's rubber knees returned and she sought the couch for support. She knew Jonathan was old...but... "You learned to play that from Mozart himself?"

He laughed and turned to stare at her. There were no lines around his eyes. His face had the unblemished skin of a young man. "I've been alive for over three hundred years, Sharon. Amadeus and I were the same age when we were in Vienna." For a moment his eyes closed as he resurrected that memory. "He was brilliant. The most wonderful musician."

Excitement filled her. He'd never spoken of his past before, avoided any questions when asked — maybe tonight that would change. "You knew him well?"

"As well as anyone, except perhaps his wife." He turned off the keyboard and sat facing her on the narrow bench. Clasping his hands in front him, he gazed downward, his mind deep in memory's well. "He was so serious about his music and it was so much a part of his life. You've seen the movie they made?"

She remembered it, the silly, giggling man who became earnest when his music was played. "*Amadeus*? Yes. Was he like that?"

A soft chuckle escaped him. "At times we all were. It was a heady time to be at the emperor's court. Hard to stay focused when there was so much life around. But he was a musician and a composer, first and foremost. Music was his life, he lived it. Breathed it. At times he'd have trouble sleeping because the notes were so frantic to escape his mind, they'd keep him awake. It was nothing for him to wake in the early hours and run to his writing table to pen off a section of a concerti or a quartet."

He rubbed the back of his head and raised his gaze to stare into her face. "Do you want to hear about me, Sharon? About my life…who I was…who I am?"

"Yes." Her answer was heartfelt. She wanted to know this tall, dark stranger who'd become so important to her. She had questions about her part in his world. Perhaps if she knew him better, she'd know what her part should be. What she might want it to be — or become.

He nodded. "Very well, I will tell you. But there are two conditions. First, you must tell no other. It is known well enough that I'm unlike other men, but confirmation of that should never come from a companion. You understand that?"

"I understand." She would never tell anyone. If they believed her, he might be in danger. If they didn't, she'd be locked up as a lunatic. "What is the other condition?"

"That you do me the same honor. Tell me who you are, what your past is. What is important to you? I wish to know you as you would know me."

That was a high price. There were things she'd told no one, could tell no one. She gazed into his pale blue eyes and saw the strength there, the compassion. "I—I will tell you what I can. Some things, I'm not sure I can tell anyone."

"If we mind linked, I would know these hidden truths, right, *meine Süsse*? Is that why you fight so hard to keep me away?"

She couldn't answer him. He didn't press it. With an elegant wave of his hand, he dismissed the question. "Very well. We will have a partial meeting of minds. You will tell me what you can—I will say what I wish to. Perhaps, someday, there will be complete honesty between us. Acceptable?"

Mutely, she nodded.

He moved from the bench to the couch, next to her. The fine, light blue silk shirt he wore matched his eyes, and the sleek black pants molded to his legs and rear like they were painted on. A rush of awareness of him caught the breath in Sharon's throat.

Some partial link already existed between them—he knew his effect on her. She knew because he glanced over at her, his half-smile dangerous, his eyes alive and molten with passion. "Whatever truths come out, let this be the first one— I wish to love you this night and have you stay with me during our time of rest."

The direct answer to her unspoken question completed her blush, a fresh wave of heat burning her cheeks. He was unlike any man she'd ever known. "But you want to talk first."

Head tilted, he seemed to listen to some unheard sound then returned his attention to her. "It is just past two-thirty in the morning. We have several hours until dawn. Yes, I wish to talk—first."

She glanced past him at the small clock on the VCR, the only timepiece in the room. Unlike most such appliances, it was set correctly—Jonathan had no trouble understanding technology. He also was dead on with the time. "How do you do that? Know the time without a clock."

He smiled, a genuine one that didn't hide his fangs. It occurred to her that he rarely tried to hide them from her anymore. She'd gotten so used to them that she barely noticed.

"Long practice. It isn't so much the time I worry about, but the position of the sun. I always know where that is. It would not do for me to be caught unawares."

"If you did...would it kill you?"

"It would be most unpleasant. My skin is hypersensitive to the sun. I cannot take the direct rays at all. The one time it happened, it took many days for the skin to regenerate and that was just on one arm." He held out his left arm and flexed it, stared at his fingers. "I couldn't use my hand for a month."

His palm landed on the back of the couch, behind her back. Not touching, but the option was there and awareness of that possibility distracted her. She almost missed the rest. "To answer your question, if enough of me was burned, I would likely die. This body of mine has a delicate balance to it. Much of it works as it did before I changed—as you already know." He wiggled his eyebrows and Sharon giggled.

Then he sobered. "Other parts are different. My blood pressure is very low and my heart beats slower. Digestion is limited. I can't tolerate most foods. Some pure substances, such as alcohol, I can manage but sugars, proteins and starches are very difficult for me to handle in any quantities. For example, I can drink vodka, but not a screwdriver, unless it's made with serum."

The image of Vanessa running for the outdoors after two mouthfuls of her contaminated "Los Niños Sunset" came to mind. That really had been a dirty trick to play. Sharon felt a surge of sympathy before remembering how nasty the nightwalker had been.

A mournful expression came into his eyes. "I can't have chocolate. The one time I did, it was so delicious, I was deliriously happy. The most luscious food on Earth...until the stomach cramps hit. I spent the rest of the night ill."

She concealed her amusement, but Jonathan seemed to sense it anyway. The arm behind her wrapped around her shoulders and pulled her into him. He nuzzled her neck, nipping without drawing blood. "That's why I like your taste. You are nectar for me, my sweet indulgence."

They embraced for a while, passion lurking, in danger of taking over the conversation, then Jonathan loosened his grip and wry expression filled his face. "You have this effect on me. I asked you here to talk, and I end up loving you instead." One arm slipped to hold her waist. "What was it we were discussing?"

"You were telling me about Mozart."

"Ah, yes. So sublimely talented. The greatest composer, the greatest musician."

"He died young."

"He did." Jonathan rested his head on her shoulder, deep sadness radiating off him. She felt it through his skin, through the link into her mind. Tears formed in her eyes for a man who'd died three centuries earlier. One she could never know, but who'd been Jonathan's friend.

"His music fell out of favor at court and he grew poorer, then ill. A fever overtook him and he died. There is a contemporary song that features a line, 'The Day the Music Died'. That's what it was like for me to know he was gone—all that bright music still in him, never to come out.

"It was why I became a vampire."

The admission startled her. Not only because of his reason, but that he'd used the title he so disliked. "How so?"

"I had known for some time there were odd things about the Countess Du Lea. She was young in appearance but seemed so much older. We all kept our skin powdered, so the paleness wasn't obvious, but she never indulged in outdoor games or daylight events. Her parties were always held at night, gay events more self-indulgent than anything you'd see today. She forever had a glass of wine in hand but never sat to dinner. In the ten years I knew her, she never changed.

"There was a young man who attended her, with pale hair and similar habits." A sly smile crossed his face. "You know him now as Sebastian. He is older than me, fifty years or more. Older, wiser," Jonathan laughed, "at least in his own mind, and therefore, my prince."

"He's your prince because he's older?"

"Not really. It is mostly that he commands respect in the parafolk world—besides for some reason he wants the job." Jonathan laughed. "We choose who governs us very carefully as they are likely to be with us a long time, and then he chooses others to help him." He seemed about to say more, but instead waved his hand as if dismissing any further comment on the subject. Sharon wondered what else he'd been about to say.

"So, now he is my prince, but at the time I met him, he was merely a young man who lived with the Countess. They seemed devoted to each other, but as much like mother to son as lovers. It was all—very odd. When Amadeus died they attended the funeral, were some of the few who did. I wasn't myself that day, and when the ceremony was over they invited me to their home."

His voice became so quiet she had to strain to hear it. "We poured wine and toasted Mozart's life, his accomplishments. They told me that his music would live forever. I said…"

His voice broke off and he turned to bury his face in her hair. Sharon wrapped her arms around him, pulled him closer, waited until he was ready to continue. "What did you say?"

He pulled back, a wistful smile playing across his lips. "I said 'if it were all the same, I'd rather I live forever and not my music'. The Countess and her friend looked at one another and told me it could be arranged."

"So you became a vampire so you could live forever?"

"In a sense. I didn't want the music to ever die, Sharon. I said it was Mozart's life, but it was mine as well."

She stroked his arm, took his talented fingers into hers. She'd seen the way he could play a guitar or the keyboard. The man was a consummate musician. She would believe anything he said about that.

"When I was a boy I lived on a farm but I never felt at home there. My father tried to teach me the ways of his forefathers but it was always music that called to me. I spent more time in the church with the parish priest than I did with the cows and pigs. The church had an organ and the priest felt it was his duty to educate me in the written chord. I could play anything on that organ, always felt close to God when I was at the keyboard."

"You believe in God?" Sharon asked, a little surprised at the thought of a god-worshiping nightwalker.

"I believe in a supreme being, of course...what else could have made such a wonderful world?" His eyes crinkled in merriment. "Oh, I understand, more old vampire lore. In truth, I don't mind crosses, I love old churches and holy water simply makes me wet. I'm not evil, Sharon, any more than a flea or a mosquito is evil. I'm just different."

Sharon had never really thought of Jonathan as good or evil, but it was nice to have confirmation. At least she wouldn't have to worry about crazy vampire hunters with squirt guns full of holy water harming him.

He leaned closer to her and grinned. "There's a church in Los Angeles that has a very fine German pipe-organ provided by an 'anonymous' donor back in the thirties. I have a letter from the bishop that gives me special permission to play it whenever I'm in town." He sighed. "It's been a while since I was last there. I hope it's still in good order."

He closed his eyes and leaned back, the smile of happy memories on his lips. Sharon watched his face. "Did your father object to you learning to play the organ?"

Eyes opened with a wistful expression. "No. In fact, he encouraged me. I was the older son, but my younger brother was far better suited to farm life than I was. Father was a forward-thinking man who believed in the greater destiny, that mine was not to live the life he led. When the priest recommended I go to Vienna, he concurred. Sold his best *milchkuh* — that is his milk cow, to pay my way there."

One hand played with a lock of her hair, escaped from its clip. "Still, I don't think he had the Countess in mind when he did it."

He held the lock of hair higher, turned it so it caught the light from the table lamp. "Did you know that your hair is the color of sunlight, Sharon?" He dropped it. "I haven't seen the sun in over three hundred years but I remember the color."

A look of quiet reflection crossed his face. "That day, the day of Mozart's funeral, was the last time I saw the sun. When I went to the Countess' home, it had already set and I'd never see another sunrise."

Sharon studied him. Did she really want to know how it had been done? He'd promised to tell her all, but...did she dare ask? Part of her did want the knowledge of how a human man became a nightwalker. Sharon gathered her courage, but before she could say anything, he continued as if she'd spoken the question aloud.

"You wish to know how it is done. The ceremony was simple. She took me to her room and had me sit on her bed, not unlike the way I had you sit on the desk. Then she linked with me, mind to mind, and took blood from my neck—a lot of blood, enough to drain me near death. Then, while I was gasping, my heart stuttering and nearly stopped, she bit her arm and put it to my mouth. I drank. It was like nothing I'd ever tasted, more potent than the finest wine or ale. It tasted of life—the essence of life. The weakness passed and I grew strong, then stronger, much more so than any time in my past. I broke off from her, lay back on the bed. My senses improved during the change. First colors flew by, then sounds. She lay next to me and I put my arms around her. She'd become the most glorious thing I'd ever know."

His grip tightened across Sharon's shoulders. Even from within his arms, she felt a pang of jealousy. "You loved her?"

A sad laugh escaped him. "In a way. She was more than any woman—she was my sire. Yes, I made love to her, that night and the many that followed. It was how she kept me alive and fed when I was a fledgling—during the act we'd exchange blood. Some nights she'd share with Sebastian instead. Then I'd hunt to feed."

"Did you ever kill anyone?" There were so many stories of vampire kills. Not all of them could be legend.

He stilled. Eyes closed, he held her hand firmly pressed against his lips. "In the beginning, a new vampire has very poor control on how he takes blood and inevitably accidents happen. I was careful, though. In all places there are those who do not deserve their life. When I had to, I preyed upon them. I never killed anyone who didn't deserve it, at least a little bit."

He opened his eyes and stared at her, his face agonized. "Believe me on this, Sharon. You do not live with that kind of monster."

She did believe him. Jonathan was nothing if not moral. If he said he didn't kill the innocent, then he didn't. He seemed to read her acceptance and kissed her hand again, gratitude in his face.

"What happened to her, the Countess? Is she still alive?"

He sighed. "She was an ancient, even then. Sebastian and myself, we were distractions, but even so, she sometimes spoke of being weary of eternal life. One day she avoided my bed and his and watched the sunrise. We found her the following evening, still in her chair on the veranda, her skin blackened and burnt."

Sympathy overwhelmed her. "How awful."

"It isn't all that bad. We all have to make that choice eventually. When life no longer means enough." He looked thoughtful for a moment. "I've known others to do it when they lose someone close.

"You see, a normal person dies when their body wears out. As a nightwalker, that doesn't happen. We die when our souls have given up. I think, with the Countess, she'd decided that she would never find someone worth living for. I've felt that way from time to time. Then, only the promise of eternal music has kept me from the dawn."

What had he gone through to become a vampire. Now she understood why. He'd seen a close friend die and didn't wish to share the same fate. She remembered Mozart's doom, dying in ignominy, buried in a humble grave. Of course Jonathan would want to avoid something similar. But to give up his humanity…

"Are you ever sorry that you accepted her offer?"

He studied her hand, his face a quiet mask. Then emotions flitted across it, some positive, others not. "I accepted it, knowing what it would mean. It hasn't been all good, but overall it hasn't been bad either. I've met people I'd have never met otherwise, musicians from every century. Heard music of all sorts, so different from what we knew in Vienna."

Pulling her hand to his lips, he kissed it gently. "Another thing—if I hadn't taken her offer, I'd never have met you. I'd have been dust long ago. And I'm very glad that I met you."

Sharon warmed to the tip of her toes. Jonathan was a loving man, even if he wasn't quite human anymore.

He smiled. "And now, I wish to know about you. Who are you, Sharon Colson, other than a woman who's stolen my heart?"

What did she dare tell him? "What do you want to know?"

"We could start at the top. What happened to make you unwilling to mind link with me?"

Ruthlessly she pushed away the truthful response to that question—one answer she'd never give. "Perhaps I could start with something easier."

His mental sigh was so loud she could have sworn it to be audible. *I didn't think it would be that easy.* But he was kissing her neck, his lips too busy to bother with words.

She pushed him away. "Stop that. Speak aloud or I won't tell you anything."

His smile looked smug. "But you promised you would." He read the determination in her expression. "Oh, very well. Tell me why you were so desperate for money that you would let me bite you."

"I told you. My landlord had locked me out of my place. I slept in the park and the sheriff told me to try for work here."

"Why were you so strapped for money? You're a good bartender, an excellent singer. You should have no trouble getting a job."

"Maybe in Los Angeles or San Francisco. The truth is, I haven't sung in a while. The other evening is the first time I've sung in public since my dad got sick."

"Ah yes. You told me he'd died." Concern wiped away his teasing expression. It helped, knowing he really cared.

"It was up north. We lived in Los Angeles, but when he got sick I had to take him to where they could treat him. It was a special program, experimental. It even almost worked." Sharon remembered that. There had been a couple of days when he'd gone into remission and even felt good enough to walk around. They'd even talked of releasing him from the hospital. But then he'd relapsed, and his death had come soon after.

"We were in San Francisco, at the VA Medical Center. The government paid his medical bills, but living expenses were so high they pretty much wiped out everything we had saved. I sold what I could, even my guitar, just to cover the funeral costs. After that, I threw the little I had left into my car and headed back to Los Angeles. I figured I'd get work when I got down there."

"How did you find yourself here? In Los Niños?"

She had to laugh. "It was my own fault. I wanted to see the ocean, the coastline. I decided to take the scenic route from San Francisco. Trouble is, my car might have made the trip if I'd gone inland, but it broke down just south of Big Sur. I didn't have the money to fix it, so I sold it to the mechanic that came with the tow truck. He gave me just enough to cover my first couple nights at the boarding house. I was thinking of hitching my way down the coast, but the first couple of days I went out on the highway, I couldn't get anyone to stop. One trucker did, but…" Her voice trailed off.

"You didn't like the way he looked?"

"Something like that." She hesitated. "There are times when I know when it isn't safe."

"And yet you are with me." He sounded amused.

"With you, I feel safe."

He moved her close, enfolding her in his arms. "May you always feel that way, sweet one." He kissed her and after that no further words were necessary.

## Chapter Eleven

Again Sharon woke in his arms at sunset—smooth sheets around her unclothed body, thick pillow under her head, unbelievably comfortable. Her head was clear, instantly alert from the best rest she'd ever known.

One thing was certain, if this kept up, she'd never need sleeping pills.

Jonathan stirred behind her, his breath starting with a thin gasp, chest jerking before settling into the slow rhythm of breathing. The arms over her tightened into a hug and he leaned forward to whisper into her ear. "Good evening, my sunshine."

Long fingers trailed down her side and under her arm, stopping on the soft curve of her breast.

Lingering, they stroked the bare skin, setting off ripples within her. "Isn't this better, to wear nothing to bed? Much more convenient."

She'd put up a fuss about settling into bed naked. After all, she'd never slept with a man that way before. Not that she'd slept with too many men. But after they'd made love last night, Jonathan had simply waved his hand over her eyes and whispered softly to her, words she hadn't understood but that her body knew the meaning of.

Sharon tried to conjure some indignation for that trick of his, to put her to sleep without her permission. But it was hard to be annoyed with a man whose touch kindled such desire within her.

At this point, Jonathan could do pretty much anything he wanted, and she was ready to learn whatever he could teach her. About the life of a nightwalker and companion—about the secret underworld of the paranormal.

She turned to see his eyes, ice blue but aflame with waking passion. His smile was sensuous but sweet and loving. There was pleasure in the way he looked at her, in the way his fingers caressed her face.

But there was more. She sensed his hunger, both sensual and physical, and realized it wasn't just sex he desired. True hunger, for blood, raced through him, filled his mind as well as his body. Thirst. She could see it in his eyes, feel it through his skin, in the rapid beat of his heart.

"You need to eat." For once, she felt no fear. Jonathan would not hurt her. She was his companion and it was her duty to feed him.

He stilled and the smile on his face slid away, leaving wonder in its place. "You feel that, do you?"

"I feel it." She raised her wrist to him. "It's all right. You can drink."

Gratitude mixed with amusement colored his features. Then his eyes glowed brighter and his smile returned with new vigor. He kissed her proffered wrist and laid it aside. "Not like that, this time. You should learn more about how our kind make love."

A thrill slid through her. Jonathan seemed different this evening. A little alien—somewhat feral. Perhaps she should be frightened by the change, but she wasn't. Somehow she knew that no matter what, he would not harm her.

Their lovemaking last night had been wonderful, fulfilling, but not unlike that of normal people. Now it was different. He wanted her, wanted to make love to her, but there was more to it than that. It was not a man's embrace she felt this time, but that of the true nightwalker Jonathan was. And he was going to show her what that meant.

His hands moved possessively over her, leaving trails of electric sensation in their wake, his teeth sliding along her neck, his tongue tasting the skin beneath. Possession was in his mind, in his heart.

Not wishing to be left behind, Sharon moved her hands down his chest, feeling the hard muscles underneath. He wasn't heavily built, but his muscles were hard as iron.

As his hands played with her breasts, cupping and molding them, she fingered his nipples until the tiny nubs hardened to pebbles under her hands. She moved one hand to cover his stomach, feeling the solidness there. Jonathan's high-protein meals left no opportunity for fat to accumulate on his body. Three hundred years of a liquid diet, and he had the body of a male gymnast in his prime.

Sliding one hand farther down, she wrapped her fingers around the part of him most like that of a normal man. Hard, but the skin covering it was like velvet to the touch. She stroked it with trembling fingers, rewarded by his low moan of pleasure. "Yes, like that," he whispered, his voice thick with desire.

Encouraged, she continued to stroke him, feeling his heartbeat accelerate—his hunger with it. Abruptly he twisted on top of her, pressing her into the bed. One hand slid between her legs and fingered her folds, stroking her. At his touch, the initial embers of desire she'd experienced flamed and intensified into an inferno of the senses.

A million sensations flooded through her at his touch. Loving, sweet, the ultimate pleasure. His tongue on her neck made that area an erogenous zone all by itself. When his teeth nipped along the vein, it drove her crazy with need.

Need. Crazy. Yes, it was crazy what she needed. She needed his teeth in her neck, she needed to feed him, now, as a part of all this. Every time he drove the pinpricks of his canines into her skin, it was like a tiny explosion detonated within her, a precursor to a far greater pleasure still unknown.

This was what he'd promised, to show her how their kind — nightwalker and companion — made love.

She was ready. Jonathan loved her. She loved him. She was ready to be anything he wanted. Provide anything he needed.

One exception. No full link. She felt his mind touching hers, saw the golden glow of his presence outside her window-blind shield. Never before had she felt such temptation to open the blind and welcome that warm glow into the room of her mind. But it was still too soon.

She loved him. She trusted him. How she wished she could open her mind to him. It just wasn't possible. She trusted him with her life — but not her mind.

Instead she focused on enjoying what he did to her, the way he touched her. She cupped her hand around his arousal and stroked him in return, feeling the slide of skin under her hand, dewy drops weeping from its tip. He gasped when she enfolded him, his heart matching hers in speed.

He couldn't be harder. She couldn't be more ready.

He pulled from her hand, placed himself between her legs, just outside her core, probing her gently, not quite ready to enter. She fell back on the bed, opened wider. Plaintive at his teasing, she cried to him. "Now, Jonathan!"

He didn't need more. One thrust took him within her, his body covering hers. Pale blue eyes gazed into hers, alive with passion, with fire. "Sharon." Just her name, burning from his lips.

Then a withdrawal, and a thrust. Then another. And another. A rhythm he set, and she met, with her own hips. Intensity built between them.

His mouth again, at her neck, the fangs scratching. Nipping. Teasing. The hunger she felt in him rose further, the need for satisfaction, for feeding. Each new stroke left her more needy as well, wanting more of his mouth sipping from her.

Finally she could stand his teasing no longer. She twisted her neck against him and his fangs dug in. Hot blood erupted from her and he groaned and fastened his mouth over her flesh, sucking it from her, drinking deeply. The pain was minimal, irrelevant.

It was the ultimate fulfillment. Jonathan's penis deep within her, his mouth on her neck, the rhythm between them intensely satisfying. She loved him. She trusted him. Jonathan would never hurt her.

The rhythm between the bodies quickened. Tension built within her, wonderful, exquisite tension. An orgasm of monumental proportion coiled within her. She leaned back, one hand cupping his buttocks, the other at the back of his head, holding his mouth firmly to her neck. The crest of pleasure overcame her and she cried out, loud, her spirit flying in the euphoric breeze.

Jonathan stiffened, mouth still on her neck, then emptied himself within her, his own cry muffled.

The aftermath found her floating, peaceful, tranquil. She was tired, but it was as it should be. They'd made love and he'd fed as much as he'd needed. Her head fell back into the pillow, and darkness lingered on the outskirts of her consciousness, keeping company with his golden glow. She felt his tongue gently closing the holes in her neck. Warmth encompassed her. Relaxed, she smiled into his loving eyes, ignored the red blood that stained his lips — her blood.

Trust was a good thing. Jonathan would never hurt her.

Then it became too hard to keep her eyes open. She closed them and surrendered to the darkness.

\* \* \* \* \*

Sharon woke in her bedroom. It was dark, the only light from the small Tiffany lamp next to the bed. She tried to lift her head, but dizziness followed, and she collapsed back onto the pillow.

A dark shadow moved just beyond the light. "Jonathan?" Even her voice sounded weak.

The shadow moved into view and solidified into Marcus' form. He took position on a stool next to the bed and soft concern filling his features. "Hey, Shari, how're you doing?"

"Okay. Just a little dizzy. What happened?" She tried to sit up again, only to have the man's big hand land on her shoulder, forcing her back down again.

"None of that. You need to stay still." Another shadow appeared at his side, handed Marcus something, then disappeared from view. A white cotton ball appeared in the cook's hand, and he carefully swiped down her arm with something that left the skin chilled.

Abruptly Sharon realized that she was still naked under the covers and cold to boot. A deep shiver ran through her.

"Hold still, Shari. This is going to sting." With a move a professional nurse would have applauded, Marcus drove the end of a large needle into her arm, finding the vein with the skill of an expert. The pain was sharp and she bit down on her lip to keep from crying out.

A long tube extended from the needle, ending at a plump, squared-off plastic bag filled with a dark maroon substance. After securing the needle in her arm with tape,

Marcus hung the bag from a stand that had somehow appeared next to the bed.

He opened a clamp on the tube and checked the flow with a certain grim satisfaction.

Sharon watched the whole procedure in a daze. "I lost too much blood," she said finally.

He shrugged. "You're down a couple of pints. That's all. Too much for one time…so we put some back in. Not as good as what you've got, but it will make you more comfortable. You'll replace the rest in the next day or so." One meaty hand patted her arm gently. "Don't worry, you're going to be okay."

Her lips were dry. Thirsty, she licked them, eyes on the flow of blood heading into her arm.

"Want some juice?" When she nodded, he rose from the stool and started for the door.

"Marcus?" He turned. "Where's Jonathan?"

The big man hesitated then looked toward the dark window on the far wall. A shadow loomed there, just outside the reach of the lamp. It moved closer and was revealed to be Jonathan, wearing a red silk robe.

"I'm here." An ominous note edged his voice, no warmth in it, no emotion at all. He nodded to Marcus, all cold politeness. "Please. Fetch her something to drink."

When the cook was gone, Jonathan came closer, his eyes ice blue embers in his pale face. The bright red silk of the robe clashed with his pallor, making it more drawn than usual. Suddenly Sharon had another image of him, his lips red with her blood, the same color as the robe. The latent chill grew worse, and she shivered, once, then again in rapid succession.

Jonathan disappeared outside her field of vision and returned with her nightgown in his hand. He drew back the covers, and wrapped it around her, working quickly. Careful not to dislodge the needle in her arm, he re-secured the blankets tightly around her. With the addition of the nightgown to hold in her body heat, some of the chill wore off.

He sat on the stool and watched impassively as her shivers gradually died away. Numbly she stared at him and wondered at her own lack of fear — or any other emotion.

Marcus reappeared with a glass of juice. While Jonathan watched, the big man eased her up into a sitting position and allowed her to sip until she'd drained the glass. He checked the IV then headed for the door. "I think you need to talk, so I'll get out of the way. Jon, let me know when the needle should come out."

At the doorway, he stopped. "You want me to call Ralph?"

Jonathan startled, as if his mind had been far away. He nodded. "That would be best."

Sharon watched the nightwalker's face, the distant look on it that faded into something else, some memory he was reliving, over and over again. From the pain in his eyes, it wasn't a good memory, either.

"Jonathan. What happened?"

His shrug was eloquent, but his words stuttered and started. "I...I took too much blood."

"Too much? But you had a link to me. You could tell." That's why he'd wanted a link with her, why he'd taught her to screen rather than shield her mind.

"You're right. I should have. It was while I loved you. Sometimes I'm unable to control myself that way. When the blood lust is on me."

A new phrase, one she hadn't heard before. "Blood lust?"

"The need to feed. Particularly when having sex, it can be potent. Hard to control." He met her eyes, his own rueful. "Hard to know when to stop."

"I thought you said only young vampires have that trouble."

"Most older ones don't… They can tell when they've had enough, and their…prey is in danger." He seemed to use the word carefully. Prey. That's what she was.

His eyes grew bleak. "I cannot, always. It's a failing on my part."

"Why did you move me here? From your room?"

Something that could have been a laugh erupted from him. "The sheets on my bed were—messy. I did not wish you to wake to find your blood covering the pillow."

"I see." The response seemed inadequate. Fear crept into her. How would she have felt, seeing her own blood on the pillow? This was bad enough.

She glanced up at the emptying bag. Blood, nourishment for him, now for her as well. Some of the dizziness was gone. She could lift her head without feeling faint.

His own eyes were drawn to the bag as well. "I am grateful that Marcus knows how to do this. It has come in handy from time to time."

"Was he a nurse?"

"He was a paramedic for a while. When we were in LA."

Somehow Los Angeles was a part of all this, why he lived in Los Niños, in isolation, away from his own kind. "You don't talk much about your time there."

He stood up and moved around the room, restless. "I left there several years ago. I needed to get away for a while."

She sat up, ignoring the dizziness that threatened to overwhelm her. "Jonathan, please. Sit down. Tell me what's wrong."

Outside of the lamp's reach, he stilled. The lower edge of the robe gleamed bright red. "I lied to you."

At first she wasn't sure she'd heard him. "What?"

He came into the light so she could read his face, see the sorrow, the shame there. "I said, I lied. I told you I'd never hurt anyone undeserving. It wasn't true, it was a lie."

Her voice came out as a hoarse whisper. "Who...who did you hurt?"

His face turned so it was half in shadow, light limning his profile. "Someone I loved. Angela. She died..." He choked, the last word nearly a sob. His fist pounded at his thigh.

He swallowed, seemed to collect himself. Face now turned toward her, he stared, his blue eyes demonic in the dim light. "She was with me before Marcus. Angela was my companion...and my lover. She died..." his voice broke off.

"She died as you almost did tonight."

A ghost of a whisper came to her. *Jonathan will never hurt you.* It was a lie—he would and could hurt someone.

He could even kill.

"Oh." She had no other response. What could she say to this? He'd lied about something so basic, that he'd never taken innocent life. Yet he'd taken the life of a woman he'd loved.

And she could have been next.

He sat down again. "Now you understand. I thought that with a link it would be safer, that I could control it, but I couldn't." Eyes closed in pain. "Even with a simple link, the thirst got beyond me. I couldn't stop feeding, even when I felt you growing faint." He reached out to her hand, fingered the needle in her arm. "I couldn't stop, not even when I felt you slipping toward unconsciousness."

The memory of his mouth on her neck, the erotic pleasure of it, tore at her. Maybe that was it, the danger of his feeding during sex, that caused her so intense a response.

"With Angela it was the same. At first I could control it and she was a strong enough companion that I could feed from her frequently without harm. Not all are like that. But one night it went further than normal. I couldn't stop at first, and when I did, she wasn't breathing."

He fingered the transfusion bag. "They didn't have these then, but it wouldn't have mattered. She was dead before I could have gotten help. I didn't even have the opportunity to offer her my kind of life."

A quiet horror filled Sharon. That would have been the option for her if he'd taken too much. To become a nightwalker like he was. "Would you have done that to her?"

A sad look came into his eyes. "You would not want that for yourself, I suppose. Neither would Angela. But I would have offered, to give her some sort of life."

He sighed. "It has always been such with me, the thirst I can't control. It was the reason I had to leave LA. I met a woman on the beach one night. Not a companion, not enough mental powers to create a link, but still she was desirable. I liked her. More, I wanted her and she wanted me. We saw each other for a while, quietly. I don't think Marcus even knew.

"One night I went with her to her room. We made love, as mortals do, and it was good. But then I wanted her again, and this time it was more than I could manage. I wanted her body and her blood. My control slipped and the blood lust overcame me. I didn't kill her — I managed to stop before that happened, but she was hardly breathing when I stopped. It was a full moon... I flew with her to the emergency room, told them some lie about finding her along the road. I slipped away before they could question me further.

"The next day the papers were filled with stories of a madman who drank the blood of virgins. I suspect my friend thought that was pretty funny. She was scarcely a virgin. That night I told Marcus we were moving here. Anything to get away from the temptation."

Bleak eyes stared into hers. "I can't help it, Sharon. When I start to feel close to someone, I put them into danger."

A creeping dismay filled her. Being with Jonathan had been as close to having a love affair as she'd ever experienced. Being his friend, his lover had made her feel wanted. If he couldn't be close to her, what did that do to their future?

Fearful of his answer, she asked the question anyway. "So what does that mean?"

He grabbed her hand, pressed it to his lips. His face was intense, pain-induced furrows lining his forehead.

When he opened his eyes, there was a grim resolution to him. "It means there can be no us, *meine Süsse*, not any longer. I told you before, I won't endanger you." He released her hand. "We can no longer share a bed or our bodies. I can't be certain that what happened today wouldn't happen again."

Rising to his feet, he walked away, each movement that of an ancient being. At the door he paused, one hand on the knob. "I'll send Marcus in. Ralph will tend bar tonight, you should rest."

He left her alone with the dim lamp and the emptying bag of blood, her emotions as tossed as her bedcovers.

By ten that evening Sharon was heartily sick of being in bed. She'd waited until the cook had removed the IV, then against Marcus's wishes she'd dressed in her jeans and a sweatshirt, leaving behind the nightgown Jonathan had left tucked around her.

Once dressed, she moved to the comfortable chair in the corner, turning on the rest of the lights in the room as she did.

She might be a pint shy, but she wasn't an invalid. No staying in bed for her!

Going through her bookshelf, she found some new paperbacks she hadn't noticed before. With titles like *Life among the Dead* and *Love among the Dead*, the books caught her eye. Pulling one off the shelf, she perused it out of pure boredom but soon found herself immersed in a fantasy tale of a brave heroine and her noble vampire lover.

The purple prose left her choking with laughter at times, but the bulk of the writing was well done, the plot engaging, and it was a wonderful diversion from her current set of troubles until the section in chapter eight when the good-hearted heroine saved the hero's life by cutting her own arm, risking not only becoming a vampire as he drank too much of her blood but also a nasty case of tetanus from the rusty knife she'd used.

The joke wore a little thin at that point. Marking her place, Sharon put the book aside to focus on the problem at hand.

What was she going to do about Jonathan?

His point-blank confession of killing a former companion had caught her off guard. All she'd been able to think about at the time was that it could have been her, particularly when he'd mentioned nearly doing the same thing to another woman in Los Angeles.

But now she'd had a chance to think about it.

She loved Jonathan. That was the truth, simple and real. She'd never known anyone like him, she'd never found anyone close to being his match. She never would.

In some sense, he was her first lover. She'd never known pleasure at anyone else's hands, not like what he'd given her. And more. In all her life, no one had ever taken care of her as Jonathan had. Just her presence in this room was proof of that.

Her room. She glanced around, ignoring for the moment the IV stand still by the bed. Instead she focused on the lovely lamp on the table next to it, the heavy quilt on the bed and the exquisite painting on the wall above her head.

When she'd moved in, she'd thought it was a copy of a painting by an old Dutch master. Now she knew differently.

Jonathan didn't own copies.

These were things from his own rooms. All the little touches that had gone into making a place for her in his home. In his heart.

The Martin in its case seemed to call to her. Carefully Sharon pulled it out, mindful of her lingering weakness. Strumming the strings, she adjusted the keys, tuning them into perfect pitch.

Her tentative strum produced a rich tone. Once again the enormity of this overwhelmed her. A Martin guitar. One of the finest instruments ever made—and hers because a nightwalker loved her.

Jonathan loved her. He'd said it before, both in actions and in words. Even this evening, when telling her she could no longer share his bed, he hadn't taken that back. He still loved her.

And that was critical.

But what of the woman he'd killed, the other he'd harmed to the point of needing to send her to a hospital? What of her as well? Could she trust Jonathan again, enough to share his bed and love him again? He'd be able to take blood from her, so long as it was the sexless act they'd engaged in before. But not during the act of love. It was too dangerous, he'd told her. He'd never let that happen again.

He said he had a problem. He couldn't control how much blood he took, not when it was part of the sex act. Even before, when he'd first marked her, he'd had trouble, taken more than he'd needed. Then he'd blamed it on the lack of a link, but even with a partial link he'd been unable to control himself this time. Would a full link have helped? He hadn't said if he'd done a full link with his companion, Angela.

A trickle of jealousy slipped through her. Angela. A beautiful name. She'd probably been as beautiful as well. And Jonathan had loved her—until his problem killed her.

She shook her head. Jealousy wasn't the issue, loving Jonathan was. For every problem, there must be an answer. She played a few chords, an old melody in her head. *To everything, there is a season, and a time to every purpose under heaven. A time of love, a time of hate, a time you may embrace.*

A time to refrain from embracing.

That was the answer Jonathan thought—refraining from embracing and keeping their relationship out of the bedroom. That would work for now.

Sharon sighed and put away the guitar. It would work for now, but not forever.

## Chapter Twelve

In the midst of the noise and chatter of the All Night Inn's main room, Jonathan sat at his usual corner table and absently studied his vodka and serum on the rocks.

For the first time since Sharon had come he felt alone. She'd brought something into his life, a new beginning, a promise. For the past four weeks, she'd kept him company, either in person or in his thoughts. The intimacy they'd shared had been so precious.

And he'd ruined it—gotten greedy and lost control. He could have kept the blood lust at bay—all it would have taken was a quiet feeding first, just as she'd offered. Instead he'd gone for a true mating and hurt her. The image of Sharon's pale face as she'd lain unconscious on the pillow haunted him.

*She'd smiled at him—just as Angela had.* Another face, surrounded by red hair instead of golden, filled his mind. A similar smile, sated...before her eyes had gone wide and her head had fallen back. Moments later the breath had left his Angel's body and she was gone.

"Where are you, Jonathan? You're a hundred miles away, and I've come nearly as far just to visit you."

He turned his attention to the petite brunette at his side. The serum-laced frozen margarita she held was nearly gone. "Sorry, Natasha. I'm not good company tonight."

One elegant black eyebrow rose. "And does your lack of attention—to me of all people—have anything to do with this mysterious new companion of yours?" She made a big show of looking around the room, eyeing everyone, in particular the shapeshifter, Ralph, working the bar. "A companion that I was told was a genius at making drinks."

Jonathan stared at her near-empty glass and a wry smile crossed his face. "Was there something wrong with yours?"

"No, it was—adequate," she conceded. "But I was hoping to meet this new lady of yours. Sebastian had so many things to say about her."

"She isn't feeling well."

Now both eyebrows arrowed up. "A companion? Ill?" Her nervous glance took in the bar and her gaze fixed on the tall muscular blond eating a hamburger. "Nothing catching, I hope."

"Not ill." He searched for the words. "An accident."

A knowing look came into her dark eyes. "Hmm...dare I ask what kind of *accident*? Could it be one that has befallen before?"

Jonathan groaned. "Leave it be, Natasha. It was a mistake and it won't happen again."

"Oh?" The female nightwalker didn't look convinced. "Does that mean you're celibate again?" She shook her head sadly. "Jonathan, that isn't the way."

"It's the only way I know," he said bleakly. "I won't risk it happening again."

The door to the back hall opened and Sharon, dressed in jeans and a sweatshirt, slipped through. Jonathan watched her progress, her movements tentative as if she still suffered from dizziness. Pale as she was she had a resolute look on her face. From the middle of the room, she glanced at his table. He saw her eyes widen at the sight of the woman he was with. A flash of anger crossed her face and she took off for the bar, more determined than ever.

He cursed quietly. Next to him, Natasha perked up and followed his gaze. When she turned back to him, she had a bright, totally inappropriate smile. "Looks like I get to meet her after all."

He rose to his feet. "Excuse me for a moment."

Within a few steps he caught Sharon by the elbow, turning her to face him. "What are you doing here? You should be in bed."

She faced him with a haughtiness he didn't expect, pride shining from her eyes. For an instant he questioned his decision to remove her to safety. All he wanted was to enfold her into his arms and kiss those pouting lips.

"Stay in bed? That's a cold and lonely place at the moment. I wanted to see what was going on out here." She cast a hard look at Natasha, now beaming at them from the corner. "I see you wasted no time in finding some amusement."

"Natasha is a very old friend, nothing more." His fingers touched her neck, covering the marks. "*Meine Süsse*, I only want to protect you."

Sharon couldn't believe his arrogance. She jerked her elbow from his grasp, ignoring the startled look on his face. "Don't you dare call me 'sushi', or 'sunshine', or anything else right now. I'm a big girl, I don't need your protection, nightwalker."

Ignoring the astonished look on his face, she strode purposefully to the jukebox. *How dare he tell me to stay in bed while he dallied out here with some bloodsucking bimbo.* It was Jonathan's fault she was so weak. Her original idea was to get a beer to take back to her room, but now she felt a new plan slide into place.

The All Night Inn jukebox held the most eclectic collection of music she'd ever seen. Early Jackson Five mixed with Devo and Metallica, not to mention Bonnie Raitt, Steely

Dan and Sting. It boasted a great selection of old soul favorites. Sharon went directly to that section, picked a couple of songs, slow and sultry, perfect for close dancing.

As the first few notes filled the room, she headed for a table where a familiar figure with a golden-brown ponytail nursed his beer. He startled when she laid one hand on his shoulder. "Hi, Chucky. How'd you like to dance?"

Chucky stared at her hand as if it were a scorpion, then shot a glance over at Jonathan who glowered ominously at him from his corner. Sharon leaned over to whisper into his ear. "Don't worry, I won't let the nasty nightwalker eat the big, bad wolf."

She pulled on his arm and dragged him, barely resisting, to the dance area in front of the jukebox. Still looking nervous, Chucky put his arms around her and they danced to the rhythmic wail of deep contralto accompanied by a moody saxophone. To her surprise, the shapeshifter was actually a proficient dancer and she began to enjoy herself.

The song ended and the next began. Chucky smiled but kept a watch on the nightwalker's table with a cautious air. "Maybe this isn't such a good idea, Shari. I don't want to get caught up in something."

A deep rich voice interrupted. "Perhaps you'd let me dance with the lady?"

Sharon took one look at the newcomer and willingly let the shapeshifter return to his table. Tall, blond, with the build of a lumberjack, this hunk was far better nightwalker-bait. Chucky fled with the air of a man escaping a fate unknown.

Her new partner drew her into his arms and gently guided her around the floor. "I'm Daniel."

"Sharon." She glanced over at the table in the corner and was surprised to see Jonathan's date laughing, while the nightwalker himself appeared far more relaxed than he had when she was dancing with Chucky. Disappointment slipped through her. Maybe Jonathan didn't care anymore.

Daniel followed her gaze and his lips twitched. "You needn't be jealous of Natasha and Jonathan. There's nothing but old friendship between them."

She tried to rally her indignation but failed. "Oh? And how would you know?"

Taking one hand off her back, Daniel pulled back the long hair covering his neck, revealing the narrowly placed scars — old, ancient-looking scars. "I know because Natasha is mine and I am hers. She's my mate." As Sharon recovered from her surprise, he twirled her by one hand, collecting her back into his arms for the rest of the dance.

When the music stopped, Daniel led her to the bar, returning to a plate of potato chips and a half-consumed bottle of Heineken, and directed her into the seat next to his. After ordering a beer for her, he picked up his and took a deep swig. "I must thank you for that. It's been a while since I've been on a dance floor with anyone but Natasha, and," he leaned in to whisper, "don't tell her this, but she has a tendency to lead."

Sharon laughed in spite of herself. "I guess I should thank you for keeping me from making a fool of myself." She took a small taste out of her bottle. Already lightheaded, she knew it wouldn't do to drink too much.

Daniel shrugged his broad shoulders. "We're all fools for love sometimes. I rather like it that you would do such a thing. It shows spirit, a willingness to fight for what you want." He glanced wryly at the pair in the corner, now deep in conversation. "With Jonathan, I think a fight is needed. He has too often given up rather than work for what he wants."

"What does Jonathan want? It isn't me anymore."

The man smiled wryly. "Somehow I doubt that. But as to what he really wants, it's what most of us desire — someone to be with who can make our lives less lonely. Can you imagine what it is to live so long, to see everything and everyone around you grow old and die? Nightwalkers live very lonely lives unless they get lucky and find someone special."

What did that mean? Even a companion aged, if slowly. "Like another nightwalker?"

"Not necessarily. What they all want is a mate. Like what Natasha and I are. Bloodmates."

"Bloodmates?" She hadn't heard that term before. "You mean you're her companion."

"Yes, but more. I provide blood for her, she takes it when we love each other." He finished his potato chips and asked Ralph for a chocolate sundae. The shapeshifter grinned knowingly and relayed the order back to the kitchen.

Daniel returned his attention to Sharon. "I have to eat more, to keep up my strength. We're on vacation and that means more opportunity for loving and feeding."

"But isn't that dangerous?" That's what Jonathan had tried and why he'd rejected her. The pain of that rejection still hurt.

He took a long swig of his beer. "Not with a full link. One I control. If she forgets, I remind her."

Oh. So that was how it was done. A full link controlled by the companion so that she could stop him. She mused over what that could mean. "You're her only companion, and she doesn't need anyone else."

He gave her an understanding look and patted her hand gently. "That's what I mean. This is what most nightwalkers want. A mate they can depend on, who will stay with them. I'm that for Natasha. Because I get drained more often, I even age slower than most companions." He grinned. "How old would you say I am?"

It was too hard to tell. She made a guess. "Thirty?"

He laughed. "Well, I was that old when I met Natasha. But I've been with her over a hundred years."

*Over a hundred years.* And he still looked young. "Suppose something happens to you?"

For a moment he lost his cheerfulness and a quiet sorrow dropped into his eyes. "We've talked about that. She says she'll meet the sun at my death. I...I don't want her to." With a flourish, Ralph slid a chocolate sundae, layered with rich hot fudge, onto the bar in front of him. Daniel brightened immediately.

"That's one of the reasons I take such good care of myself." He gave Sharon a mischievous look and pulled the frosty treat in front of him. "Now, watch Natasha." He took a big spoonful of ice cream, dark with fudge, and put it into his mouth.

Over at the nightwalker's table, the dark-haired woman sat up quickly, her eyes widening with delight. Her gaze locked on Daniel, carefully helping himself to another spoonful. She licked her lips and smiled.

Daniel chuckled under his breath. "She loves chocolate but it's too rich for her stomach to handle. If I eat it, she gets to share the flavor."

Realization hit fast. "You have a full link with her. Even now?"

"Yes. She and I spend a lot of time in each other's mind. It's to the point that I don't always know if it's my thoughts I'm thinking or hers. Not that I care much either way."

*Jonathan loved chocolate too.* The idea of being able to share that kind of experience seemed so attractive.

He gazed at her. "Doesn't Jonathan touch your mind?"

"Not today. Not since..." Her voice trailed off.

"Not since he slipped up earlier."

"You know about that." She played with her bottle. "He told me he'd killed a companion that way."

Daniel made a rude noise. "That's what he said at the time too. I don't believe it, though."

Hope blossomed. "You don't think she died that way?"

"Angela died all right, and in Jonathan's bed. I just don't think Jonathan was responsible for it." He pushed aside the sundae. Sharon looked over to see Natasha's look of disappointment before returning her attention to her own beverage.

His hand tapped hers, demanding her attention. "Here's the problem. You know how much blood is in a normal human, right?"

"Um. Eight pints?" she guessed.

"More like eight quarts. Now, can you imagine drinking that much?"

"No…"

"Neither can I. Natasha couldn't do it. Nor Jonathan. He took about two pints today, right? And you're new, so it made you faint."

She began to see what he was driving at. "How much would he have had to take before he could have killed her?"

"For a longtime companion, at least a quart. We're real resilient to suffering a blood loss. One of the reasons it's harder to turn us." He glanced at her. "I bet you didn't know that either. Few companions become nightwalkers. We can't be drained enough for another's blood to transfer over. But that's why I don't think he could've lost so much control that she would have died. Imagine drinking a quart of milk, all in one sitting."

The truth lit up like a full-moon sky. "You're saying that his taking blood couldn't have killed her. It would have taken too much. So how did she die?"

"I don't know. Back then, we didn't have the tests we do now. But something wasn't right." He went back to eating his dessert, sucking the fudge off the spoon. "Something similar happened just a few weeks ago in LA."

She sat up at that. "Another companion was killed by a nightwalker?"

"That's what they are saying but again the situation was suspicious. It was Laura, the City Chief Esteban's companion. Unfortunately he killed himself afterward. They are examining Laura's body but haven't pinpointed the problem yet."

"So you think that something similar happened with Angela?"

"I think someday the truth will come out, but I don't think Jonathan was responsible for anything."

Sharon nursed her beer and mused on that for a while. When she glanced back at the nightwalkers they were intent in conversation, the slight smile on Natasha's face the only sign she was aware of the treat her companion was indulging in. Jonathan's face was tense by comparison, his mouth drawn down into a frown. Intense words poured from his lips. It was hard to tell but she thought he was talking in German.

"What are they discussing? Jonathan doesn't look very happy."

Daniel shot a glance to the corner. "Probably Los Angeles. Bad stuff has been going on in the city. There have been deaths in addition to the city chief and his lady, both parafolk and norms. We live in Santa Barbara but we hear the news." He took a big spoonful of fudge, licked it carefully. "Sebastian was after Jonathan to return and take over. Clean things up."

Excitement grew in Sharon. "Sebastian asked Jonathan to move to LA? What did he say?"

He finished licking the spoon and placed it back in the dish. "He said no." Grimacing, Daniel examined the interior of the Inn with disgust. "He said he'd rather stay here than take on the responsibility of a city. I can understand his position. This is a great place and Jonathan has a nice quiet life here. But he's needed. As an ancient, he should take on the responsibility, and frankly, he's shirking. If something isn't done soon, it could jeopardize all of us."

Daniel's earnest eyes stared into hers. "Nightwalkers aren't all-powerful. They can be killed by cutting off their heads or with a stake through the heart." A grim look took over his face. "Or simply being tied to a chair out in the sun. And there are norms that would do such things if they felt threatened. For example there's been an upswing in membership in the Paranormal Watchers society. Most people consider them a joke but if they ever got control, we could be in a lot of trouble.

"Los Angeles is becoming a hotbed of unrest, young nightwalkers without adult supervision, shapeshifters who don't respect anyone but their own clans, spellcasters who don't listen to anyone. The place needs an ancient, good with local politics and able to sway others." He returned his attention to the remaining fudge.

Sharon watched him and considered. Jonathan would be perfect for that. He had the residents of Los Niños fully on his side. He kept the peace between the different factions of the parafolk, quite a feat when usually werewolves and werepanthers didn't even like to be in the same room. Yet the All Night Inn regularly hosted everybody, with all on their best behavior.

Sharon tried to ignore her own reasons for wanting to return to Los Angeles. She could find singing jobs there and get back into the entertainment business. It was where the action was. Even more than her desire for her dark-haired boss, Sharon wanted to return to performing. Singing the other night in the Inn had reawakened that old dream in her.

"Maybe he'll change his mind," she said wistfully.

Daniel's eyes crinkled in the corners, a gleam of hope within them. "Maybe someone will help him change it. I'd hope you might see it that way." He ate the last of the ice cream off his spoon, a distinctly satisfied look on his face.

"Daniel, don't you think you should introduce me to your friend?" A sweetly melodic voice with a heavy accent, Russian perhaps, came from behind her. Swiveling on her seat, Sharon found herself face to face with Natasha. Up close the brunette was stunning, her dark eyes shining with nightwalker power. Unlike Vanessa, Sharon felt no mental leakage from her. It must have been tied up in her link to Daniel.

Daniel slipped an affectionate arm around his lady's waist. "This is Jonathan's new companion, my love. Sharon, this is Natasha." He kissed the nightwalker's forehead and they smiled into each other's eyes.

Sharon sighed at the obvious affection between them. If only she and Jonathan could be like these two.

Pulling her gaze from her mate, Natasha held out a delicate hand to Sharon. "I'm so glad to meet you."

Taking it, Sharon discovered the woman had a surprisingly powerful grip—she couldn't pull free. Also, while there was no touch against her mental shield, a number of emotions passed through the handclasp, into Sharon and back again. Curiosity, caring, concern, then finally, hope.

Natasha was a touch empath, could transfer and read emotions through her hands. When Sharon finally pulled hers away, the other woman smiled and nodded approvingly.

"Jonathan has done well," she murmured, "you're an excellent choice." Her eyes glazed over and she seemed to see much further than the end of the bar.

"Much will happen. There will be an offer, a compelling one. Fortune and fame. An unveiling of a hidden truth that forces a change." She stiffened and her eyes widened. "Fear. Danger. A betrayal."

Natasha shuddered and blinked then stared apologetically into Sharon's face. "Much will happen. But I think it will be all right."

"You can see the future?" Sharon found herself shaking, her dizziness making a comeback. She set aside the rest of her beer.

Natasha gave an elegant shrug. "Only glimpses. Now and then."

She smiled up into her mate's face, stroked his sudden concern from his mouth. "We should go, my love."

"Where do you go from here?" Another familiar voice came behind and Sharon startled. Jonathan had come up behind her, unheard as always. His breath ruffled the hair on the back of her neck. To her disappointment, he made no move to touch her.

Daniel nuzzled Natasha's hand. "North," he said. "Along the coast to Monterey. There's a place near the beach where we'll stay during the day." He grinned at Jonathan. "You know the place—it's quiet and discreet." A nod in Sharon's direction. "You might even think about going there yourself sometime. It would be great for a honeymoon."

*A honeymoon?* Sharon glanced at Jonathan's pale face. Right. He was too scared to even bed her right now.

Oblivious to their discomfort, Daniel continued on. "It's a great night. There's still enough of a moon for a well-lit drive. I may even put the top of the car down."

That seemed to overcome Jonathan's moodiness—he actually laughed. "Natasha, only you and Daniel would own a convertible."

"Darling, it isn't just any convertible, it's a Mercedes and just the thing for a drive on a windy coastal highway in the middle of the night." She tapped her companion on the arm. "Come, we have hours on the road." Her eyes gleamed in anticipation.

Sharon went outside with Jonathan to watch them leave. The sleek black convertible did seem like the perfect car for a drive in the moonlight. Before climbing in, Natasha pulled Sharon aside while the men examined the high-powered vehicle, enthusiasm born through shared male interest.

As she wrapped a long scarf over her hair and secured it, she spoke quietly. "One thing to remember. He does care for you and he truly needs you. Be patient with him."

"I'll try," Sharon promised.

She waved as they took off down the road in a cloud of dust.

## Chapter Thirteen

Jonathan stood with Sharon and watched the Mercedes head down the winding road, Daniel at the wheel, Natasha beside him, her hand on the back of her lover's neck. He could hear their joint laughter over the sound of the engine as it disappeared around a curve.

His friends' departure left him with mixed feelings. Pleasure, regret, envy. He recognized some of his discomfort as restlessness. The All Night Inn had been his home for a long time, become comfortable, a place of refuge. Peaceful. Safe.

Peaceful and safe as a tomb.

Turning, he stared at the structure behind him, the heavy wood frame and shingled roof. No windows broke the long walls, only the one door. The only spot of color in the darkness was the dimly lit sign over the door.

A place of safety, the safety of a tomb, as his overactive imagination had labeled it, but he didn't belong in a tomb. As he'd told Sharon long ago, he wasn't dead.

A thin breeze sifted through the trees, making the leaves whisper, bringing fresh smells into the gravel-covered clearing that served as the Inn's parking lot. Not a breeze from the ocean, but from overland, distant smells of places far away.

Places he hadn't been to in a very long time.

He explored the restlessness that assailed him. He wanted to go somewhere new, do something different. A road trip perhaps. Take the van out for a few days and leave the Inn to the shapeshifters' management. Maybe he and his companions could take a trip up to San Francisco and on to the Napa Valley where Sebastian kept his home. Or maybe give in to Marcus' dream of visiting Las Vegas.

Or maybe he'd just take Sharon someplace and let his older companion visit the desert city with Kevin. He glanced at her fair hair gleaming in the pale moonlight and imagined her in the seat next to him as they drove the van on the long winding highway along the coast. They could travel far during the dark hours and be in Monterey long before daybreak.

*Or Los Angeles.* That idea tugged hardest. The City of the Angels — he'd called the place home for so many years, from the early twenties when the first filmmakers had arrived. He'd come with them from New York, to a land of constant sunshine, perfect for making films that required a lot of light. Ironic that, since he could not walk in the sun, but the evenings there were also fine, hardly ever cold and harsh the way New York had been. And he'd loved the ocean, walking the beaches at night, flying over the hills in the full moon.

He'd watched during the years, as the city grew and expanded, seen firsthand the growing pains of a mighty metropolis and enjoyed the free spirit that permeated the people there. Flappers and zoot-suits had evolved into hippies with long hair and gentle eyes. When he'd left, the fashions were bright colors and the hair sleeked back. Now they wore black clothing and metal studs in their noses, and their hair bore the vibrant colors their parents once used to dye their shirts.

All the same, though. Still just young people searching for a meaning to their lives.

Just as he was. Centuries old, and he hadn't found an answer yet. At least not much of one, beyond the music he loved. Sometimes he listened to the radio and heard the current sounds. There was the internet, a new way to broadcast information, including sound and pictures, using computers. So many intriguing ideas out there.

Maybe he needed more than a vacation. Perhaps Natasha was right. She'd argued with him to accept what Sebastian had offered, to move back to LA and take the position of city chief.

Some of the stories she'd told had worried him. An ugly element was raising its head, jeopardizing their way of life. Something malevolent adrift in the city. Evil. Threatening to nightwalkers and those who traveled with them.

Like their companions.

He cast a glance at Sharon, still standing under the moonlit sky. She didn't look back, didn't seem aware of his presence at all. He listened to her heartbeat, the rapid pace of it, measured with secret skill the volume flowing through her veins. Nearly recovered already. Miraculous, really. Even Marcus after all these years couldn't replace blood that fast.

She could even be fast enough for him to love her as Natasha loved her bloodmate. The hope of that idea warmed him as nothing could. But then, no, he'd watched her faint earlier. It was only the transfusion that made it seem like she was recovered so fast from his feeding. Even now, he could feel the weariness dragging her down, slowing her mind and body. She needed rest.

"Sharon."

She deigned to acknowledge him, her face wary as she turned to face him. Silently she stared at him. He read it, the hurt in her eyes from his rejection, her fear from his confession. And something else he couldn't quite make out, some warm regard he was unused to.

Still, she didn't speak. He held his hand out to her. "Come, I'll see you to your room."

He allowed himself the small pleasure of his arm around her waist as he led her around the Inn to the back entrance. So nice, the feel of her, the warmth of her skin under his hand. How easy it would be to forget his promise and seek more of that warmth, lead her to his own bed and not hers.

Would she come? Something told him she would... And that was the most frightening thing of all. If anything happened to her, it would be his responsibility.

Responsibility. To Sharon. To his prince. To Natasha and Daniel, to Marcus. To all the others—nightwalker, companion, and the norms that served them, to the parafolk in general. That's what LA meant.

Sebastian had said Jonathan could make a difference there, could preserve the uneasy peace threatened by unknown forces. Natasha had said much the same, but even more, that things were far worse than their prince had known. She'd intimated that public revelations of their kind's existence was imminent. The authorities already knew the truth but kept it quiet in exchange for minor considerations.

But for the general population to uncover the truth that vampires existed would be disastrous. As city chief it would be his job to stop that, make certain the truth stayed hidden.

For twenty years he'd avoided responsibility. Now he looked into a young woman's heart and realized he could be responsible for her life. Or death.

When they reached the door to her room she turned under his hand, spoke her first words to him since earlier in the bar. Her eyes didn't meet his. "Could you come in? Please? I..." Something swallowed her words then she stared into his face, resolution evident. "I think we have something to talk about."

He followed her through the door.

She stood by the bed, awkward, as if not sure what to do. Jonathan took the opportunity her silence afforded to gaze about the room. His glance fell on a book lying on the small table. The lurid cover drew his attention, a tall, blond god of a man, fangs showing, with a buxom, auburn-haired beauty supplicant at his feet. Suppressing a grin, he collected it from the table.

He read the cover aloud. "*Love Among the Dead*, by Estelle Roberts." He noted the position of the paper she'd used as a bookmark. "You've gotten quite a way through it. How are you enjoying it?"

Sharon shrugged. "It's rather fun. Entertaining, but not very realistic. I'm surprised you have a copy of it."

"It was a gift from Sebastian. He's very fond of the books by this author, owns all of them. I think he finds them amusing. Once he threatened to find the author and see if she might want to write about a real nightwalker." He thumbed the pages before putting it down. "How did you like my friends?"

"I liked them a lot." She hesitated. "Daniel said he and Natasha were bloodmates."

"And he explained what that was?"

"Yes. It sounded nice," she said, her voice wistful.

*Nice?* Ruefully, Jonathan nodded. It was more than nice. The loving pair had celebrated their hundredth year together three years ago. He'd long ago dealt with the envy he'd felt over their union. How could you envy someone else's happiness?

She stared at him with her blue-green eyes. "Have you ever thought about taking a bloodmate?"

Of course he had. Angela...once she'd been his chance for that kind of love. A single woman to be his mate, provider for the sustenance he needed. But then she'd died and he'd known he could never have a bloodmate. No one person would ever be able to keep up with his thirst.

"It isn't possible for me. Angela was proof of that."

"But Daniel said…"

He interrupted her with an angry wave of his hand. "Daniel says many things, but he was not there. It is not possible."

She stared at him. Was there disappointment in her face?

"Daniel also said that Sebastian wants you to return to Los Angeles."

"Is that what you were talking about?"

"Some," she admitted. "We talked about a lot of things." Her demeanor grew bolder. "Are you thinking about going to LA?"

"Perhaps."

"Would you want me to come too?" Her words came out in a rush.

He blinked, surprised. "You are my companion. Of course you would come. Did you think I would leave you behind?"

"I didn't know. This is all so strange. I don't know anything, Jonathan, not even how I feel about you."

*Sharon admitting to feelings?* "How do you think you feel?"

"I…I care for you…"

From some deeply buried place inside him, emotion spilled and overflowed. Too precious she was, so much of him had become tied up with her. Not since his Angel had he felt so for a woman. If he could have touched her mind he would've been able to tell her, to make her see.

Instead he had to use words, inadequate at best. "I know what I feel. I love you, my sunshine. I think I always will."

He gave in to the need to hold her, captured her in his arms and drew her to him. "You know what I think? I think maybe you care a lot more than you say." He drew his finger down her neck to rest on the marks. "I think you feel as I do. I think you love me too, my sweetness."

She tried to move away, but he stalled her with his arm. "Have you read that from my mind?"

*No. I can't see your thoughts.*

She slapped ineffectually at his chest. "Stop that. Talk to me, don't think at me."

"Very well, I will talk. You were angry with me earlier. Perhaps you even thought Natasha was more than a friend? I think you tried to make me jealous by dancing with that shapeshifter."

He leaned in and narrowed his eyes in what he hoped was a threatening gesture. "I did not like seeing you dance with him."

His threat was ineffectual. Her eyes glinted with hidden amusement. "You didn't mind my dancing with Daniel."

"Daniel is not now nor ever would be a threat to what I want."

She lifted her chin. "I wasn't trying to make you jealous. I simply wanted to dance."

"When you wish to dance I will dance with you. I didn't know you had such a desire. Besides, tonight was not a good night for dancing—you were weak and needed to rest."

"I don't feel weak now."

She was right. Her blood volume was near what it should have been. Barely a companion for a month and she was producing nearly enough to feed him several times a week. The transfusion might not have even been necessary, although it was best to be prudent.

"Perhaps we should dance then." He slipped one hand around her waist, began to lead her around the cramped interior of the room.

Sharon smiled at his gentle humor. "There's no music," she protested.

Then there was. Through the screen of her mind, she heard a delicate waltz, Chopin, perhaps. Jonathan's arms tightened and his movements adjusted to the rhythm of the dance. Around the room they turned, sharing in his mental melody.

*And she shall have music wherever she goes.*

Laughing, Sharon gazed into his face. "You are a wonderful dancer."

"Well, you do something long enough…" he began the familiar litany then stopped to hold her close. The waltz faded away from her mind. "We have so much time to be together. Time enough to fix all problems, time enough for love. Everywhere I go you shall be with me. Where I stay, I will have you by my side. For all time."

*For all time?* Suddenly Sharon realized how serious he was. "Jonathan, how long do you expect me to be here?"

"I told you." He leaned forward to kiss her—only to be met with her hand on his mouth.

"How long, Jonathan? How long am I to be with you?"

Pulling his hand from her hair, Jonathan stared. "What is it, sweetness? Why do you ask this question? You are companion to me. You will stay as long as I want."

"As long as you want?" Sharon's gaze sharpened, and her voice to match. "I didn't think you were my master."

"A poor choice of words. I meant as long as we both wish, of course."

Sharon pulled away. She'd known he was possessive, but to hear it was something different. "That is how you see me. As your servant. Your property." Suddenly worn out, she collapsed onto the bed. "Suppose I didn't want to stay?"

His voice softened. "We have just now declared love for each other. You would leave me, knowing I love you and you me? How could you do this?"

A deep melancholy rose within her. She could stay with him, as his beloved companion. He'd feed from her once in a while as he had before. Maybe they would even share a bed, when he could trust himself not to kill her. But that wasn't enough.

It wasn't like she'd ever be his bloodmate. He'd made that clear enough.

She was a singer. She couldn't stay in Los Niños forever, no matter how much he wanted her to. Not with the terms he was offering. "How can I live my life as servant to another, my wishes and desires never to be respected? I'm not a slave, Jonathan."

"No one said you were!"

"Then when can I leave?"

"When I say you can!" He crossed the space between them and grabbed her upper arms, pulling her off the bed. In his face was a strange fury and she felt the pounding of his heart. Her arms ached where he held her. She whimpered and he eased off, gripping her less tightly. Still he held her close, her struggles useless against his strength.

Fear of his anger assailed her, but she would not give in to it. "And when will that be?" Her voice was a whisper.

Jonathan shut his eyes and loosened his hold, letting her slip back onto the bed. For a long moment, he stood, until his rapid breathing slowed. He blinked, once, then twice.

"It will be when you wish. When the time comes, when you want to leave, you will tell me and I'll remove the marks. You will go back to how you were before, a normal human and no longer my companion. And then you may leave."

He turned and left the room.

## Chapter Fourteen

๛

A week after Natasha and Daniel's visit, Sharon woke in her own bed. The light coming through the window blinds was deep amber. There was one advantage to not sharing Jonathan's bed. Without him to put her to sleep, she now woke a couple of hours before dusk.

For once, the light outside beckoned to her. Foregoing for the moment her usual wake-up shower, she dressed in jeans and a light sweater and fetched her hiking shoes from the depths of her closet. After nabbing her coat, she paused in the hallway and heard the sounds of Marcus rustling about in the kitchen. If she went that way, she'd be conscripted into helping, or at least forced into a meal. For once, her stomach seemed content with its state of emptiness. She needed fresh air and sunshine more than food.

Moving along the hallway to the front of the inn, she left through the main entrance.

The air outside was more than fresh—it was exhilarating. For the first time in what seemed like a lifetime, the golden warmth of the sun touched her face. The light nearly blinded her and she shoved on a pair of sunglasses, cutting the glare down to something bearable.

A trailhead opened off the parking lot, up the mountain behind the Inn, leading to a lookout with a western view of the ocean. She'd been up it a couple of times at night, with Jonathan or Marcus, but never during the day. With the sun behind her, she took the trail, followed it up the steep hillside until she reached the top. The heavy woods that filled the narrow canyon thinned out here, leaving a clearing backed by trees.

A large fallen log served as a bench, the bark on the top edge worn away from the rear ends of the many hikers who'd passed this way. Still breathing heavily from the climb, Sharon sat and contemplated the view before her.

To the west, the canyon walls stretched in a narrow funnel, leading to the navy-colored ocean beyond. The sky, a deep, rich blue decorated with thin wisps of clouds, made a soothing backdrop. With less than thirty minutes until sunset, the sun was a distant red-gold ball high above the horizon. It had been months since she'd last watched a sunset. Sharon settled in for the wait.

The breeze picked up and tugged at her hair, which she'd worn loose. A long, unruly strand swung down along the side of her face, and her gaze was drawn to it. She collected the stray lock and pulled it further into view. The setting rays colored it a reddish hue.

Jonathan called her his "Sunshine". He'd said her hair reminded him of the sunlight he'd known as a youth and that he hadn't seen the sun in over three hundred years.

A deep melancholy flowed through her. Jonathan used the endearment because it meant something to him. That she "brought sunshine" into his life. Daniel had told her a nightwalker's life was lonely unless he or she could find someone to share it with.

She tucked the wayward strand behind her ear, felt along her neck to the narrow pinpoints on her neck. *Jonathan's mark—his proof of ownership.*

In their fight a week ago, she'd accused him of treating her like a slave...but it wasn't true. Even when she'd said it, she'd known how false the comment was.

Jonathan loved her. He'd said it often enough. More, he'd shown it, in every way he could. Making a home for her in the Inn. Buying her the finest guitar available to play. His patience ...waiting for her to serve him as a companion should, waiting for her to be ready to partially link minds with him so he wouldn't hurt her.

The only times he'd hurt her had been the first time without a link and the last, when he'd taken too much blood. A thrill slipped through her. Even that hadn't actually hurt...not unless you counted ecstasy as intense as pain an issue. Sharon sighed. Now that she'd known that kind of pleasure, how could she ever consider settling for anything less?

For two days after their argument, he'd kept his distance but working and living at the same place had made it impossible to stay apart for long. By popular demand, she'd sung again on Friday and Saturday nights, Ralph taking her place as bartender as she entertained. Both times she'd felt Jonathan's warm gaze on her during her sets, his intense interest in her music...and herself.

By last night, Sunday, they'd gone back to their old relationship, friendship with sexual tension on the side. Jonathan had invited Marcus and her to a horror film mini-festival in his room and welcomed Kevin to the party as a special guest. They'd sat around and drunk wine coolers, Jonathan's made with his special blood-based mixers, and roared with laughter over the campy antics of the movie monsters.

At one point, while the celluloid creature had crept up upon the helpless maiden in the film, Jonathan had mimicked the action with Sharon, to the amusement of the other men. He'd crouched behind the divan and playfully pounced upon her, eliciting from her a scream almost as ear-piercing as the one onscreen. But instead of feasting on his powerless victim, he'd tickled her, leaving her convulsing with merriment.

In the end he'd collapsed in laughter next to her. She'd been surprised by how normal he looked, how his fanged smile no longer struck her as unusual. It was just Jonathan's smile. He'd stayed beside her for the rest of the movie, one arm around her shoulders, his hand playing with her hair from time to time.

In the morning, Marcus and Kevin had taken themselves off to the house they shared while Sharon reluctantly sought her own room. When Jonathan had bid her good morning, she'd seen his own lack of enthusiasm at her departure, clearly wanting to have her stay with him and share his bed but unwilling to allow her to do so.

That was a very good sign. Maybe he was rethinking his position on their relationship, a return to the passion they'd shared. If that were true, then perhaps in time they could become bloodmates as Natasha and Daniel were. She certainly hoped so.

She wondered about how to improve her ability to link minds with him. What Daniel had said about her controlling the link made sense, but she'd never had any training in using her mental powers. Her fear of being controlled had always been too great, since that time...no, even now, she couldn't think about that night.

Could she find someone to train her now? Jonathan might be able to do it, but she didn't want to ask him, not now. Not when things were just getting back to normal.

Around her the light changed. Shadows grew longer as the sun slipped further down in the west. Light flickered off the distant waves, white with hints of red. As the disk of light touched the edge of the horizon, a pathway formed across the water, yellow-white at first, then crimson. Red highlights lit the waves and the shadows of the trees in the overlook also took a reddish hue, echoing the sky as it darkened.

Sharon watched the giant disk slip from sight, down past the edge of the world into the waiting ocean. When the last of it was gone, her sadness intensified for a moment. It had been beautiful. *And something that Jonathan would never see.*

*What won't I ever see, meine Süsse?* In her head, a sleepy voice spoke, the mind behind it just gaining consciousness. Another thought, more intense this time, curious, concerned. *You are not in the inn...where are you?*

Delight filled her. It had been over a week since Jonathan had "talked" to her through their link. She'd begun to think he'd severed the connection, but apparently it had merely lain dormant. For some reason, now, he'd finally opened it and peeked into her mind, seeing her internal commentary. She made a note to keep her more private thoughts to herself when the sun was down.

She tested her own mental voice. *At the overlook. I watched the sunset.*

*Ahh...* A soft note of regret colored that thought. *You are right, of course...it has been a while since I saw the sun kiss the edge of the world.* There was a pause. When he continued, humor was in his thoughts. *Perhaps you'd like to watch a movie with me after we close? I have a pristine copy of* Gone with the Wind. *Wonderful sunsets.*

She couldn't help it. She laughed. *Not tonight.* Another idea appealed instead. *What I'd really like to do is visit the beach.*

*Another moonlight stroll? No, there will be little moon tonight, but we could build a fire.* His mental voice warmed rapidly to the idea. *Perhaps Marcus can make us a picnic. How does that sound?*

Sharon let her mental laughter accept his invitation. Around her the dusk grew rapidly, and removing her sunglasses, she peered through the advancing gloom at the trail leading downward. *I'd better get going before it gets too dark to see. I'll meet you in the kitchen.*

His "voice" was soft, pleased. *Take your time…and if you need a guide, call. I'll be waiting.*

\* \* \* \* \*

Marcus was more than happy to provide a picnic for them. He threw in a pair of thermoses, one of hot chocolate, the other cold serum, plus some special cheese and smoked salmon sandwiches for Sharon.

Jonathan grumbled as he hauled the heavy basket out to the van. "You'd think we were going for a week, not just a couple of hours."

Sharon giggled at him. "Well, it was your idea. And Marcus says he's under strict orders to fatten me up."

His expression grew wry. "I did say that. Not that there is anything wrong with your current shape." His burning glance told her much the same thing, and she began to hope for a lot more from the evening than a simple stroll on the beach. She checked to see if there was a blanket in the car suitable for lying on the sand and was gratified to see there was.

He drove the van down the long road to the ocean side, heading for one of the small overlooks that had a trail down to the beach. Unlike the last time, he couldn't fly directly there, and they would have to make their way to the shore the way others did, through wheels and their own feet.

Sharon rolled the window down for the trip and breathed in the fresh sea breeze as they grew close, the spicy scent of ripened seaweed mixed with the sharp tang of the salt-laden air. She felt Jonathan's speculative gaze on her.

"You really love the ocean, don't you?"

She nodded. "Always. I've often wanted to go out on it, on a ship." She glanced at him in curiosity. "You must have done that…how else could you have come here from Europe?"

Self-consciously, he laughed. "Well if you want the truth I came as cargo on a freighter with a pair of others, in the early nineteenth century. It was about the time that Napoleon was making such a nuisance of himself and all of Europe was involved in one conflict or another. There was no time for music then, except for that of the military. And I've never been that fond of bugles, drums and marches."

"How did you survive such a long journey?" Visions of the "death ship" from the movie *Dracula* came to her uneasy mind.

"We had a couple of companions with us, riding as passengers. They provided what they could for us. And then there was the crew." He cast a sidelong glance at her. "I could approach them as they slept in their bunks and control their minds while I fed."

She couldn't restrain the revulsion she felt at that confession. He'd taken from unwilling victims, just as all other vampires had.

He must have sensed her horror. One hand departed the steering wheel to pat hers on the seat. "For what it's worth, I took only enough to survive. No one was harmed by my crossing the Atlantic to this new world. And my prey those nights had very pleasant dreams."

His dry humor overcame her revulsion. "I might have known you'd do that, make pleasurable such an experience."

He shrugged. "It costs me little to do it. And I take satisfaction from the comfort of others."

The van turned onto the highway. "I arrived in New York City and spent many years there before coming to California. There I met Natasha, and eventually Sebastian joined us. I also met Vanessa…"

His voice trailed off and Sharon wondered what he was going to say. But then he pulled the van into a roadside parking area, adjacent to a publicly accessible beach. Killing the engine, he sat quietly for a moment and when he turned to her, his face was guarded. "Let's go."

Grateful she'd worn heavy boots, Sharon clutched the blanket and followed Jonathan who'd taken the basket as his own burden down the treacherous hillside to the sand below. For the first time, she realized how improved her night vision was. Even with a mere sliver of the moon to provide light, she was able to see the trail in front of her.

Of course as a creature of the night Jonathan had no difficulty at all seeing his way through the dark to the waiting shore.

One of the more established beaches, the one Jonathan had chosen for their outing, actually boasted a fire-ring, deserted at this time of night. Sharon gathered driftwood for their campfire while he cleared the ring of rubbish and accumulated debris and soon they had a blazing fire, cheerful and soothing. Sharon spread the blanket nearby and they sat together, sipping their refreshments from their respective thermoses. Sharon helped herself to one of the sandwiches. The night air was bracing and made her hunger more intense.

The salmon and cheese filling was delicious, although an odd accompaniment to the rich taste of the hot chocolate. She caught a glimpse of Jonathan's face as she took her first sip, the longing there, and wished that like Daniel, she could share the flavor with him. Again she resolved to find a trainer for her mental powers. Maybe soon she'd be able to link minds with him on her own terms.

As she nibbled, she watched the now quiet nightwalker at her side, his eyes fixed on the fire. In their light blue depths she saw flickers of other flames, not necessarily the ones reflected. He was nostalgic tonight, reminiscing about his life both to himself and to her.

Once more she breathed in the fresh sea air, now seasoned with the smoke from their fire, mixing with the other smells of the seashore. The churning sound of the surf vied with the soft crackle of the flames, a medley of sorts. Under the crescent moon, the sand glistened white, except where the sea dampened it, and then there was the white surf that faded in and out of view at the edge of the dark ocean. While the breeze blew cold, she was dressed warm enough in her coat and jeans, and the fire took the rest of the chill from their surroundings.

"I guess it would be hard to take a long ocean trip these days," she said, making conversation. Jonathan startled and stared at her, as if suddenly surprised to find her with him. His mind must have been far away.

"Why is that?"

"Well, with passports, fingerprints. Tight controls over immigration. How could you manage it?"

He gazed out over the ocean. When he spoke his voice was soft but focused. "If I wanted to go overseas, I could. There is little that enough money can't buy…and I've enough to satisfy that sort of need.

"Besides, if I wanted to go very far, I'd probably simply take an overnight flight rather than a ship. Or a private jet if I couldn't avoid flying during daylight hours."

"You own a private jet?"

"I don't. But Sebastian does." He smiled, his narrow fangs glinting in the dark. "He's a pilot, after all."

She stared in disbelief. "A pilot? An airplane pilot?"

Jonathan nodded. "With a license to fly most kinds of planes, including the Lear jet he owns. It took a bit of doing to pass the tests, but it allows him the freedom to move around at night. Sometimes I envy him. He can fly even when there isn't a full moon."

She couldn't avoid chuckling over the wistful tone to his voice. "I suppose you could learn to fly a plane too."

"I could…he's offered to teach me." He eyed her thermos with intense interest. "I don't suppose you'd let me have a taste, would you?"

"I thought this was bad for you."

"Just a sip?" he begged.

Sharon handed him the flask and tentatively he let just a small amount cross his lips. Rolling his eyes in ecstasy, he moaned dramatically, "It's hot, but so good."

With clear reluctance he handed the flask back to her. She capped it to save the rest for later.

They settled into an easy silence, listening to the surf, the fire, feeling the steady beat of the waves on the shore. Whimsically, Sharon thought of it as the heartbeat of the Earth. The steady regularity had a feel to it similar to the beating of her heart — or Jonathan's. One of the reasons she loved the ocean was this feeling she got from it, of belonging, of being home. She sat with a creature that should have been alien to her, but in truth they were both children of the earth.

Two hearts beating, with if not the same rhythm then with similar passion, while around them the world encompassed and held them close. For a moment she felt like she and Jonathan were the only two people alive.

"I told you there was someone here." From the darkness came a harsh voice, male, more than a little drunk, the words slurred. Looking down the beach, Sharon saw three figures staggering toward them.

Beside her Jonathan stiffened, his eyes narrowing as the three came within the throw of the light from the fire.

Definitely drunk, and strangers to the area from the looks of them. Jeans and leather jackets, not unusual clothing for a deserted beach in early spring, but the condition of these clothes were clean and relatively new. These weren't bums, but bikers on tour, probably from further south. No doubt harmless but their presence on the otherwise deserted beach was still a nuisance.

Sharon tried to control her annoyance at the interruption.

All three leered at her, ignoring the man at her side, and apprehension filled her. Perhaps they weren't as harmless as they seemed.

One, whose jacket bore a set of fancy chains, crouched on the ground next to the blanket. "What's a pretty girl like you doin' here?"

"Just enjoying the beach," Sharon replied. She caught a whiff of his breath and grew queasy at the smell. "Or at least I was."

"She's with me and you will leave us alone. Now." Jonathan's deadly quiet voice should have struck fear into their hearts, but the three were too full of themselves—and beer—to notice the menace in his tone.

"Well, yes. I can see that she's with you," Chainman said, not taking his eyes off Sharon. "But the way I see it there're three of us and one of you, and you aren't in any position to be giving us orders."

He eyed Jonathan's slight frame with a dismissive look. "If we decide to help keep the lady company, there isn't much you can do about it, is there?"

One of his buddies moved in on the other side of Jonathan. His leather jacket had an assortment of patches on it. The third man Sharon promptly dubbed Zipper, due to the plethora of decorative fastenings on his jacket front. He took position behind them, leaving Jonathan and Sharon surrounded.

In spite of her nightwalker escort, Sharon felt a surge of nervousness. She let down her shield and allowed herself a moment to read Chainman's mind. The images he held there included her, naked... She gagged over what he had in mind for her and slammed her mental shield shut.

She pulled the thermos of hot chocolate to her, uncapping it carefully.

*Don't be afraid, meine Süsse.* Jonathan's mental voice was calm, reassuring. She glanced at him, and he gave her a wry smile before his hand indicated the flask in her hand. *If it makes you feel better, go ahead and use that.*

She tensed and waited.

It happened fast. Chainman reached for Sharon, while his buddies both jumped Jonathan. The uncapped flask in her hand, Sharon threw the steaming hot contents into her assailant's face.

His hands flew to his eyes protectively, and his scream echoed across the sand. "You bitch! I'll do you for that."

Meanwhile, Patches and Zipper had their own troubles. Jonathan's slight form had seemed an easy target, but now they found themselves with his hands on the back of their necks in a vise-like grip. There was a sickening crunch as Jonathan banged their heads together and the pair collapsed onto sand.

A switchblade knife appeared in Chainman's hand. Sharon raised her arm defensively as he slashed at her. Burning agony ripped down her arm and a deep cut ran the length of it, blood pouring from the wound onto the blanket. Terrified at the extent of the gash, Sharon cried out.

Her scream was answered by Jonathan's battle cry. Having dispensed with the others, he'd turned just in time to see Chainman's knife cut into Sharon's arm. Fury distorted his face and voice, rage driving him to seize the man who'd injured his companion.

In the instant, one hand had the man by the throat, the other grasped the arm wielding the knife. There was a hideous snap, and the man groaned in agony as the knife slipped to the sand. Broken bones protruded from the skin of his forearm, crushed under Jonathan's grip. He would have screamed, but the nightwalker throttled his throat shut. Low moans were all he could manage.

Sharon stared at the pair—the now terror-filled features of the man who'd hurt her, the furious mask Jonathan's face wore. Horror filled her. He intended to kill the man who'd dared attack them and who'd injured her. As she watched Chainman's scalded face darkened, his breathing becoming ever more labored.

Jonathan's hand had closed his windpipe—the man was suffocating. With a little more pressure, he could crush the fragile bones under his hand and stop the man ever taking another breath.

With more effort than she expected it to take, she rose to her feet, clutching her injured arm to her, the blood staining her blouse. "No, love. Don't."

Jonathan's voice was low, even and furious. "He hurt you." Using his strength, he raised the man higher so his feet no longer touched the ground. Barely conscious, Chainman's feet kicked helplessly.

"Don't kill him. I'm hurt, not dead. Please don't take his life."

With an oath, Jonathan flung the man to one side. Chainman hit the sand hard, but Sharon could hear his still-labored breathing and she said a silent prayer of thanks.

*Wasted on that scum.* Jonathan's mental voice filled her mind and his face lost some of its woodenness as his fury receded and more gentle emotions could take hold. He came to her, tenderness in his eyes as he pulled her arm away from her body to examine the damage. More fury evidenced itself in his eyes before he reined it back in.

*A total waste of a good prayer*, he told her, in a weak attempt at levity. *Let me in, Sharon. Let me take some of the pain so I can heal this properly.*

She closed her eyes and in her mind the window formed, the wooden slats of the blind indistinct. The whole thing was fuzzy, the pain from her arm too intense to allow her to focus as she wanted. She tried to visualize instead an open window, Jonathan's golden essence flowing through it. Her imaginary room filled with a soft golden glow, distracting her, and the ache died away.

From her arm came warmth and a soft lapping sound. She opened her eyes to see Jonathan's tongue running along the wound on her arm, cleansing it of blood. The flow ceased in its wake. The open gash was horrifying without its covering of gore, but as soon as he'd stripped it clean, he returned to the end and repeated the action. This time, the cut closed under his ministrations, his fingers holding the edges together, his tongue sealing them shut. The action took but a few moments and when he was done, there wasn't even the hint of a scar on her arm.

From her mind the glow exited, and in its wake was a simple promise. *No pain, no injury will I allow you.* Sharon collapsed forward into his arms and he lowered her onto the clean part of the blanket.

She struggled with the events of the last few minutes, trying to keep the faint she knew waited just outside her senses from overcoming her. She'd lost a lot of blood from that wound. The blanket was soaked with it, as was her blouse. But it was the shock of the attack, and not the blood loss, that caused her to feel faint. She stared at her unblemished arm and wondered how much she could lose without it becoming a problem. Finally, she closed her eyes and allowed the world to slip away.

Around her, Jonathan moved quickly, putting out the fire, repacking their basket. He dragged their attackers further up the beach, out of the tide's range, verifying that their injuries, while serious, weren't immediately life threatening.

Not that he cared that they might die, but his companion did. He'd call the sheriff from the Inn, when he'd secured Sharon there. Sheriff Green owed him more than a couple of favors. Taking care of this scum wouldn't be a problem.

He returned to Sharon and lifted her into his arms, her weight negligible to his strength. Cradling her, he carried her to the van then returned to collect the rest of their belongings.

One of the men had gained consciousness, the one with patches on his jacket. Fear coated his features as he stared at Jonathan, who was calmly folding the blanket into the basket. The look turned to terror when the nightwalker strode over and knelt on the sand beside him.

"You going to kill me?" he asked, his voice quivering.

Jonathan allowed a small smile to creep across his lips. "No. But only because my lady wouldn't like it." One hand touched his forehead. *Sleep. And forget what happened this night.*

He repeated the action on the other one then turned to Chainman. He touched the man's mind, listened to his fevered thoughts.

*Vampire! That's what he is. I'll tell the Watchers, that's what I'll do.*

Grimacing at the ugliness of the man's mind, Jonathan took a moment to compose himself then erased from the man all knowledge of the evening, adding a little something else to Chainman's compulsion.

It would be a long time before the man would ever able to think about riding a motorcycle without breaking into a cold sweat.

## Chapter Fifteen

ಐ

Marcus sat in the kitchen with Kevin and startled when Jonathan carried the barely conscious Sharon through the door. The big man's concern turned to fury as Jonathan told him in short, tense words what had happened on the beach. Only the nightwalker's reassurance that the three who'd dared attack them had already been dealt with kept him and Kevin from returning to the scene and dispensing a little retribution of their own.

Instead, Marcus called the sheriff to report the incident while Jonathan took Sharon to her room. After hanging up the phone, Marcus grabbed a bottle of cold water and followed them.

When he arrived at the room, she was sitting on the big armchair, wrapped in her robe. Her blood-soaked clothes lay in a pile on the floor.

From the bathroom came the sound of running water. Jonathan appeared in the doorway. "And the sheriff?"

"He'd said they'd deal with it." Marcus handed him the bottle. "She should drink this."

He turned his attention to Sharon. She clutched the robe across her breasts, her eyes open but far away. Gently he gripped her shoulder. "Hey, Shari. How's it going? Talk to me."

Her gaze turned to him. In the depths of her normally calm eyes dwelled bleakness, their color a green as intense as the emotions churning within her. A shudder ran through her.

"They were going to..." Her voice trailed off, broken, and it hurt to see her that way.

The big man put one arm around her. "It's all right, Shari. No one's going to do anything to you. Jon and I'll see to that."

Jonathan came over to them, opening the bottle and handing it to her. "Drink. It will make you feel better."

She did, consuming a near third of the bottle. The liquid did her good, some of her color returned. "I... I reached out and touched his mind. The Chainman, I saw what he wanted to do to me."

"You touched a stranger's mind?" Jonathan asked, looking astonished that she'd been so bold.

"I had to. I had to know if they really would...before I could...I just had to know." Tears flooded her eyes.

Jonathan moved beside her, put his hand on her chin, lifting it. "And even so, you wouldn't let me kill them."

She shuddered. "Killing isn't the answer."

"Perhaps...but it would have given me great satisfaction to have done the job."

Jonathan's voice was dark. Marcus had never seen him so angry, not in the thirty years he'd known the nightwalker. The big man eyed Sharon with a half-smile. It wasn't just a companion Jonathan wanted to protect. Deep feelings were involved here, at least on the nightwalker's side.

Sharon smiled slightly and raised her head. Her changeable eyes, so green before, had mellowed back toward blue. They were aqua now. "There are better ways to find satisfaction, Jonathan."

Marcus felt a little smug satisfaction of his own. *Okay...it wasn't just Jonathan's emotions involved.* Standing, he gave her shoulders a squeeze and both pairs of eyes turned to stare at him. "I can see that I'm not really needed here." He grabbed the bundle of bloodstained clothes. "I'll just put these in to soak and call it a night."

He paused on the way through the door. "No more bloodletting tonight, okay? I need some time off."

In the kitchen, Kevin waited for him, his handsome face intent with concern. "Is she okay?"

"Yeah, she will be. I think what she needs most is some tender loving care, and Jonathan is just the guy for that."

Kevin gave a rueful laugh, folding his arms across his narrow chest. "I guess the real thing is pretty hard to give up, once you've tasted it." He cast a sly glance over. "I know it's been that way for me."

Marcus smiled, warmed by his friend's words. Since Jonathan had taken Kevin out of the food chain, the younger man had been much more attentive. For the first time in thirty years, Marcus felt like settling down, spending his life with just one person.

His agreement with Jonathan allowed him to ask for removal of the marks at any time. Up till now he hadn't felt the urge to do so. Jonathan had needed at least one companion, and Marcus had enjoyed the benefits—good health, a virtual fountain of youth.

But now… He saw Kevin and realized what he'd been missing. Someone to care for, to live with—to grow old with. Giving up virtual immortality might seem like a bad idea to some, but what good was a long lifetime spent alone? Jonathan had his love, he had his own.

Marcus hefted the bundle of bloody clothes in his arms. "Help me get these into the laundry, and then we'll go home, Kevin. There's something I want to talk to you about."

\* \* \* \* \*

"Sharon…" Jonathan's voice was soft, gentle.

Wakened from her brief doze, she smiled up into his face. "You were drawing me a bath."

"I thought it would be good for you. You felt so cold when we got back." He brushed his fingers along her cheek. "You were close to shock and that can be very bad, even for a companion."

She examined her arm, running her finger along the place it had been sliced open. Not even a scar marked the location. "If I hadn't been a companion, this would have killed me. Too much blood loss."

He grasped her hand, lifted it to his mouth. Closing his eyes, he kissed it, the pinpricks of his fangs a brief reminder of who he was. But it didn't matter at all.

His voice was a harsh whisper. "I would never have allowed your death, *meine Süsse*."

She reached over and stroked his near-black hair, soft and fine under her fingers. "I know."

For a moment they simply gazed at each other. He managed a smile, his attempt at reassurance. But there was still too much darkness in his eyes, evidence of past sorrows not forgotten. "What about that bath?"

Her smile felt more natural. "I'd love a bath. But isn't your tub bigger?"

At last his smile reached his eyes, dispelling the ancient sadness. His mouth widened into a grin that revealed all his teeth, fangs included. Once again Sharon was surprised at how natural it looked.

*It was just Jonathan's smile. And she loved him.*

He laughed. "Why, *meine Süsse*. I didn't realize you liked my smile. I'll have to smile more often."

She felt her cheeks redden, knowing he'd no doubt heard all of that mental comment. She really did need to be more careful around him.

"Yes, I heard that. But not to worry, I won't hold your good taste for loving me against you."

He stood, pulling her with him. In addition to the humor, intensity burned in the depths of his blue eyes. "You made an excellent point about my tub. Perhaps we could both use a bath. And then to bed, I think."

His fingers slipped through her hair, letting it catch the light. "I have missed your presence when I wake."

Mind made up, he lifted her into his arms and carried her from the room.

She was close to laughter by the time they reached his lair. Jonathan watched it in her eyes, now intently dark blue.

"I could've walked, Jonathan."

He lifted her higher into his arms, leaning in to indulge in her scent. She still carried the fragrance of the beach, the scent of seaweed and burning driftwood in her hair.

"Perhaps, but I prefer to keep you close to me." He didn't put her down until they reached his bathroom. Then he placed her onto her feet, keeping close watch to see she didn't fall. He could have left her on the couch in the lair, but he didn't want her out of his sight for even as long as it would take to fill the tub.

She wobbled a little before settling onto a small bench next to the tub. He noticed she still clutched the bottle of water he'd given her. "Finish that. It will help replace the fluid loss."

Obediently, she did as he turned on the water in the large sunken tub. When he'd first moved into the Inn, he'd had the basement space redesigned to his exact specifications, including the bathroom. The tub, a total indulgence of marble and Jacuzzi jets, he'd designed with two in mind, patterning it after the one Natasha and Daniel owned. In twenty years of living here, this was the first time he'd use it with a guest.

Once the tub was filled, he helped her out of her robe. Leaving it on the bench, he directed her into the tub.

She eased into the warm water and glanced over at him, running her gaze along his still dressed body. Her bold stare left him aching, as if she'd touched him with her hands instead. "Aren't you planning on joining me?"

He felt her stare as he pulled off his shirt and unbuttoned his jeans, pulling them off with a minimum of fuss. One nice thing about modern clothes was the invention of the zipper.

A lifetime of good habits caused him to fold his clothes and place them on the bench next to her robe. She had her hand over her mouth trying to hold back her giggles as he finished.

"You are the neatest man I've ever known."

A prick of jealousy assailed him. "And how many men have you known?" She hadn't been a virgin when he'd taken her to bed. She'd known other men before, as he'd known other women. That hadn't bothered him…until now.

Her eyes changed from blue to green—a perfect barometer for her moods. She hadn't liked that question.

"I haven't had as many lovers as you have, I imagine. And no, you can't ask about them."

He wasn't in the mood for a quarrel. "I wasn't going to," he said, trying to placate her. Slipping into the tub beside her, he reached for her, pulling her warm body closer to settle in his lap. She relaxed against him, silky skin and hair against his chest, the softness of her breasts under his hands. It was just as he'd imagined it the first time she'd bathed in his home, when he'd wanted to join her but hadn't dared.

Now he dared anything.

His body tightened in reaction to hers, desire cutting through the lingering fear. He could have lost her tonight...the wound had been deep and across several blood vessels. As she'd said, only the fact that she was a companion had saved her. The mark he'd given her had kept her alive. The mark that showed she belonged to him.

*She belonged to him.* That thought echoed through him, opening doors in his being he'd thought closed forever. As they opened, the truth poured forth, filling the gaps of his existence.

Parts of him had known it all along. She belonged to him, for him, with him, part of him. Part of him. She was his lady, his lover. More than a companion ever could be.

*Bloodmate.* That was the answer. She'd even proposed it before but he'd refused, not wanting to risk her life to his thirst.

But now...he had to try. When she'd been injured, it was as if a part of him had been ripped asunder. He could no longer consider her leaving him. As his bloodmate, she never would. In return, he would learn to control his thirst. He'd have to.

It was still too soon, though. Tonight she'd proven she could suffer a significant loss without more than a little lightheadedness. It wouldn't be long before he could claim her that way, bind her to him. And once he did, he'd never be alone again.

She leaned back into him, her head on his shoulder. He felt her weariness as if it were his own. Between the blood loss, the injury and healing, and the shock and violence of the attack, she needed rest more than anything else.

In response, he wrapped his arms even more tightly around her, cuddling her closer, willing his rebellious body to relax. Tonight was a time for comfort and love, not lovemaking.

Very close to sleep, she murmured into his ear. "Don't leave me alone tonight, Jonathan."

"Not to worry, *meine Süsse*. I won't." If he had his way, he'd never leave her alone again, nor allow her to leave him. He'd keep her with him, safe, for as long as she lived. And when her life was over, he would end his.

From his long memory, he dragged something the Countess, his sire, had told him not long before she watched her final sunrise.

There had been a great party that night and he'd entertained a pair of young ladies, feeding a little but enjoying himself a lot. He'd rejoiced afterward and the Countess had smiled quietly at him.

"Ah, yes, young Jonathan, you must please yourself, of course. But in your pursuit of pleasure don't forget that the man who seeks only his own gratification will rarely please others enough to keep them beside him. And what good is that? If we must have eternal life, the last thing we want is to live it alone."

When the women he'd been with that night refused any further contact with him, he'd understood what she'd meant. After that he'd put the desires of his lover first.

But even so, he'd never found someone who completed him the way Sharon did. To make her his bloodmate, he'd brave anything, even risk losing her.

After all, what good was eternal life if you must live it alone?

## Chapter Sixteen

෨

Five evenings later, Sharon sat in the kitchen, sipping a cup of coffee. A bottle of water sat on the table next to her, only partially touched—the great thirst from her blood loss on the beach was pretty much gone.

The days since the incident on the beach had been interesting. Five nights spent with Jonathan, either in the bar or in his room. Five days spent in his bed, his arms wrapped tightly around her.

Five of the happiest—and most frustrating—days and nights of her life. Five times she'd awakened in his arms, opening her eyes to see Jonathan's loving regard. He'd leaned forward to kiss her, gently, sweetly—on the forehead.

And then disentangled himself from the covers—and her—to rise and dress for the evening.

Not once in the past few days had he come close to making love to her. She could feel his love in the way he held her, looked at her, touched her. But not since that night two weeks ago when he'd fed from her during sex had he made love to her.

Frustrating. That's what it was. Clearly he wanted her but was wary of losing control while they were intimate. Tonight when they'd woken she'd tried opening her mind to him as she had on the beach. For a moment his eyes had linked with hers and she'd felt the warm golden glow within her.

But then as he'd come closer, she'd panicked and backed away. The glow had died away and his kiss had been even more poignant than usual.

If only she could make a complete link with Jonathan. She'd done it on the beach, when he'd needed it to help heal her. But since then each attempt at a full link had resulted in failure. She had to improve her ability to link minds. It was the only way she'd be able to open up to him, the only way to control his thirst.

It might be the only way she'd get him to make love to her again.

Sharon put her cup down and turned her attention to Marcus, who was stirring a big pan of spaghetti sauce on the stove. A pot of boiling water rested on the back burner, waiting for the noodles. She sent out a tentative tendril into Marcus's mind, felt him startle.

*What is it, Shari? Something I can do for you?* Dark brown amusement filled his eyes.

She struggled to control the link. *I need to know how to do this better…could you help me?*

He laughed. Shaking his head, he dumped the noodles into the steaming pot. "You're already far beyond me. I'm not that strong a talent."

"Oh." Disappointed, she picked up her cup again and drank the cooling brew.

He turned the burner down to simmer and grabbed a seat opposite her at the counter, eyeing her near-empty cup. "You want a refill?"

"No, thanks."

He seemed to read her tangled emotions. "So how are things with our 'master'?"

Sharon groaned. "I don't know. I haven't seen him since dusk."

The big man's confused look didn't make her feel any better. "Listen, Sharon, it isn't any of my business…"

"…but you want to know what's going on?" She grimaced. "Believe me, I wish I knew. He wants me with him… Just not *with* him."

"You're spending the night in his bed." He laughed at her shocked glare. "Sharon, your bed hasn't been slept in since your run-in with those goons on the beach. I haven't been prying, but some things are just too noticeable. Particularly when one of my jobs is the laundry."

"He may have me sleeping in his bed, but sleeping is all we've done…and no, abstinence hasn't been my idea. That's why I need to learn to open up more. Allow a full link."

"You think that will help?"

"It couldn't hurt. That's the problem, that he doesn't link with me."

"Why not just ask Jonathan for lessons?"

Why not? It was a fair question. "I think some of the problem is that he always takes the lead with the link. I want to learn to control it myself." Her head sank onto the table. "I don't feel comfortable asking him."

"Well, if you want to ask someone else, I'd try Callistra. You know her?"

A tall, red-haired woman with a sweet face came to mind. Callistra was one of the spellcaster set, a regular at the bar, if not one Sharon had actually spoken much to. Since Sharon had stopped using a shield, she'd been able to identify the others with mental powers as if by voice. Callistra's mental voice was soft but had depth, as if holding hidden power.

"I've heard her…" Sharon began.

"I imagine you have. She's a very powerful psi, although you wouldn't know it to talk to her. Plus, she's a teacher."

"A teacher?"

"Yes, at the local elementary—fourth, fifth, and sixth grades. Good with the kids...and with the parents. Knows how to be subtle with her touch. I think you have the power, Sharon, but you need training. She'd be a good person to ask."

Amber wandered in and opened the refrigerator, looking for raw meat to feast on. Her presence ended the conversation but not Sharon's thoughts. It was Friday night and she was scheduled to play and sing. Callistra would likely be there, with the rest of the spellcasters. Sharon should be able to talk to her between sets.

She was still mulling her decision when Jonathan arrived.

From her position at the counter, a piece of raw chicken in hand, Amber grinned at him, then at Sharon in anticipation of some malicious fun. "So who's on the menu tonight, Jon?"

Sharon suppressed a groan. Since the last full moon, when seeing Jonathan and her together had prompted Ralph to declare his intentions, Amber had become almost friendly. But that hadn't stopped her from teasing Sharon about her distaste over his blood-donating friends.

Jonathan paused in the middle of fetching a glass of serum. Abruptly Sharon felt his mental touch, testing...something. She couldn't tell what he looked for, but it was not in her mind.

*Her blood pressure?* Could he tell how much she had to spare, just by probing?

His touch scooted away, then returned. It became a gentle caress, similar to how he'd played with her shield.

Sharon's attention riveted to his face. He still seemed to be studying the glass in his hand, but inwardly...

"Actually, I wondered if Sharon would attend me tonight. It's Friday and you were going to play anyway, so Ralph will be here to tend bar." His eyes locked with Sharon's. "If that's all right with you?"

She couldn't help her triumphant grin. "I'll be happy to. Before my first set?"

"That will be fine. Come to my office when you're ready." He smiled reassuringly before leaving, taking his drink with him.

* * * * *

*Was she ready?* Sharon paused outside the door to the office then raised her hand to knock.

*Come in, meine Süsse.* Jonathan's mental voice sounded amused.

She grimaced. Of course he'd known she was outside the door. Not bothering to knock, she turned the handle and stepped inside.

He waited for her. Lean, male. Handsome. Her vamp…that is, her nightwalker lover. Waiting for the blood she could give him. He smiled at her, his fangs obvious, and held out a hand. "Come to me, my companion."

She stepped to him and his hand clasped hers firmly. A touch of nervousness assailed her. "Jonathan…"

He raised her hand to his lips, the tips of his fangs lightly imprinting against the sensitive skin. "It's all right, my sweetness. Just as it should be." Leading her to the couch, he guided her down to sit at one end, taking his place next to her.

His ice blue stare studied her face. "Why are you so nervous? You have nothing to fear from me."

"I know. It's silly." She glanced around at their surroundings, the place he usually fed. "I'd hoped…"

Why couldn't she just get the nerve up to suggest they go to his bed? She didn't want a sterile feeding like before, she wanted his love. She wanted his mouth on her neck while they made love. She wanted…

She wanted what she couldn't have.

Disappointment furrowed his brow. "You don't want me to feed? I will find another if that's the case."

"No, I do want you. I just…I just want to feel more than satisfaction. I want more…"

"Ah, you want *more*. That's fine." The disappointment fled, replaced by gentle humor. He kissed her hand again. "I'm very, very good at *more*," he said, his voice teasing.

Before she could question his intentions, Jonathan moved off the couch to kneel beside it and directed Sharon to lie prone. "Just relax. Let me into your mind."

Carefully she cleared her doubts away. Envisioning a room with a window, she omitted the blinds across the opening, leaving it free for him to enter. Jonathan's golden glow rested outside the frame, soothing, gentle.

She barely felt the prick of his teeth in her neck.

The glow entered and filled her. It was beautiful, glorious, a pleasure to experience. Satisfaction became overriding, joy followed. Golden contentment built, overran all her senses and overcame all lingering resistance.

*All resistance.* She was helpless in his mental thrall.

The pleasure started. At first small, a twinge, a stroke, a touch. As if invisible fingers played against her skin, at first soothing, then arousing. The sensation became more distinct then more centralized.

She'd asked for more and he was giving her what he'd thought she wanted. Caught in the strength of his mental hold, she couldn't protest, couldn't stop him. Could do nothing but experience what he wished.

The pleasuring touches increased. Sharon felt as if gentle but insistent and highly trained fingers explored her body. Some stopped and caressed her now swollen and hard nipples. Others fled further and toyed with her feminine core. Invisible fingers stroked and guided and led her most sensitive parts to a state of full arousal in just a few seconds.

In her mind, she heard soft whisperings then saw erotic images she could never conjure on her own, silken limbs, bodies entwined, hers and his. Already provoked, this forced her into a new state of heightened sensation, one she'd never known outside of Jonathan's bed. Everything was emphasized, the feel of his hand behind her head, the workings of his mouth on her neck, the hard smoothness of the leather couch beneath her back and legs.

The feel of Jonathan's mouth on her neck, drinking deeply of her crimson nectar, the blood he needed and she created for him. Passion rose, in part from the manipulation of her senses, enhanced by her desire for him.

She wanted Jonathan. She wanted his body, his love. His teeth on her neck, to feed him, to serve him. Part of her knew some of this need was manufactured by his link into her mind.

But without the link, it would have been the same. She would have still been there to serve him. And that's what hurt the most. She didn't need that false desire. She had enough of her own but he hadn't seen that, felt it or trusted it. Instead, he'd imposed on her what would get him what he needed…a cooperative companion.

A writhing and moaning companion who fed her master while he drank his fill, and experienced pleasure at his hands and mind.

The first wave of ecstasy struck her, like the swell of the ocean, rising and falling. Then the next hit, then another, and another. Like waves of passion, of pleasure, of satisfaction, one after the other, in an unending string of orgasmic delight.

Sharon rode each one, felt each as a separate thing. Gasping, crying out, overcome with the experience he gave her. It was glorious—pure rapture.

The last wave rolled through her and she rose and fell on it, grinding her hips into the couch. She felt his tongue on her neck, licking the place he'd pierced the skin, closing the holes to leave no mark.

Her body still shuddered under the passion he'd released and sought to satisfy with his mental touch. He leaned back, one hand still on her hair, stroking it. Sharon struggled to sit up, her body cooperating with difficulty. Part of her still wanted to be back in that ocean of pleasure.

The rest was hopping mad. She stared at Jonathan, wondering if he knew what he'd done. How could he have treated her as he did his other friends, insulted her this way?

Jonathan stared down into her face and laughed. "How did you like it?"

The flat of her hand caught him across the cheek. Off guard and off-balance, Jonathan fell to the side, shock coloring his face.

Jumping to her feet, Sharon glared at him. "You bastard, how dare you treat me like one of your stupid clients? I trusted you. I let you in, totally, and this is what you do—jerk me off when I asked for love. How could you?"

Tears, unbidden and unwanted, flowed from her eyes, leaving her madder than ever. Shaking, furious, she ran for the door. Once there, she turned and faced him, aiming a mental probe as powerful as she could right into his brain. She barely registered his flinch at the blow.

*Don't ever touch me again.*

Once she was gone, Jonathan pulled himself onto the couch. His face stung from the slap, his mind from that last strike. Once opened, her mind held incredible power. He was no expert, but he could measure the push she'd given him. And she was untrained...who knew what strength she'd wield if properly developed?

He was so stunned by it that over an hour passed before it occurred to him that he'd drunk his fill, much more than he would have taken from one of his regular clients, and then his dinner had not only slugged him but had run from the room as if she'd suffered no blood loss at all.

* * * * *

She sang in the corner, the spotlight turning her pale hair silver, her voice melodic bliss accompanied by the rich mellow tone of the guitar.

*So beautiful...* He watched, wanting and wishing. Wishing he hadn't pulled so stupid a trick, wanting the true passion he knew she was capable of. Watching her spin her siren song, enthralling the audience, paranormal and human alike. The room was hushed, what conversation taking place occurred in whispers in deference to the singer's spell.

Sharon, the Entertainer. Sharon, the songsmith, whose words and music diverted concerns to places unknown, raised emotions in healthy ways. Made her audience feel good about who they were, those they were with, what they could do. Gave hope. Gave comfort.

Sharon's songs were wonderful. Sweetness and light—peace and tranquility. She sang of far-off rivers and forests nearby, of places she'd been to, and beaches she'd never see. But when she sang of them, the audience saw them and heard those distant shores in their own minds.

For a moment, Jonathan wondered at that. How could a woman so talented have ended up stranded here, in his town? Of all the taverns in all the towns, why his?

Perhaps it was luck...perhaps it was fate.

He believed in God. With all he'd seen, how could he not? With very little effort Jonathan could believe that divine providence had led Sharon to his door, allowed him to pull her to his side.

*She loved him.* That was the message he'd chosen to take from her outburst earlier in the evening. She loved him and didn't appreciate being lumped in with the rest of his meals.

That was fine with him, although she was wrong about one thing. He'd felt every passion-loaded moment of their encounter. His groin still ached with unfulfilled need, something that never happened with the others.

Why should it? She was his companion. He'd taken her as his lover, more than once. Of course his body ached for her.

He'd known for some time she didn't care for his dining practices. With luck, he'd eliminate any need for additional blood sources...eventually. It was just too soon to do it now.

The song stopped and those in the audience applauded, even Amber by the bar. It had been a love song, and the shapeshifter had needed to free her hand from Ralph's who was acting as bartender. Tender passion for each other colored both their faces, the result of Sharon's skillful song.

In the doorway to the kitchen, Kevin stood with Marcus, one arm around the bigger man's waist. Discreet enough...not that anyone here cared.

*Why do I have to be the only one without a mate?* Jonathan thought bitterly. *Surely after all this time I deserve someone to love.* Even though he'd never admit it, he envied his friends and their lovers.

Her set finished, Sharon turned off the spotlight and put the guitar back into its case. She stowed the instrument behind the bar then asked Ralph for something.

Jonathan smiled when he saw her open the bottled water and take a deep swig. Ever the dutiful companion, taking care of herself to feed him better...even when angry.

Her next action confused him. For the first time, she entered the spellcaster corner of the room and stopped in front of a table with several regulars to address a red-haired woman. After a moment, the pair moved to an empty table and soon were deep in conversation.

What did Sharon want with Callistra, one of the local schoolteachers?

\* \* \* \* \* \*

"Why ask me, Sharon? Why not have Jonathan train you?"

Again that question. "Whenever we're together, he's the one in control. I've tried, but I can't seem to initiate the link, and as soon as I open..."

"...he jumps in and takes charge." Callistra's elfin face broke into a smile. "Typical male," she said wryly.

"Marcus told me you were a teacher."

Callistra nodded. "And so you thought I could teach you. I can...for a price."

Startled, Sharon spoke quickly. "Oh, I'll be happy to pay you. Since I got here, all my wages have gone into the bank." She'd accumulated quite a savings in the last couple of months, nearly enough to give her a fresh start in Los Angeles. Not that she was thinking of leaving, at least not yet. She was angry with Jonathan over the trick he'd pulled, but not enough to leave.

Throughout her set she'd felt his steady gaze on her, the warmth of his mental touch, just beyond her reach. There was an apology in the distance he'd kept, in his expression.

No, she wasn't quite ready to leave...yet.

"Sharon?" Callistra's voice, laced with amusement, penetrated her internal musings. "You look like you were thinking very hard. I hope not about how you were going to pay me...because it isn't money I want."

"What then?"

"A song. You write them, I've heard the ones you've done for the shapeshifters, but you've never sung of the Goddess or that which gives us all life. I want a song from you of celebration. Something I can use with my students. Could you do that?"

Delighted, Sharon smiled into the other woman's earnest face. "I'd be happy to."

Callistra leaned back in her chair and sipped at her garlic-laden wine. "It's a deal then. Can you meet me tomorrow? In the afternoon?"

It would mean avoiding Jonathan's bed in the morning... But she'd planned on doing that anyway after his stunt in his office.

Sharon nodded. "Just tell me where."

## Chapter Seventeen

"Sharon...you're forgetting to breathe."

Callistra's soft voice broke through Sharon's mental haze, bringing her back to the here and now, the here being the overlook above the All Night Inn, the now being two hours before sunset.

It was the most daylight Sharon had seen in weeks, and she wasn't sure she liked it. The intensity of the sun was blinding and she was developing a headache. Plus, there was so much wildlife around, birds everywhere, insects, biting flies...she batted away one of the larger ones tormenting her, satisfied to see it speed to the other side of the clearing and collide with a tree. *One for her.*

Another one bit her on the leg. She swatted at it and missed. *And one for them.* It was hopeless—she was outnumbered. Sharon cast Callistra a desperate look. "Do we have to do this up here? Why don't we just go back to the Inn—no one is around."

"No one but Jonathan."

"Who is asleep and won't wake for two hours."

"He might be asleep, but I suspect he's still aware of what is happening around him. Nightwalkers, particularly ones as old as he, aren't completely incapacitated during the daylight hours." The red-haired spellcaster leaned in. "I thought you wanted this to be a surprise."

Sharon slapped at another fly. "I did, but I'd rather not be eaten alive."

"Oh? I would think you were used to that by now."

A dirty look was the only reply Sharon offered on that. "What I don't understand is why they bother me and not you."

She watched with envy as a new cloud of bugs sped through the clearing, parting into two streams that bypassed Callistra completely. Meanwhile, several of the newcomers joined the group plaguing Sharon.

Callistra smiled beatifically. "They don't come near me for two reasons. One, most insects don't like garlic. Second, my aura pushes them away."

Sharon perked up. "Aura? Can you teach me to do that?"

"Well, it's outside the realm of what we discussed..." Callistra's voice trailed off as she watched Sharon battle the flying pests. She sighed. "But if it will make you more comfortable. Here, take my hands."

Through her mental window, Sharon saw Callistra's spirit, deep purple in color rather than Jonathan's gold. It hovered, then entered. Images came into her mind, the key to adjusting her aura to repel insects.

*Oh!* she thought delightedly, *that's how you do it!*

When they dropped hands, the air around Sharon was bug-free and in fact, the entire clearing had become insect-proof. Sharon let loose a cheer.

"Maybe I'll write you two songs!"

Shaking her head, Callistra laughed. "If you feel the need, I'll not turn it down. But let me earn one first. Close your eyes and breathe deeply."

Sharon did as ordered, and in minutes a deep calm permeated her. She tried sending her mental voice. *Must I always do it this way?*

Callistra's mental voice came back, surprised and pleased. *You have a strong power. Very strong... I'm surprised you've gone so long without training. To answer your question, no. You will be able to create a link without the calming exercise in the future. But now you need focus and this is the best way to achieve that.*

*So what do I do now?*

*I will open my mind. It will seem like a bowl on the horizon. Reach for the bowl with your spirit.*

There it was, shining as if in sunlight, although their minds were in a place where day and night did not exist. Jade green in color, the rim thin enough to be translucent, as if the bowl was made of porcelain. Sharon sent a tendril of herself to the bowl like a thin deep blue tentacle, allowed it to run along the edge, as if she were running a finger on the rim of a glass.

*Now enter the bowl. Fill it. See what's inside.*

The space inside seemed cramped, but Sharon slid over the rim into it. Images formed along the inside, moving images, of the ocean, the sky. Memories of things and places Callistra had been and seen. Open fields and deep forests.

One picture caught Sharon's attention—a full moon with the silhouette of a man superimposed across it, a woman on his back, both suspended in the sky.

*From our last ceremony.* Callistra's amused mental voice said. *We knew then that Jonathan had found someone he cared for.*

Longing filled Sharon. That had been the night Jonathan declared love for her and on the next rising, he'd made love to her for the first time. He'd been her boss, then her friend, and then her lover.

Now? Now he was her world and she wanted that world to continue. It was the reason for her learning what she'd never wanted to know before. How to control this power inside her—how to harness her own mental strength.

*How to be good enough to control the link and be his proper mate...his bloodmate.*

*And to do that, you must learn control—and trust*, Callistra thought. *Open to me, as wide as you can. You are in control but you must allow me entry. Think of pulling the bowl into your mind.*

Sharon imagined the bowl in her mental room. She visualized a table and set the bowl down with invisible fingers. The Callistra-bowl hovered then disappeared into mist, a deep purple cloud. The misty cloud flickered for a moment then slipped around the interior as if examining the furnishings. The walls lost focus and displayed images that Sharon recognized from her past. *What are you doing?*

*You're showing me who you are. It's a natural thing, part of being linked.* The mist hovered near one set of images, featuring a pale, dark-haired man with pointed teeth. *You care for him very much.* A purple tendril pointed to the image of Jonathan from last night, the humor on his face right before she'd slapped him. *Even when he hasn't been on his best behavior.*

No, Jonathan hadn't been on his best behavior last night, but the truth was he'd thought his actions would please her. How was he to know that induced pleasure hadn't been what she wanted—or needed? How was he to know how much it would bother her when she'd never told anyone the truth?

Older images showed up. Ones from the hospital when her father had been so ill. The mist grayed and thinned. It was sad, but there was so much love as well. His passing had been too early, but it was peaceful. He was content.

As Callistra's mist moved to another part of the wall, Sharon contemplated what she'd thought. Her father had been content at the end of his life. It had been too soon for her to lose him, to lose the one person she'd had left in the world to care for.

*Until Jonathan.* Suddenly Sharon realized what she was showing Callistra. Images of caring, of trust, of times when she'd loved. And been betrayed.

*Callistra, wait...* Too late. Much older images showed now, from a time Sharon thought she'd relegated to the deepest well of her mind. Images of a man, limbs intertwined with hers, in a bed, her mind not her own, held in a foreign thrall.

The purple mist intensified, almost black in places. She could feel the horror in Callistra's mind. *Does Jonathan know about this, that you were forced into passion? How could he have thought to do the same thing?*

Sharon willed the walls blank and the window open. *Go, please.* The mental room faded, the mist gone, the connection broken...and by her will. She'd controlled the link.

She'd celebrate that fact later. At the moment she was cold, shivering in spite of the warm afternoon sunlight filling the overlook clearing. Callistra hovered nearby, her face grim.

"Well, at least I now know why you haven't been trained in spite of your power. After being raped, mentally and physically, it must have been all you could do to even admit you had the capacity." She stood, dusted off her pants and moved to the log-bench. "Did you ever report it?"

Sharon shook her head. "It would have involved my brother, he'd be held responsible too."

"He was, though, wasn't he? It should have been reported. Something should have been done, Sharon..."

"It's over!" She used a thread of power to reinforce that comment, arrowing it at the spellcaster. At Callistra's paleness, Sharon felt a surge of regret.

*No. Don't ever apologize for being who you are.* The spellcaster pulled herself to her feet, rubbing her temples. "I should not have been pushing like that. It is your business…but someday I hope you find that man and at least do to him what you just did to me," her last comment was tempered by her smile.

So strange. She'd never told anyone about Stuart's "friend" and what had happened on her eighteenth birthday. Shame was what she'd expected to feel but instead she felt—relief at Callistra knowing. Some measure of freedom.

And more. That man had been able to take advantage of her through her mental powers, but now she knew how to control them and no one could ever dominate her again. Eagerly she leaned forward. "Should we try the link again?"

"We should. And this time I'll not pry into your deepest secrets."

An hour later, Callistra climbed wearily to her feet. "You've learned everything I have to teach you. I've never seen a pupil as quick as you are. When you get to the city, there are some names I can give you of spellcasters who can show you more."

"The city? Who said I was going there?"

Callistra smiled. "Sharon, your talent is far too great for you to stay in Los Niños. You want to return to Los Angeles…it's clear in your thoughts when you speak of the place. There's only one thing you want more. I hope he's worth it to you."

The spellcaster shook her head. "You should never let your ambitions be thwarted by another's wishes, no matter how much you love them. If they love you in return, it will work out."

Sharon hoped she was right. She did want to return to LA, but not without Jonathan. At least not at the moment. Now she was ready to try linking with him. Ready, even, to act as his dinner tonight. If he could be persuaded to let her control the link.

She grasped the spellcaster's hands. "I owe you a song or two."

"Right now, I'll settle for a glass of wine."

"That can certainly be arranged. One garlic special, on the house of course."

Anticipation winged through Sharon as she followed Callistra down the hill.

\* \* \* \* \*

"Where did you go with Callistra today?" Jonathan's voice seemed to come from nowhere.

Calmly, Sharon raised her head from her pre-opening inventory to face him, suppressing a triumphant smile. For once he hadn't been able to sneak up on her. As he'd moved silently through the bar, her new sensitivity had told her he was in the room long before he was close enough to speak.

"We went to the overlook. She was teaching me...oh, never mind," she said, suddenly apprehensive. Maybe it was better he didn't know everything she'd learned.

Jonathan hesitated, the words coming slowly to him for once. "I made a mistake yesterday. I thought..." A glance at her face, and he returned his attention to his serum glass. "I apologize for that...I will never do it again."

*No... you won't*, she thought smugly.

He blinked, his attention riveted on her now. "That was strong, Sharon. You've gotten more powerful."

She allowed a smile to cross her lips. "I've taken some lessons. You may not be able to take control again."

"I see." He didn't seem terribly happy about it, but then he probably wasn't used to his dinner fighting back. This would be a new experience for him.

Sharon moved from behind the bar and approached him, putting her hand on his chest. *We can make love again, Jonathan.*

He spoke aloud, as if she wasn't linking into his mind. "No, my sweetness, I'm sorry. It's still too dangerous." Taking her hand, he kissed it regretfully. "I won't risk your life, and I can't control myself with you. I've tried so many times in the past."

"But you won't need to try anymore. I'll control the link, I'm strong enough now…"

"No!" Jonathan's pale blue eyes went wide and he dropped her hand, stepping back from her. "I won't let that happen."

Confused, Sharon stared at him. "I don't understand."

"I won't let anyone control a link to me. No one, not even you. I've been there before."

It was too much like her declaration when he'd first tried to link with her. "And why not, Jonathan? What happened to you?"

He wouldn't look at her. "Vanessa…that's what happened. That conniving, little…she always kept control. I could barely feed when I was with her. To let you do the same. No…I won't allow it." Anger suffused his features, turning them to stone, his emotions locked deep within.

All of her hopes died. Jonathan had as many hang-ups about mind-linking as she did. Still she had to try. "I'm not Vanessa, Jonathan, and I don't much like being compared to her. I'd never leave you hungry. When I talked to Daniel, he said it was the only way to control the thirst, that I had to take control."

Some of the stone of his face melted, allowing a measure of sorrow to filter through. "Sharon…I know what Natasha and Daniel have is desirable to you. It is for me as well. But there are other ways. You will continue to get stronger, produce more blood each time, and someday I'll be able to control myself better. We will be able to love then…"

"Will we? Or will you make more excuses to keep me away? I can control the link now. We could make love tonight if you'd let me…"

"I said no, I don't want that."

She watched his face, saw the conflict. "You don't trust me."

The widening of his eyes told her she'd guessed the truth. "It isn't precisely that," he tried to tell her.

"It is exactly that. All this time, you've told me I can trust you, but now that I have, it's you who doesn't trust me."

"There are things you haven't told me…"

He was right. She hadn't told him everything, about her brother's betrayal, why she hadn't trusted anyone for so long. But now things were different. Callistra had seen the truth, and all she'd felt was anger. No fear, no shame. It hadn't been her fault, not that she'd ever believed it had been…exactly. But she hadn't wanted anyone to know. Even her father hadn't learned the truth. And as for Stuart, what he recalled of that night…well, she doubted he remembered much anyway.

She loved Jonathan. She could live with him knowing the truth now.

"There are things you've kept from me too. But I'll open my mind to you now and you can see everything. All I ask is that you allow me to control the link next time we feed." It was a brash promise, but she was ready to fulfill it.

For a moment he hesitated, weighing her words. Breathlessly she waited for him to make his decision then watched deflated as he shook his head.

"No, *meine Süsse*. If that is the price I'd rather not know your secret. We'll wait until you're stronger and see then. I won't give you control."

He turned and slipped from the room as quietly as he'd entered, ignoring the first heartbroken tear that trailed down her cheek.

## Chapter Eighteen

ಐ

Jonathan helped Amber carry a heavy case of beer into the tavern's main room. It wasn't like the shapeshifter couldn't have managed the weight by herself, but the case was an awkward size and he didn't want the contents on the floor.

Even so, she was hardly appreciative of his assistance. Once again, it was virtually all he could do to keep his temper at her insolence as she snarled her thanks. Only the realization that Amber wasn't really his problem kept him from firing her on the spot.

No, firing Amber wouldn't help. Truth was, nothing would. He rested his arms on the bar and watched Amber effortlessly tug open the case.

He missed Sharon. She had gone into town with Marcus to pick up a few supplies they were short on. Lately she'd been spending a lot of time with the cook and if Jonathan hadn't known the man's commitment to his sexual preference, he'd have been jealous of the pair.

He wasn't jealous, but he was envious…and lonely. And more. Restlessness plagued him, a desire to get out, to spend time away from the inn. He'd gone into town a few times in the early evening and later spent time on the beach after closing hours.

Occasionally he'd found himself outside Sharon's door, listening to her performing mysterious female rituals when preparing to rest. Sometimes she'd sing, as she had that first evening while taking a bath. It was a torment to hear her voice, to know she was so close, so available—and so forbidden to him.

There had been no repeat of their last encounter. Even though he'd left the room, he'd heard her crying afterward. But no matter how much his body ached for her, he wouldn't let her control the link…and she'd refused to do it any other way. He hadn't even taken blood from her.

Jonathan watched Amber unload the bottles into the mini-fridge behind the bar. It was a popular brand, a best seller. He'd tried it in the small quantities he could handle. It didn't taste nearly as good as Sharon did. Nothing ever would.

Not even chocolate.

Suppressing a sigh, he leaned over the bar. "Do you need any further help?"

The shapeshifter glared at him. "No. Thank you." She leaned back on her haunches, her golden eyes glaring at him. "Don't you have something else to do?"

Suppressing yet another wish to send her looking for a new job, Jonathan pushed back and headed for his office.

The front door of the tavern opened and a man entered, thin frame encased in worn khakis and a button-down shirt that had seen better days. The clothes hung on him, as if purchased for a heavier man—or maybe he'd just lost a lot of weight recently. A thin blond beard covered his cheeks, matching his close-cropped hair.

The stranger's entrance into the tavern was tentative but determined. Something about him was familiar, but Jonathan couldn't place what it was.

The newcomer spotted Jonathan and must have known who—and what—he was. He paled and took a step back, but then something kept him from what he'd clearly wished to do, flee. Instead, he drew himself up taller and swallowed. "Good evening."

Folding his arms, Jonathan offered his best glower. "Good evening. I'm Jonathan Knottmann." He could tell the name meant something from the other man's ill-concealed shudder. "Can I help you with something?"

Under the nightwalker's steady glare, the man became more nervous than before. "I'm looking for Sharon Colson."

"Are you? And you would be?"

"Stuart Colson." The stranger took a deep breath and then met Jonathan's gaze. He stared into the man's eyes and at the blue-green color of them, and Jonathan knew why the man looked so familiar. "I'm her brother."

\* \* \* \* \*

Sharon returned from town and helped unload the van into the kitchen, carrying the bag of limes that had been her principle excuse for the trip. After all, she couldn't very well make margaritas without limes.

Truly though, she'd just really needed the trip away from the Inn, away from Jonathan and his brooding stare. Away from the place with its memories she couldn't reconcile herself to.

*Jonathan didn't need her.* The last several days he'd made a point of avoiding her. When he'd tried to control the link, she'd brushed it off. If he wouldn't do it her way, she wouldn't do it at all.

But now she paid the price. He might never come to her again. Pausing in the doorway from the kitchen, she fingered the twin scars on her neck. Jonathan's mark. She might as well not even carry it. She was hardly his companion anymore.

Pushing through the swinging door from the kitchen, she entered the main room. Jonathan sat at the bar next to a stranger with blond hair, a beard and a cold beer in his hand. The pair were engaged in a lively conversation, and there was more animation on Jonathan's face than she'd seen in a long time.

Her heart throbbed painfully. Was Jonathan looking for another companion, a replacement for her?

She forced a smile. "I see we have an early customer. Who's your friend, Jonathan?"

The blond swiveled on his stool and her knees went weak. "Stuart?" Her voice sounded like a screech.

"Hey, Shari. How're you doing?" He pulled himself off the barstool and came toward her. Standing a few feet away, he held his arms open. "What, no hug for your big brother?"

Stunned she allowed herself to be drawn into his embrace. His body felt thin, sick. After being around super-healthy parafolk with their innate vigor, it was a shock to experience his mortal frailness.

"I didn't think I'd ever see you again," she managed.

His answering wry grin was pure Stuart. "Ah, you know me. I'm the bad penny. I always show up."

She pushed aside the thoughts that comment raised. Instead she kissed him on the cheek, the haphazard beard rough under her lips.

He examined her with a critical eye. "Man, Shari. You look great. I don't think I've ever seen you so healthy."

Healthy, happy and sane. Well, two out of three wasn't bad. "Thanks. You look…thinner."

He held out the waistband of his pants. "Yeah, I've lost a little weight." One hand rubbed the underside of his nose in habitual fashion. "Been kind of a tough year."

No doubt. She knew exactly what he'd been doing with his nose—the same thing he'd been doing fifteen years ago when…no. She wouldn't finish that thought.

Sickened, she pushed away from him, took a seat at the bar. Amber held an unopened bottle of beer toward her with a questioning look. Sharon shook her head fiercely and the shapeshifter returned the bottle to the fridge.

Amber stood, a speculative look on her face, her gaze glancing between Sharon and Stuart. "If you don't need me, Jon, I'll see if Marcus wants some help." At his nod, she took off for the kitchen.

Jonathan sipped his serum and watched. Something was very wrong—he could feel it in his blood. First Sharon's brother—one she'd only mentioned once before, when she'd first come to the inn—had shown up, now she acted as if she wasn't happy to see him.

It was clear Stuart was her brother. Now that Jonathan had a close look, he could see the same sunshine color in the man's hair, the same shape to his blue-green eyes. Older, yes. Much older.

In fact, the brother was pretty seedy looking. From the way his nose kept bothering him, he was battling at least one kind of drug problem. But there was more than that to their estrangement. Something about the way she'd kept him at arm's length. When she smiled, it didn't quite reach her eyes.

Yes, something was very wrong. Jonathan watched them and waited for some sign of what to do.

"How did you find me?" Sharon was asking. "I'm not exactly in the phone book."

The man's gaze darted around, and Jonathan felt a lie forthcoming. "A mutual friend told me he'd heard you singing, said you'd come to work here. I was surprised, I thought you were still in San Francisco."

"I left there two months ago, Stuart. After Dad died."

"Oh, yeah. Dad." He had the good taste to look embarrassed. "I was so sorry about that. It really broke me up that I couldn't make it to the funeral."

Agitation tightened her voice. "I tried to reach you. You didn't contact us at all while he was in the hospital."

"Well, you know. I was busy. Doing deals. You know how this business is."

Her temper finally broke. "For six months? You couldn't get away from LA for a couple of days in six months?"

His hands went up, placating. "Geez, Sis. I know. I'm sorry, I really am. But that's why I'm here, to make it up to you."

"Excuse me," Jonathan broke in smoothly. "What business did you say you were in?"

Stuart's thin chest popped out in self-importance. "Show business. I'm a promoter and agent. I book acts…used to have some big names until they got too big for their britches and signed with other agents." There was bitterness in his tone. "I even used to manage Sharon. Got her some good exposure back in the old days." He took a long pull on his beer. "Man, that really hits the spot."

Jonathan nodded grimly. That explained something. This odious little toad had been managing his sister's career. No wonder it hadn't gone anywhere in spite of her talent.

For a moment, he wondered what sort of promotion he, himself, could do for Sharon. He'd done work of that sort from time to time. Maybe assemble a group to back her up, piano, drums and bass. Perhaps he could even serve as the keyboard player. It had been a while since he'd been on stage, but…

His thoughts engrossed him so that he almost missed Stuart's next words. "Of course, this new gig I've got for her has all those other places beat."

For the first time, Sharon's eyes lit up. She leaned forward. "You have a job for me? A singing job?"

Leaning back, Stuart smiled. "What would you say to working at The Music Box?"

Her jaw dropped open. "The Music Box. But that's one of the best clubs in Los Angeles. How could you get me in there?"

"*The* best club, not just one of them. I know a guy who knows the owner, convinced him to give you a tryout. He needs some backup singers, is willing to let you do solo work as well."

Even Jonathan had to admit to being impressed. Not too many unknown artists worked that club. "When would she need to be there?"

"Right away. I'm here to fetch her back, tonight." He pointed the near-empty bottle at her. "This time tomorrow, I'll have you singing on the hottest stage in town."

Jonathan shook his head. "Tonight? That's not possible. There's too much to do, I couldn't possibly get away."

"Hey, who said you needed to go?" The beer had made Stuart bold. "Sharon's a big girl. I've got a car outside and can take her."

Sharon's excitement was so palpable, it broke Jonathan's heart. "It isn't possible for her to go alone. She's my companion and she belongs with me. And I can't go to LA tonight." He turned to her. "I'm sorry."

Sharon stared at him. "You're sorry? The opportunity of a lifetime, and I can't take it because you can't get away? Jonathan, you can't ask me to give this up. I've waited years for a chance like this."

"There will be other chances. I'll take you myself and introduce you to the clubs."

"When? This year—next? When?"

"When I say!" How dare she argue with him as if he didn't know what was best. He'd had centuries to practice patience, knowing when to keep a low profile. "It's too dangerous in LA right now. Too unsettled."

"You could do something about that. Sebastian asked you to."

"Sebastian wants many things from me, but I make my own decisions. I won't go to the city now, and I won't let you go without me."

Sharon lifted her chin, her eyes near green with anger. "You don't own me. I don't have to answer to you."

Her stubbornness shredded his patience. "You do so long as you wear my mark."

Stuart interrupted them. "Hey, hey. I didn't mean to get into the middle of something. Listen, Sis, if you can't come, that's all right."

Sharon glared at both of them. "No, it's not all right. Jonathan, you expect me to wait years if necessary. I'm not like that."

"Don't you understand? You have years…many more years than you had before. Plenty of time to do this."

"And in the meantime, I sit here. I play on weekends. I wait, and wait, and wait for you to decide how things are going to be between us. I must be patient, I must trust. But you don't trust me…not enough. We could be together now if you did."

Her accusation hit him, the truth like an arrow into his heart. An unexpected heat warmed his face under her steady glare. "It isn't that I don't trust you…" Desperately he cast about for an excuse. "But there are things you haven't told me." He glanced over at Stuart. "I hardly even knew you had a brother. You've mentioned him only once, and I'd gotten used to thinking you had no family."

Stuart looked hurt. "Hey, I know I haven't been the best brother, but that cuts, Sharon. I mean, it wasn't really my fault…"

Her face twisted, fury making a mask of it. "It was completely your fault, you bastard. Just because you were stoned…"

Jonathan grabbed Sharon by the arm. "What is it?"

But she didn't answer him. Instead, Stuart waved his hands, his voice developing a irritating whine. "I wasn't that stoned. For all I could see, everything was okay. I mean, a girl's got to lose it sometime, and Izzy was a good friend. You'd always talked about him like that. How was I to know what he'd done?"

Coldness clutched Jonathan at Stuart's words. *A girl's got to lose it sometime?* He turned Sharon to face him. "Come with me."

Seconds later they were in his office, the door closed behind them. "What did 'Izzy' do, Sharon?"

For a moment he wasn't sure she would answer him. Then her shoulders squared and her chin lifted. Anger colored her eyes, a brighter green than ever and before he could react, her mind opened, the link strong and under her control. His discomfort at that was swallowed by the images she showed him. In his mind was a replay of the events of her eighteenth birthday party, her brother showing up with his 'buddy', Izzy, a man near thirty with dark eyes and a scraggly brown beard. The man's slight build gave the impression of weakness, until one saw the intensity in his gaze. *Spellcaster, a strong one.*

It had started with a kiss for the birthday girl, visiting her brother at his in-town apartment. But somehow during that brief touch of the spellcaster's lips, another connection had been made. Jonathan felt Sharon's horror at the mental invasion, the link that had enthralled her, made her brother believe it was her idea to head for his bedroom in Izzy's arms. The false passion that had overwhelmed her senses, making her the man's willing sex slave.

She'd learned much that night...about how seamy sex could be. There had been pain, more than the usual for a deflowering. Fury filled Jonathan as he realized how much pain she'd endured. Izzy had been inventive... With all his experience, Jonathan only recognized half of the positions. Some didn't look comfortable for the woman at all.

Afterward, the spellcaster had choked her unconscious and left her, bruised, bleeding, her brother passed out from "recreational" drugs in the next room. When Stuart sobered up, he'd driven Sharon to the doctor who'd reported it as an unknown rape. They'd never seen their "good friend Izzy" again.

She hadn't been able to look at herself in the mirror for months afterward. Izzy had fed his visions of her into her mind during the act and whenever she'd seen her face it was twisted into a passion-induced mask from her memory.

Horror gripped Jonathan. What he'd done to her, just days ago—it had been similar to Izzy's attack. No wonder she'd been so angry.

*I'm so sorry.* He fed his remorse to her and silently resolved to find the man who'd hurt her. He rarely killed— but he would make an exception in this case.

*And yet, even after that, I trust you.* Her eyes were calmer now, returned to their familiar aqua shade. *And you don't trust me.*

He dropped his hands from her shoulders and cut the link. "We've had this discussion."

"And now it's over." Sharon stepped away, laying her hand on the bar. "Jonathan, you've seen the worst thing in my life, but it doesn't hurt as much as your rejection does."

She took a deep breath. "It all comes down to trust. At first I didn't trust you. My experience with Izzy hadn't left me able to let you into my mind, but as I grew to know you better, you earned my confidence. I knew you would never hurt me deliberately. I knew I could rely on your promise, the one you made the night you marked me, that I have 'your protection and support'. I learned to trust as well as love you. But have you learned to trust me?"

He had no answer for her. How could he, when the answer was...she was right.

Her nod held regret. "No, I don't think you have. I know you love me, but even with normal people, trust must be a part of a couple's bond. With nightwalker and companion, that goes double. It isn't just our hearts we risk with each other, but our minds and our lives. I can't stay with you if you can't trust me."

"It isn't that I don't want to, Sharon. I do. Perhaps with more time—"

"No, time isn't the answer. You've had three hundred years to learn patience, but there are other lessons you've failed. You don't trust me because you don't trust anyone, not really, not even yourself. You won't take Sebastian's job...why? Because you don't trust that he's right, that you'd be the best person to do it. You'd let someone less fit become chief rather than trust his judgment.

"You only keep one or two companions, even though you should have far more since you don't have a bloodmate. You'd rather rely on your 'clients' because they can come and go and you can control them easily and you don't have to trust a group of companions."

She took a deep breath. "Finally, you won't be my lover because you don't trust yourself not to hurt me. And that's the worst of all. You don't trust yourself and you've had three hundred years to learn to do so. A man who hasn't faith in himself…how can he have confidence in anyone else? And how can he commit to a relationship?"

She faced him, her aqua eyes bright with unshed tears. "That's what I want, Jonathan. I love you too much to have anything less than a relationship with you."

"We have a relationship."

"Not the one I want. Give me your trust or…or I'm leaving."

Fierce possessiveness touched him, burning his soul. "Not while you wear my mark."

She took a deep breath and closed her eyes, and he was reminded of how she'd looked the night he'd marked her. The same pained resolve in her face and tension in her body.

Her eyes opened and she stared directly into his. "Remove the mark."

At first he wasn't sure he'd heard her right. "Sharon?"

"I mean it. Remove the mark. You promised you would when I asked."

Sudden anger singed his blood. "This singing job means that much to you, that you would leave me?"

"Your lack of faith in me means more. I wouldn't do this if we were bloodmates. But yes, this is an opportunity I can't miss. Not when you offer me so little to stay."

For a moment Jonathan hesitated. "You don't mean that."

"I do. Remove it as you promised."

Pain filled him, colored the world in shades of red. When he focused on her again she tried to link to him. He brushed it aside, but the intensity of it hurt. *Don't do that again!*

*Then remember your promise and release me.*

"As you wish!" He grabbed her upper arms and dragged her to him. Eyeing her neck, he sank his fangs into the exact spot of the marks, reopening them. Sweet, hot blood erupted into his mouth, and for a moment he forgot what he was doing. He drank deeply, hungry for this last taste of her.

*Stop!* The command cut through the haze in Jonathan's mind, jerking him back to reality, the bloodlust fading. He paused, swallowed, shuddering against her.

He looked at her mind and saw the deep blue glow of her spirit. Strong, intense. Her spirit, her essence... He'd never seen it before. He'd always been the one to create the link—all he'd seen was the bare room she'd fashioned. Now she was as strong as he was.

*You can control me.*

*I can.* Her mental voice rang clear in his mind, as poignant as her singing voice. *But I won't, not unless I need to.*

A memory came into his mind, of Vanessa forcing him away from her, leaving him empty, hungry. She'd always said it was necessary.

She'd laughed when he'd complained...told him to find someone else to feed from. He had—Angela—and it had been very good. Shortly afterward, Vanessa had appealed to Sebastian, asking to be converted into a nightwalker, and then cut her wrists when he'd said no. In a moment of weakness his prince had never exhibited before, the other man had agreed. Vanessa had left him and Angela in peace...but then Angela had died in his bed.

Private thoughts he couldn't share whisked through his mind. *All my women leave me. Vanessa because she was selfish,*

*Angela because she wasn't. Now Sharon...because she wants what I can't give her.* But it was better this way.

Jonathan spoke into her mind. *Even so, it's too much, I won't let you control me.* He pulled away, cleaned her neck with his tongue, letting the holes close afterward. When he was done there was no sign they'd ever been there.

For a moment he gazed into her face and found her eyes fastened shut. A single tear escaped and Jonathan watched its progress down her cheek. He collected it with his tongue, tasted its salt.

Bitter, this last taste of Sharon.

He released her, stepped away. "If you're leaving, then go."

She stood, her stride unsteady, taking her to the door.

"Take the guitar with you."

Sharon turned in the doorway. "The Martin? I couldn't..."

His voice was harsh, bitter with disappointment. "Take it, please. I'd never play it again, and it belongs with you. Take it...to remember me."

One hand on the handle, she spoke over her shoulder. "I don't need a guitar for that, Jonathan. I'll never forget you." She closed the door quietly behind her.

*And I'll never forget you, Sharon, not as long as I live.* However long that would be.

Right now, it seemed far too long.

## Chapter Nineteen

☙

"What kind of an idiot am I, Marcus?"

The big man paused in the middle of polishing the bar and examined Jonathan, as if giving the question serious merit. "Hard to say," he said finally, returning to his task. "I haven't known enough idiots to be able to classify them."

Jonathan winced and returned to sipping his "screwdriver", serum mixed with vodka. "She's gone. I really loved her, and now I've lost her. What am I going to do?"

Sharon and her brother had packed her few belongings into his car and left around ten. They'd be halfway to Los Angeles by now.

Marcus didn't even pause in his cleaning. "Go after her," he suggested. "That's what I'd do."

Through his mild alcoholic haze, Jonathan considered that option. It had potential, but it was a little late to be setting out. "I couldn't get there before dawn."

"We could take the van. I'll drive while you sleep. It's only a five-hour trip." Finished with the countertop, Marcus turned his attention to the beer taps, polishing them like Sharon usually did. Ruefully, he stared at the results of his efforts. "I miss her already."

Suppressing a groan, Jonathan took another gulp of his drink. It didn't taste nearly as good as the ones Sharon made. Not that he'd point that out to Marcus. The man was already put out over his fellow companion's departure and how he'd had to play bartender this evening.

At the rate Jonathan was going, he would have no companions at all. That was a dismal idea.

On the other hand, the thought of seeing Sharon on the stage of The Music Box... That was an idea well worth exploring. He could visualize her wearing her little red dress, her sunshine hair adrift around her face, beautiful under the spotlight. He let out a heartfelt sigh.

Marcus threw the rag down on the counter. "Seriously, Jon. Let me call Kevin. We can pack a few things and take off well before dawn. I've been promising him a trip anyway. Amber and Ralph can run the bar while we're gone."

Such a tempting idea. But then he'd still have to face Sharon's ultimatum. Run their relationship her way...or there wouldn't be a relationship.

In three hundred years, he'd only once let himself be led by a woman. And look at the result—Vanessa. There was no way he would allow *that* to happen again. Better to stay here than to make a fool of himself chasing after her.

"It's no use. I don't think she'd be that pleased to see me."

Marcus leaned his big body against the bar. "Okay, Jonathan, let's talk about what happened. Why did Sharon leave?"

He tried to shrug off the question. "Her brother brought her an opportunity she couldn't refuse. I told you that."

"Yeah, you told me. But she never would have gone if you hadn't done something to make it impossible for her to stay. She had the mark removed, when five days ago she asked me how she could learn to control the link better so she could become more than a companion. Like Daniel is to Natasha."

Jonathan squirmed at the mention of his friends. Marcus wasn't happy with him, but those two would be even worse.

In the short time she'd been there, Sharon had managed to endear herself to everyone around him. Even Amber had left the Inn in a huff after her shift...and she was the one person he'd expected to be pleased at the news of Sharon's departure. Instead she'd called him a fool to his face.

No one was happy. Certainly he wasn't.

"So...you gonna answer me? What did you do?"

"Nothing...I didn't do anything."

Marcus glared at him. "Somehow I don't believe that." Then comprehension struck, his eyes widened and jaw dropped open. "You mean that. You didn't do *anything*." One meaty finger pointed accusingly. "You rejected her."

"I didn't reject her. I want her to be my companion, I just don't want her to control the link. It would have been too much like Vanessa."

Astonishment segued into anger. "Vanessa? Is that what this is about, you were comparing Sharon to that she-devil? They aren't the least bit alike!"

If there was one truth, that was it. Sharon wasn't anything like Vanessa who'd never been a proper companion to him. Just the thought of her made him thirsty, remembering the lean times he'd experienced. He took another gulp of his screwdriver and wiggled the near-empty glass. "Think you could make another for me?"

All he got in response was a dirty look. If possible, Marcus was even more disappointed in him. "You don't need more of that. What you need—"

"I know what I need, and it isn't a babysitter. You'd think after all the times I sat with you through a break-up, you'd be a little more understanding."

"Believe me, Jon, this is 'understanding' compared to what I'd like to do to you. Of all the lame excuses, comparing Sharon to..."

Behind them the door flew open, the lock Jonathan had carefully set at the close of business no longer operational. Both men turned and stared as Vanessa appeared in the doorway, with a cheery, fanged smile curving her too-red lips.

"Surprise!" she called gaily.

Shock was more like it. Jonathan stared as she glided into the room with Alex close behind her, a couple of bundles in his arms. "Vanessa, what are you doing here?"

She turned to Alex and pouted prettily. It was probably intended to look cute but Jonathan's stomach twisted in disgust. He put aside the remainder of his serum screwdriver.

"Alex, darling, imagine...he forgot! The hundredth anniversary of my becoming his companion and it slipped his mind."

*Hundredth anniversary?* Well, maybe...he didn't exactly have the date engraved in his mind. Not like the day he'd met Sharon. March fifteenth. A Saturday.

That day he'd remember forever.

He cleared his throat. "I'm sorry, Vanessa. We've haven't celebrated that much in the past."

The pout disappeared. "Well maybe we should be more proactive about that. I mean, after all, if it hadn't been for you, I wouldn't be here now."

True. She'd be about a hundred and twenty, if she were alive at all. An image of what the female nightwalker might have looked like crossed his mind, her black hair white with age and her smooth skin a mass of wrinkles.

Jonathan smiled regretfully. She'd have looked like a wicked old witch, the embodiment of her inner ugliness. *Too bad.*

She took the stool next to him. "Since you've forgotten, I suppose you didn't get me anything. But that's all right, I brought you a present."

"You shouldn't have."

"Of course I should have." She gestured to Alex, who placed the bundles on the bar.

She glanced over at Marcus, who looked as dumbfounded as Jonathan felt. "Alex has something for you too. And for your little songbird." Vanessa scanned the room, appearing to notice Sharon's absence for the first time. "Well, where is she?"

The words clotted in Jonathan's throat. Perhaps if he didn't say it, it wouldn't be true.

"She's gone," he finally managed. "Went to LA."

"Oh?" A slyly innocent look crept across her face, and for an instant Jonathan wondered if she'd already known. But how was that possible?

Vanessa reached over and patted his hand. "I'm so sorry. Perhaps she'll come back."

"Perhaps." He could hope.

Sorting through the packages, she withdrew one and put it aside. "We'll just leave hers for later then." She handed Marcus a short square box, then with a flourish presented the remaining present to Jonathan.

Sitting back, she clapped her hands, looking as bright as a child on Christmas. "So... Open them!"

At a loss for a better response, Jonathan tore at the bright paper, noticing Marcus doing the same.

"Hey, thanks, Vanessa." Jonathan was taken aback at the pleasure in Marcus's response. The big man held up a tea tin. "It's my favorite brand, almost impossible to get up here."

What was the world coming to? Vanessa had managed to pick a present that delighted Marcus. Curiosity over his own gift made Jonathan tear the paper off even faster, revealing a boxed bottle. *Oh, heavens.*

It was Swansblusse, a very rare and very old liqueur, one he'd enjoyed when still a normal man. Sweet as honey, heady in flavor and pure enough that he could still drink it. His mouth watered in anticipation.

Suddenly enthused, Marcus headed off to the kitchen with his prize. "I'm going to brew some of this right now. It'll be just the thing to keep me awake for the drive."

Vanessa's delicate eyebrows rose. "Oh? Are you going somewhere?"

Halting, Marcus turned and stared at Jonathan. "Well?"

"We were just discussing a trip to Los Angeles. Sharon will be performing, and we'd thought…"

"You're going after her?" Astonishment filled her features, followed by something else, not as pretty an emotion. "She abandons you and you intend to follow her?"

Jonathan put the bottle onto the bar, irritated at her tone—and the truth of her words. "And what's it to you if I do?"

"I'm just surprised, that's all. You wouldn't have done that for me."

Jonathan suppressed a smile she wouldn't appreciate. "No, I guess I wouldn't have." He turned to Marcus. "Go make your tea. We'll need to leave within the hour."

Marcus went through the swinging door looking like he'd won the lottery.

Vanessa gave Alex a shove. "Why don't you keep Marcus company? You'll need some coffee for the trip north." After her bodybuilder companion had gone, she played with her necklace, a silver locket decorated with an intricate design. "How long do you think you'll be down there?"

"I don't know. Maybe a while."

Vanessa didn't like that answer... Her eyes flashed a red tinge. What was she so bothered by? It made no sense that she might be jealous of his relationship with another woman.

On the other hand, there was something she might be worried about. Sebastian had said she wanted to be chief of Los Angeles, but he wanted Jonathan instead. Maybe Vanessa was worried if he went to LA he might decide to take the job. Ambitious as she was, that made more sense than envy over his feelings for Sharon.

The temptation to tease her became overwhelming. "You heard that Sebastian wanted me to return to LA, to take the chief position. If I did, that would make it easy to be with Sharon. I could help her in her career." He fiddled with the ribbon from his package. "I used to know quite a few people in the industry."

"After thirty years? I doubt you know too many." Only the heightened color in her cheeks gave her anger away. "I probably know more of the real power types than you do."

"Yes, I suppose you do. Well, maybe you could help Sharon then. After all, it wouldn't do you any harm to keep in harmony with your chief by doing favors for his companion...would it?"

Vanessa took a deep swallow, visibly agitated, one hand clutching the locket so tight he thought she might crush it. Then she blinked, relaxed. When she faced him, she smiled, the narrow fangs barely visible beneath her tight upper lip. Her smile did not reach her eyes, which glared at him poisonously.

"Of course, Jonathan. I'll be happy to help your little songbird. Anything to keep the peace." She cast a glance at the unopened bottle. "I tell you what, why don't I pour us a drink to celebrate."

Smoothly, she moved behind the bar and found the narrow bowled stemware used for serving liqueurs. With practiced ease, she pulled the bottle from its box and opened it, only fumbling a little. She had to lean over and tug hard to dislodge the cap.

Her locket swept perilously close to the glasses, narrowly missing one, clinking against the edge of the other. "Oh, how careless of me." She picked up the glass and examined it, looking relieved. "Good, it isn't chipped."

Bemused, Jonathan watched her pour the heavy liquid into the glasses. Placing one in front of him, she took her own and raised it.

"To the new city chief of Los Angeles."

He chuckled and lifted his own glass. "Thank you. I'm glad I can count on your loyalty."

"Me? Of course, Jonathan." She sipped, closing her eyes as the thickened fluid hit her tongue. "Oh, that *is* good."

He tried his and was rewarded by the rich flavor, just as he remembered it. The taste brought back memories, of another time with the Countess, sipping the same drink, discussing love and its importance in life. He held the glass to his nose and savored the heady fragrance. *Wonderful.*

Vanessa was talking about Los Angeles and her contacts. "I'll have to introduce you once you're down there. Some of them who know about us, what we are…they can be very helpful. And I know Sebastian will be pleased that you've taken the job."

A hint of bitterness caught his ear. "Of course, you're pleased as well."

She leaned back, her black hair dipping across her shoulders. He remembered how he'd loved her midnight tresses. Her hair had been one of her best features but now the thought of sunshine-colored locks filled his mind.

Again he thought of the Countess. What would she have said about Sharon? Jonathan grunted as the answer came. She'd call him a fool and a half—that's what she'd say—and then she'd tell him to get himself down to Los Angeles and give Sharon anything she wanted, anything, if she'd come back to him.

The Countess was always right. They'd go to LA tonight and he'd beg Sharon to forgive him.

He took another sip and appreciated the richness of Vanessa's gift. So fitting…to toast his future lady with a wine nearly as sweet as she was.

Jonathan shook his head. *What am I still doing here?* He should be on the road with Marcus, heading down the coast. Sharon would be in Los Angeles…he could see her in the evening and somehow he'd convince her to return with him.

If not…maybe he *would* stay there. The restlessness he felt before returned. Much as he loved Los Niños, after twenty years, anyplace could become tiresome.

"Jonathan, are you listening to me?" The trace of annoyance in Vanessa's voice dragged him back to the present.

"Sorry, Vanessa. I need to cut short this party of ours. Marcus and I have things to do before we can leave." Draining his glass, Jonathan stood up, surprised at how difficult the task was. His feet felt distant, cold, like stone.

Attempting to keep his balance, he grabbed for the bar. Now his hands were cold, and he could barely feel the smooth wood beneath his fingers.

How much had he had to drink? One screwdriver with a liqueur chaser shouldn't have this much effect on him. His vision blurred, the lingering taste of the wine a memory. He couldn't even smell Vanessa's cloying perfume anymore, the one bright spot in the situation.

All his senses were shutting down. Through the static in his ears, he heard his fellow nightwalker's vicious chortle.

"My, my, Jonathan. You don't look too good. Perhaps you'd better sit down."

He staggered back to the stool. For an instant his vision cleared, and he was able to focus on the glass still in his hand. He dropped it on the bar, watched the syrupy liquid ooze from the bottom of the glass into a red puddle on the maple countertop. It looked like blood. "What have you done?" The words caught in his throat. It was hard to breathe.

"Protected my interests, as always." She fingered the silver locket, now open—and empty. "Sebastian should have offered me the city chief position but instead he insisted you take it. So long as you were unwilling, I could bide my time. But now…"

Vanessa studied him with detached interest as he struggled to remain upright on the stool. "It's a poison, of course. One of my more interesting herbal concoctions. Practically tasteless, very effective. You have a remarkably strong constitution. The others went out practically at once. Must have been something you ate. Perhaps that little songbird of yours?"

He remembered. He had fed from Sharon before she left, to remove the marks. "Companion blood is an antidote?"

"It is, as with most other ailments we have. Trouble is, one of yours has fled your pretty cage and the other…"

Horror filled him. The tea. "What have you done to Marcus?"

"Not a whole lot. He's alive, unconscious at the moment, but he'll live. You could save yourself by feeding from him. But…"

"But what?"

She uncoiled from the stool, giving him the impression of a snake about to strike. "There is one small side effect of the drug I put in his tea. If you feed from him, he'll die."

Her serpent smile and eyes reflected her amusement. "You might find this interesting, Jonathan. I've used that drug before, on another companion of yours. You remember Angela? She never told you about our tea party the day before her death. I doubt she remembered it. Temporary amnesia is another of the side effects. Marcus won't remember a thing about my visit tomorrow.

"The tea I served her has a very special set of ingredients. I was merely looking for a way to decrease the blood production in a companion, to make it easier to be turned. How was I to know that it would be so effective…that it would turn off production completely and cause the system to collapse during a feeding? It was far too strong for my purposes, but I have found uses for it since then."

Thoughts of Estaban and Laura went through his head and then the real truth hit like a hammer. *Angela hadn't died because of his thirst.*

"All this time, I thought I'd killed her." He'd blamed himself for it, had not trusted himself because of it, and it had cost him so much over the years.

It had cost him Sharon.

If he could've moved, he'd have happily broken Vanessa's neck.

She laughed merrily. "Yes, I know that's what you thought. It really was an accident. I hadn't planned it. But it did get you out of the way for a while."

He gave up trying to remain upright and collapsed to the floor. Alex appeared in the kitchen doorway. "All set, boss. The big guy is napping on the floor, and I took care of the phones so he won't be able to call anyone."

"Very good, Alex." She consulted her watch. "It's about three. We can make it to the safehouse if we leave now." She spared a single glance at Jonathan, now leaning against the underside of the bar, legs spread out.

"I'm afraid I can't stay to watch you die, Jonathan. It could take several hours, and we can't be found here. I don't want anyone to be able to say I had any part in this. When you're discovered, Marcus won't remember what happened, and yours will just be another mysterious death. Sebastian will probably chalk it up to a suicide."

"Sharon." The one word was all he could manage. His breath was too short.

"She'll be all right, Jonathan, so long as she stays out of my way. I'm not a monster, you know. Even Marcus will get to live, so long as he doesn't suffer any major blood losses for a while."

Alex looked concerned. "Shouldn't we tie him? Just to make sure? He could still feed from the big guy."

Vanessa laughed. "Don't be silly. Jon would rather die than hurt one of his precious humans. Come, we've quite a distance to go."

At the door, she paused, took a final look around. "I like this place. Maybe I'll see if I can buy it from your estate. I suppose it's too much to hope you left it to me in your will."

A low growl was his only response.

She shook her head. "I guessed not. Well, goodbye, Jonathan. Enjoy the next few hours. They'll be your last."

The door clicked quietly shut, leaving him alone.

It took nearly ten minutes to crawl to the kitchen and find Marcus, sacked out on the floor. The tea tin was missing—they'd taken it along with the wine. Jonathan tried to leave a note, but his hands shook so badly nothing on the paper made any sense.

*No evidence.* Vanessa had planned pretty thoroughly. He'd be found dead, Marcus would remember nothing, and there would be no reason for Sebastian to believe anything but that Jonathan had taken his own life.

*So it ends...unless.* He eyed the rise and fall of Marcus's chest, the pulse-point in his neck. *Blood.* Companion blood, could save him.

God help him, he was tempted. Jonathan's life would be over if he didn't. He would die, and Vanessa would win. She'd become city chief—Sebastian would have no choice but to name her, and that could be terrible for the parafolk in Los Angeles. She might even go after Sharon in spite of her promise not to.

He would be protecting the woman he loved. It would cost Marcus his life, but that was a small matter compared to everything else.

Vanessa might have even lied about the drug—but no, she hadn't. He remembered finding Angela asleep early in the evening and how still she'd been during the day. It was the same drug Marcus had been given.

What was he to do? His death would accomplish little. Marcus' would solve everything. Marcus would probably even insist that Jonathan do it.

Jonathan reached out with shaking fingers and gently stroked the fang marks on the unconscious man's neck, and the companion oath came to mind. *I take you as my companion, to serve me as long as you bear my mark. In return you have my protection and support, from this time on.*

His hand fell away.

*I always take promises seriously, my friend.*

It took thirty minutes to crawl to the office, twenty more to load CDs into the player, fighting the trembling of his hands. Classical music—Beethoven, Mozart, Brahms, Chopin—eternal music, music that would never die.

He set it up for repeat play, so the music wouldn't stop. The hidden speakers blared the opening chords to a symphony and he almost smiled. He'd heard it when it had first opened in Paris, two hundred years before. *Angel trumpets, and demon trombones*—a line from a movie he'd seen once.

The last of his strength went into crawling up onto the couch where at least an illusion of comfort could be found. After that it became impossible to move. A terrible lethargy flowed through his body.

Only at the last did he try and reach out with his mind to touch Sharon. She was too far away to hear him. They'd be far down the coast. She might have even made it to Los Angeles. But still, he had to tell her.

*Meine Süsse, I'll love you forever.*

\* \* \* \* \*

*This is ridiculous.* Sharon watched Stuart head into the rest area bathroom. It was their third stop in as many hours since they left the Inn. She'd felt like she'd seen every public restroom along the Pacific Coast Highway.

What could he be doing in there? Drugs? She'd accused him of it the last time they'd stopped, and he'd sworn he hadn't been. Still, there was that telltale nose rub and the red-rimmed eyes that got worse every time he returned to the car. She looked at the keys hanging in the ignition and decided she would drive the rest of the way after he came back.

Uncomfortable, tired of the long drive and not looking forward to the longer one to come, Sharon shifted on her seat and stared at the dashboard clock. Just after one o'clock in the morning, and they were still several hours from Los Angeles. At this rate, they'd be lucky to make it by dawn.

Dawn—when Jonathan would seek his bed. Would he miss her as he tucked himself under the covers, as much as she missed him?

Maybe. Maybe he'd even miss her enough to come after her. A fantasy played in her mind, of being on stage at The Music Box, singing to a large crowd. Looking up, she'd spy Jonathan in the audience and sing a new song, special...just for him. A tune came into her mind, and words.

Frantically she searched the interior of the car for the means to write them down. Finding an old pen in the glove compartment, and a credit card slip under Stuart's seat, she wrote quickly across the back of the receipt before the words faded from her mind.

It was the perfect song for him and she smiled as she wrote. Jonathan always inspired her best writing.

When she was done, she turned the slip over, curious. Stuart hadn't qualified for a credit card in a long time.

It took a moment for the signature at the bottom of the slip to make sense. "Vanessa Hind."

Sharon put the slip down and stared at the empty parking lot around her. Why would her brother have the female nightwalker's credit card slip in his car? Assuming it was his car...and at the moment she had serious doubts. While he'd shown considerable pride as she'd admired the late-model black Cadillac, it had taken several minutes for him to find the lights before they'd left, and several times she'd had to point out he was driving in second gear.

Why would her brother show up in a car that wasn't his own, that likely belonged to Vanessa, and offer her the job of her dreams? Her dream job and all she had to do to get it was leave Jonathan right away.

Sharon smelled a rat, a queen-sized, bloodsucking, female rat, using her drugged-up brother to get her out of the way. She glanced over at the men's restroom, where the light was still on inside, then got out of the car and moved to the driver's side.

Time to get back to the Inn.

The car left a layer of rubber as she peeled out of the parking lot and headed back up the coast.

# Chapter Twenty

The parking lot of the Inn was deserted, the light over the door out. No sign of life in the place. Sharon parked and went around to the back door, using the key she'd forgotten to return.

She turned on the light in the kitchen and found Marcus on the floor, lying far too quietly. When she couldn't rouse him she ran for the phone, only to find it didn't work. Returning to the big man, she noted his breathing was regular, even though she couldn't get him to wake up.

Nothing to be done here, she'd have to drive to a phone for help. With that thought Sharon headed for the door.

*Meine Süsse, I'll love you forever.*

"Jonathan?" His mental voice was far too weak. "Where are you?"

There was no answer. This time she used her mental power, cast it in a far reaching net. *Jonathan...*

His answer sounded surprised. *Sharon? Wo bist du?*

He had to be inside the Inn, his mental voice was too weak to be very far away. She pushed open the door to the hallway and heard the music coming through the open office door. "Jonathan?"

She found him on the couch, paler than she'd ever seen him before. Disheveled, his normally immaculate black pants were dusty. There were dirt marks on his white shirt from where he'd dragged himself. At the sound of her voice, he opened his eyes and the normally luminous blue orbs were pale, washed out. His lips moved but no sound emerged.

Instead she heard his voice in her mind. *You…are here?*

*Yes.* Sharon knelt next to him on the floor, put her hand on his chest.

His hand wiggled as if to touch her but fell back. *Didn't think to see you again. I'm pleased.*

*What happened?* she asked quickly.

*Vanessa…poison. Both Marcus and me. He will live…* His eyes shut and she felt the trembling of his heart under her hand. Fear clutched at her and she grabbed his hand. He looked like he was dying.

*Tell Sebastian. Marcus won't remember. Vanessa responsible for me…and for Angela. Estaban and Laura too. She told me, many others.*

*Vanessa?* Suddenly Stuart's appearance made sense and she thanked heaven that she'd found the telltale receipt.

His eyes opened again, and she saw some of the old flame in his gaze. *Tell Sebastian.*

*You will tell him yourself.*

*No…too late. Too much damage. Only companion blood…*

Her heart picked up speed. "The antidote is companion blood?" No wonder that female jackal had wanted her out of the way.

He barely had the strength to nod his head.

"But not Marcus," she guessed, "that's why he was poisoned."

Again that brief nod.

Then there was a chance. "Okay, you will feed from me."

The slightest shake of his head. *No—not companion anymore.*

"I was until a few hours ago, my blood shouldn't have changed that much."

*Won't be able to replace it. Need too much.*

"I'll take that chance." As she spoke she pulled off the light jacket she wore, then her sweater, a turtleneck she'd worn for the first time in months. Clad in her bra, she pulled his head toward her neck, lifting it off the couch. He didn't have the strength to stop her, but he didn't help either. His head lolled on her shoulder.

*I won't feed from you. I won't risk your life.*

*I can make you do it. I'll force you if I have to.*

*Don't.* His mental voice was firm for all of its weakness. *Do and it will be the end of things with us. Won't be controlled. You most of all should understand why.*

She did understand. He was referring to the mind-rape, but she wouldn't let that sway her. It wasn't the same thing — Izzy had forced her for his purposes and not her benefit. Frustrated, she let his head slip back to the couch, cushioning it as it fell. As she watched, he seemed to grow colder, more limp. He was dying.

It was now or never. "I'm not asking your permission, Jonathan. It's my life to risk — and my duty to take care of you. If you never speak to me again, so be it."

She ran to the kitchen, grabbed one of the wicked-looking knives from the butcher-block holder. When she returned, she held it over her wrist.

"Shall I do it the hard way, Jonathan, or are you going to do it for me?"

His eyes opened and she saw dismay in his eyes. "No." The one word was a whisper.

Her fingers tightened on the handle, pressed the edge on the tender skin of her wrist, cringing in anticipation. It was going to hurt. From somewhere she summoned the strength. The blade slid across, cutting deep.

*Shit.* The pain was sharp and worse than she'd imagined.

Bright red blood welled over the knife's edge, sliding down the blade and onto her hand. Throwing the bloody knife across the room, she pressed the open wound to his mouth, pushed a mental command into his mind. *Drink.*

Jonathan's lips moved convulsively, taking a little, but then she felt his tongue moving across the wound. She remembered how he'd healed the cut on the beach. He was going to do the same thing now, heal her before he could feed. She could even feel some of the pain slipping away.

*No!* She shouted the word into his mind and pulled her arm away.

There was no choice now. If Jonathan was to live, he must feed, and without his cooperation, she'd have to force him. She'd have to create a link and control it...regardless of how he felt about it.

Sharon took a few deep cleansing breaths, centering herself as Callistra had taught her. Closing her eyes, she imagined a golden bowl, Jonathan's mind, inches away. It formed before her, paler than it should be, and when she reached for it, she found it made of mist rather than the solidity of Callistra's. Still she took firm hold of it, pulled it into her mental room. Imagining herself as a thin blue mist, she poured herself into it, filling the bowl to the brim.

There were images there, of her, of others, but she didn't focus on those. Only one image did she look for, one of Jonathan at the height of passion, feeding without restraint. Sharon grabbed it and brought it forward, making it the only thing in his mind.

A groan rumbled through the nightwalker's chest and his body convulsed in sensuous rhythm. Sharon pushed her wrist over his mouth and his lips closed over the cut. She felt the first deep pull from the wound, painful, but not too bad. She could live with the sensation, he wouldn't live without it—and she wouldn't live without him.

*Drink, my love. Let me satisfy you, let me heal you.* She crooned that thought into his mind. Enthralled, he lifted one hand to support her arm, to keep it close to his mouth.

He fed, his mouth working against her wrist. Her own heart picked up speed as the drag on her body continued. Seconds dragged by, then minutes. She used what skill she had to test his strength, the beat of his heart. Every swallow seemed to improve things. He no longer looked as pale.

Jonathan's eyes opened and locked with hers, a strange glow in them. Then his gaze moved, took in her near nakedness, and the glow intensified, his look turned feral.

*Enough of this.* Jonathan struggled against her hold and pulled his mouth away to swipe his tongue against the cut on her wrist, sealing it.

Sitting up, he grabbed her and pulled her into his arms. Sharon felt his arousal through his pants and the harsh pounding of his heart against her bare chest. With a swift movement, he tore the bra off her, no gentleness in his hand, and no gentleness in his mouth when his lips enveloped hers.

On his lips, her blood tasted coppery sweet. *See what you taste like to me.* His mental voice commanded.

She thrilled at his kiss. *Odd, it's sweet.*

A near chuckle sounded in his mind. *So I've always told you.*

His mouth slipped from hers, sought her nipples, teasing them to pebble hardness. He suckled them and ripples of sensation slid down her body, radiating into her very core.

It had been far too long since he'd touched her this way. She reveled in the feel of his hands stroking her back, his mouth working on her breasts. All thoughts of control began to slip away under his sensuous attack.

One hand fumbled with the fastening to her pants, undoing the button but failing to budge the zipper. With a frustrated jerk, he pulled and the fabric ripped open. Seconds later the crotch of her underwear met the same fate and his hand plunged into her soft folds beneath.

The ripping of her clothes brought Sharon back to earth. She wanted no mindless passion between them. If this was their last time, then let it be as it should be. Let it be love.

"Jonathan, stop…or I'll make you stop." She grabbed his hands and forced them still. His lips and tongue stopped their wild plundering of her breast.

Jonathan's head tilted upwards and his eyes stared into hers. He was shaking, barely in control. "What would you have of me?" She startled at the wildness in his voice.

Her own wild breathing revealed her own passion. "I would have it all. But let's take it slower." She tugged on the bottom of his shirt. "Starting with this. Get undressed."

Disentangling herself, she rose, stepped away and watched as he removed his clothes, his eyes locked on hers. Shoes, socks, pants and shirt soon made a pile on the floor, his underwear lying across the top. He leaned back on the couch, his lean body gleaming in the pale light of the lamp, his aristocratic features half in shadow.

Only his eyes were unobscured. Passion enlivened them, made them glow with an unearthly light, and she felt the intensity of his stare to the core of her soul. Sharon's breath caught in her throat.

He was the most beautiful man alive.

The Mozart piece ended, and something by Beethoven began, a slow piece, suitable for making love. Sharon removed her torn pants and the remains of her panties, leaving them on the floor next to his.

He eyed them. "I'm sorry…"

"It's all right." She laid her hand on his chest, pushing him back onto the couch, leaned forward to whisper in his ear. "I'll let you make it up to me."

Holding her upper arms, he pulled her to sit astride him. Tucking her legs on either side of him, she slid against his hardness, the feel of him exquisite against her warm folds.

He threw his head back and groaned. "Oh, *meine Süsse*, I've so missed this."

She caught his mouth with hers in a kiss as gentle as his had been rough. The mating of their mouths raised further needs. The need to touch, to hold. The need to connect and become one. The need to make love as man and woman, nightwalker and companion.

Even if she wasn't a companion anymore.

Running her hands along his shoulders, she traced the contours of his torso, his flat chest dusted with dark hair as fine as silk, then reached down to cup the tip of him poking up between her legs, and revel in the smooth firmness between her fingers.

Hers to touch, this one last time. She'd overcome his reluctance with the force of her mind and he was still somewhat under her spell. When he woke, tomorrow, he would be furious with her.

She wouldn't focus on that. They might never love again after tonight, but she'd keep the memory of this one time in her heart forever.

At the moment, his rejecting her seemed far from Jonathan's mind. He ran his hands along her back to her hips, raised her buttocks to slide against his rock-hard arousal. The sensation made Sharon forget her current worries and focus on the here and now.

*Love me, Jonathan. I want you.*

*I want you too, little witch.* He caught her nipple between his teeth and suckled it tenderly. His fangs gently grazed the top of her breast.

*Don't you mean spellcaster?*

His mental snicker tickled her, made her feel playful. She teased the hardness of his arousal, rubbed her thumb across the sensitive tip and felt it stiffen even more. He groaned aloud, his mouth falling away from her nipple.

*You certainly have cast a spell on me. But be careful or the magic will end too soon.*

His hand reached between them, played with her own sensitivity, sending wave upon wave of pleasure through her. Each stroke of his fingers awoke her body to new levels of arousal. She pressed against his hand, no thought of holding back. Anything he wanted from her he could have.

In her mind came another memory, of the last time he'd fed, when he'd given her the impression of loving. His fingers now repeated the actions of his mental touching, the two in sync with one another. He'd loved her that night as he'd wanted to love her for real. As he was loving her now.

It hadn't been a false passion, but the impression of what he'd wanted all along. In his mind she saw that he'd felt every stroke, been involved, both physically and mentally. She felt his pain as she'd rejected what he'd intended to be a gift.

*I didn't realize…*

Ice blue eyes locked with hers. *I know, I should have told you or done it differently. It doesn't matter now.*

She answered with her kiss, her caress, and a mental image of them as lovers, and felt his response. Awareness, desire, was paramount now. All she wanted was to be one with him.

He slid his hands to her bottom, raised it to make their joining possible. She guided his hardness into her, the feel of penetration excruciating after the wait.

It had been too long since they'd loved. She raised herself and glided down, his shaft filling her. *Oh, yes. Way too long.*

Beneath her, Jonathan's breathing increased to match hers, his eyes closed, then opened again to stare into hers. *Far too long, indeed.* His hips moved, rising to meet her, picking up the pace, their mating the only thing on his mind.

*For the moment.*

Then she sensed another thought slip in, another need, and she welcomed it, encouraged it. He needed to feed still. What he'd taken from her arm was enough to save his life and give him strength but wasn't enough to restore his health.

Callistra had taught her how to test her vital statistics and using those techniques Sharon knew she could accommodate him. He couldn't take much, she'd have to control it, but then she was already foremost in his mind.

She leaned forward, her neck in close proximity to his mouth. "It's all right, Jonathan. I won't let you hurt me."

His answering groan seemed to rise from the deepest part of him. It filled her ears as well as her heart. Seeking her warmth, his mouth closed on her neck, and once more she felt the sharp sting of his bite, then the pull of his mouth as he took what he needed.

In far too short a time, weakness grew within her, something she hadn't felt since their last coupling when he'd fed uncontrollably. She was no longer a companion—she couldn't support his feeding much longer.

Reluctantly, she forced him to slow down, to focus instead on their joined bodies. The delight from their lovemaking filled her and through his mind she felt his pleasure and the surge of tension indicative of imminent climax.

His mouth fell back, one swipe of his tongue eliminating the holes his fangs had cut, no trace left behind. The tension in his body increased and they moved together as one, minds joined as the final moment arrived.

*Come with me, Sharon, experience it with me.*

At his mental command she found her own orgasm, simultaneous with his, both their senses overwhelmed, minds set adrift in a sea of passion but joined together. The echoes passed through the link until she didn't know if she experienced his climax or he felt hers.

Irrelevant. As the echoes died down, she rested on him, his body warm beneath her. Together they'd fought his near-death with sustenance and love and won that battle. Now they would take comfort in the aftermath.

As Beethoven's symphony became a Chopin sonata, she closed her eyes and fell into a dreamless sleep.

\* \* \* \* \*

Dawn had broken a short time ago. Sharon knew immediately, when Jonathan's breath stopped short and his eyes closed. Sleep though, not death. Not this morning.

She'd given him back his life. Her blood, strong, rich, that of a companion, although technically she no longer bore his mark, had cured him of Vanessa's poison.

Jonathan would live. Pulling herself from his arms, Sharon rose from the couch, turned to gaze at his perfect body — long pale limbs, wide shoulders, narrow waist and hips. Dark hair scattered along his chest into a narrow vee leading to his groin, hair as fine as silk.

She took a long last look, fighting the tears that burned her eyes. She'd never know any man as perfect as he was. It would be a long time before she could even think of a man the way she did him.

She couldn't believe she ever would.

*Her nightwalker.* But not really. Tonight, even when refusal meant his death, Jonathan had fought the link, refusing to trust her. Refusing to trust himself.

No, Jonathan wasn't hers and he never would be, not so long as he clung to his belief that trust was unnecessary. Even this morning he'd attempted to force her to sleep alongside him and only her control had prevented him.

Her hand slid along her neck, noting the lack of scars. He hadn't re-marked her. Was it by choice, or had he forgotten? It didn't matter. The truth remained that she was free. She could leave now, and no one could stop her.

The stereo still played, something by Mozart. She turned it off. From the kitchen she heard the sound of someone moving about. Marcus must have awakened.

Jonathan had said the drug would leave the companion disoriented and that he wouldn't remember what had happened. She'd have to fill him in.

She pulled the blanket off the back of the couch and wrapped it around Jonathan. He could sleep here today, with Marcus to guard him. She'd get the big man to call in the shapeshifters and they would take care of Vanessa and Alex if they dared show up. Jonathan would be safe.

Sharon dressed, pulling on her pants and fastening the button that remained, then her sweater, leaving it untucked to cover the rest of the damage. With her coat on, no one would notice.

She would talk to Marcus and then take off. Perhaps Stuart was still at the rest stop, or maybe he'd headed south.

Whatever, she'd find him. As he put it, he was "the bad penny," he always turned up. And when he did, she'd have a serious talk with him. He needed to get his life together.

As did she. And Jonathan. If he ever overcame his issues, he'd find her. Her breaking heart clung to that hope, even as her mind told her how hopeless it was.

Before she left, she bent and gave Jonathan's still face one final kiss.

*Goodbye, my love.*

## Chapter Twenty-One

Last set of the night. Sharon crooned the final verse of the song into the mike, the vibrations of the last chord from the Martin dying against her chest. The audience applauded steadily, perhaps not as enthusiastically as what she'd become used to at the All Night Inn, but still appreciated.

She gazed at the crowd, the faces smiling in the dim light of the table candles, more than a few sporting the fangs of a nightwalker. Happy faces, listening to her music.

As she had for the last several nights, she scanned for a particular face, thin, aristocratic, with dark hair and ice blue eyes. No sign of him and the hope she still retained died again.

It had been nearly three weeks since she'd returned to the All Night Inn and forced Jonathan to link with her to save his life. If he'd still wanted her he'd have shown up by now. She'd left him twice. Why would he come now? He had his life and she had hers.

From the audience came a steady drone, the call for an encore. She smiled at that. Stuart, sitting in the front row and looking cleaner and more sober than he'd been in years, nodded his approval. After she'd abandoned him at the rest stop, he'd had ample opportunity to think about what he'd done and had been grateful that she'd returned to pick him up hours later. He'd told her the entire story on their way to Los Angeles, that the job offer was legitimate, if obtained through Vanessa's intervention.

Stuart had promised to turn over a new leaf if she forgave him. She'd decided forgiveness wasn't enough, but that she would try trusting him as well, and that's what finally made the difference.

The fact he knew she could check up on him just by reading his mind helped him keep his promises.

After two nights of performing at The Music Box, she'd been offered a job at a different place, an after-hours club that specialized in a clientele similar to that of the All Night Inn. Along the coast, just up from Santa Monica, The Dark Water Tavern had become her new home.

So, once again Sharon found herself performing her songs of moonlight romps to faces of fang and fur. She enjoyed it, being with the parafolk again. It was almost like being back in Los Niños. *Almost.*

The crowd was still calling for an encore and Sharon searched her mind for something appropriate for the occasion. One came to mind—the song she'd written in the car, on the way to Los Angeles. She hadn't performed it yet, had been waiting for the right time.

*Why wait?* If he were going to come, he would have shown up by now. She strummed the first chords as the crowd quieted down.

*"Walker in the night, sleeper in the day,*
*Flyer in the moonlight over fields where shifters play*
*Musician through the ages, player without par,*
*Lover at midnight, holder of my heart*

*My Midnight Lover keeps me warm at night*
*My Midnight Lover takes me on his full moon flight*
*My Midnight Lover holds me while I sleep*
*My Midnight Lover, for him I'm all he needs."*

The crowd burst into full applause and Sharon nodded gratefully to them.

*Is that what you want, meine Süsse?*

Sharon snapped to attention, her eyes scanning the audience at that familiar mental touch. From a shadowed corner, a dark figure separated from the wall and stepped into the light of a nearby table.

Jonathan's appearance caused quite a stir. Those nearby, nightwalkers from their pale complexions and unusual dentition, bent their heads together and whispered urgently. From her position, she heard others in the audience saying softly, "It's Jonathan, the new chief."

His face held the slightest hint of a smile. *I asked a question…or have you lost your ability to bespeak me?*

Heart racing, she tried to keep her joy from appearing in her face. As nonchalantly as possible, she answered him. *I'm not sure what the question was.*

*The question is do you want to be all that a nightwalker needs?*

The joy she'd resisted burst forth and developed into a smile she couldn't stop. *That…would depend on the nightwalker. Did you have someone in mind?*

Jonathan actually laughed, something she'd never expected to hear again. *Why don't you come to my table and we'll discuss it.*

After placing her guitar into its case, she left the stage and moved through the crowd, the curious gazes of her audience following her.

As he'd said, he had a table, tucked away in a raised corner, secluded but with a clear view of the stage and an even better one of the sea beyond the window. Outside the full moon shone over the constantly moving ocean.

He waved her to the seat next to his, where a glass of white wine already waited for her.

"This is where the owner usually sits." She looked around for the ponytailed shapeshifter who'd hired her to work at his club.

"Yes, Garrett is a friend of mine. Brother to Ralph, actually." He glanced over at the window, at the moon's reflection on the water, a wistful smile on his face. "He likes to run the beaches on nights like these."

"Oh?" Eager for news of her friends, Sharon leaned forward. "How are Ralph and Amber? And Marcus?"

"The shapeshifters are fine. I left them in charge at the Inn. I think Amber's planning a wedding, come the fall. You'll be invited, of course."

So Amber had finally chased Ralph down. "I'm glad to hear that."

Jonathan seemed thinner, although he still wore his sharply tailored dark blue shirt and pants with elegant ease. He'd cut his hair into a shorter, more modern style and it suited him, she thought. One dark lock fell across his forehead, and Sharon had to resist the urge to reach over and push it back, to feel again the silky texture.

She had to resist touching him right now. She had to be certain with him — she could lose her heart too easily.

Not that she hadn't already lost it.

He toyed with the glass in front of him. "I took the mark off Marcus a week ago, after we were sure the drug Vanessa had given him had worn off. He and Kevin have gone to Las Vegas for a while."

Concerned, she searched his face. "Why did he leave? Was it because…"

"Because of Vanessa? No. He'd been thinking about it for some time. Kevin means a lot to him, and Marcus didn't want to live alone anymore." His blue eyes glowed at her. "I know how he feels."

Under his steady gaze, sweet happiness enveloped her. To hide it she drank some of her wine, the taste of it cold and tart on her tongue. "What about Vanessa?"

He grimaced. "She and Alex are still at large, unfortunately. Now that we know what she was up to, though, we can prepare for her better. She won't get away with that sort of thing again, not in California under Sebastian's watch. When we find her…"

She leaned forward. "Will you kill her?"

The fierceness in his look was unmistakable, his eyes narrowed and lips thinned. "If I can. Too many are dead because of her. For a while, I thought she might even come after you. And that I could never tolerate."

Pleasure at his concern flooded her. "I hear you are chief now. So you'll be here for a while?"

Jonathan's good mood returned. He stood and performed a deep courtly bow, a clear reminder of his distant past in the court of King Leopold. "Indeed. Chief Jonathan, of the City of the Angels, at your service. And yes, I'm here for some time to come. I even purchased some property in LA."

He glanced around the room, at the low ceiling, elegant fixtures and glass wall overlooking the dark ocean. "This place, to be exact."

Sharon couldn't help her surprise. "You own The Dark Water Tavern?"

"I do."

She toyed with the stem of her glass then raised her eyes to link with his, mischief in her gaze. "And does this mean that I must carry your mark to work here?"

Jonathan reached across the table to take her hand. "It isn't necessary but..." His fingers tightened. "If you would, I'd be most appreciative."

His other hand found her neck, stroked it, two fingers lingering where the marks used to be. "Do you trust me, Sharon?"

Leaning into his hand, she felt her eyes fill with tears of happiness. "I trust you, Jonathan."

But there had to be more. She initiated a link to him. *Do you trust me?*

Jonathan hesitated and Sharon's rising hope crashed back to earth. She pulled back, rose from her chair. "This is a mistake."

His hand shot out at inhuman speed and grabbed hers. "Wait."

The strain of three weeks of waiting, wishing, hoping and praying he'd come around, caught up with her and angrily she lashed at him. "You're forever telling me to wait, to have patience. What should I wait for now?"

Blue sparks seemed to fly from his eyes. "If nothing else, at least wait for my answer!"

Sharon took a deep breath, forcing herself to calm. Without relinquishing her hand, Jonathan pulled her back to her seat.

He released her and rested his chin on his folded hands, his gaze on the ocean behind her. "I've thought a lot about what you said, about trust, and you were right. I didn't trust myself, or you, or anyone. Some of it was Angela, having her death on my conscience, but not all.

"All my life I haven't wanted to be dependent on anyone—people leave. Even the Countess died, and it wasn't until I came so close to losing you that night on the beach that

I realized why she committed suicide. Without someone to love, life can be unbearably lonely."

Some of Sharon's anger drained away. "That's why you wanted me to be with you, even without sex," she whispered.

Jonathan raised his head and she felt the weight of his ice blue gaze on her face. "I wanted you close, where I could feel your presence, but it wasn't enough. When you offered me more, to become my bloodmate, I couldn't trust you or myself enough to take it. You were right to leave me then, without trust we had nothing. But then you came back."

Wonder filled his face, his eyes aglow. Sharon felt that glow clear to her toes, and the breath caught in her throat. "I'd never fully linked with anyone until that amazing last night with you. When I woke and found you gone…"

She saw the pain in his eyes and knew she'd put it there. "I didn't think you would want me after I forced the link," Sharon explained. "I was too much of a coward to face you."

"I was angry," he admitted, "for about ten minutes. Then I realized what I'd lost and it nearly tore me apart. I'd already planned on going after you, but when you left the second time I knew I had to offer you more than a life in Los Niños. Now I'll give you anything you want and all I want in return is everything you're willing to give me."

Everything she could give him—that was everything she had! Trembling, Sharon used her power to initiate a link, and he allowed it, his golden glow welcoming her. Her thoughts mixed with his, scrambled around, joined and separated, joy and desire in the mixing. One image became clear, of a bed with satin linens and soft pillows, in a place not too far away.

*Just a short flight under a full moon.* Jonathan stood and pulled her to her feet. "Come, I will re-mark you there."

Flushed, her body tingling at his touch, Sharon stared into his eyes. "You didn't answer my question. Do you trust me?"

His mind gave the answer before he spoke it.

*Forever, my love – my bloodmate. I will trust you that long and beyond.*

## The End

# Why an electronic book?

We live in the Information Age—an exciting time in the history of human civilization, in which technology rules supreme and continues to progress in leaps and bounds every minute of every day. For a multitude of reasons, more and more avid literary fans are opting to purchase e-books instead of paper books. The question from those not yet initiated into the world of electronic reading is simply: *Why?*

1. *Price.* An electronic title at Ellora's Cave Publishing and Cerridwen Press runs anywhere from 40% to 75% less than the cover price of the exact same title in paperback format. Why? Basic mathematics and cost. It is less expensive to publish an e-book (no paper and printing, no warehousing and shipping) than it is to publish a paperback, so the savings are passed along to the consumer.

2. *Space.* Running out of room in your house for your books? That is one worry you will never have with electronic books. For a low one-time c ost, you can purchase a handheld device specifically designed for e-reading. Many e-readers have large, convenient screens for viewing. Better yet, hundreds of titles can be stored within your new library—on a single microchip. There are a variety of e-readers from different manufacturers. You can also read e-books on your PC or laptop computer. (Please note that Ellora's

Cave does not endorse any specific brands. You can check our websites at www.ellorascave.com or www.cerridwenpress.com for information we make available to new consumers.)
3. *Mobility.* Because your new e-library consists of only a microchip within a small, easily transportable e-reader, your entire cache of books can be taken with you wherever you go.
4. *Personal Viewing Preferences.* Are the words you are currently reading too small? Too large? Too... ANNOYING? Paperback books cannot be modified according to personal preferences, but e-books can.
5. *Instant Gratification.* Is it the middle of the night and all the bookstores near you are closed? Are you tired of waiting days, sometimes weeks, for bookstores to ship the novels you bought? Ellora's Cave Publishing sells instantaneous downloads twenty-four hours a day, seven days a week, every day of the year. Our webstore is never closed. Our e-book delivery system is 100% automated, meaning your order is filled as soon as you pay for it.

Those are a few of the top reasons why electronic books are replacing paperbacks for many avid readers.

As always, Ellora's Cave and Cerridwen Press welcome your questions and comments. We invite you to email us at Comments@ellorascave.com or write to us directly at Ellora's Cave Publishing Inc., 1056 Home Avenue, Akron, OH 44310-3502.

# THE
# ☥ ELLORA'S CAVE ☥
## LIBRARY

Stay up to date with Ellora's Cave Titles in Print with our Quarterly Catalog.

TO RECIEVE A CATALOG,
SEND AN EMAIL WITH YOUR NAME
AND MAILING ADDRESS TO:

CATALOG@ELLORASCAVE.COM

OR SEND A LETTER OR POSTCARD
WITH YOUR MAILING ADDRESS TO:

CATALOG REQUEST
c/o ELLORA'S CAVE PUBLISHING, INC.
1056 HOME AVENUE
AKRON, OHIO 44310-3502

*Please be advised Ellora's Cave books as well as our website contain Explicit sexual content. You must be 18.*

MAKE EACH DAY MORE *EXCITING* WITH OUR

# Ellora's Cavemen Calendar

www.EllorasCave.com

# Ellora's Cavemen
## Legendary Tails

Try an e-book for your immediate
reading pleasure or order these titles in print from

## www.EllorasCave.com

### Ellora's Cave
### The Best in Today's Romantica™

# Cerridwen Press

*Cerridwen, the Celtic goddess of wisdom, was the muse who brought inspiration to storytellers and those in the creative arts.*
*Cerridwen Press encompasses the best and most innovative stories in all genres of today's fiction.*
*Visit our website and discover the newest titles by talented authors who still get inspired—much like the ancient storytellers did, once upon a time…*

**www.cerridwenpress.com**